Shadow In The Sky

Marcus McGee

PEGASUS BOOKS

ISBN – 978-0-9826936-8-1

LCCN: 2010930833

Comments about *Shadow In The Sky* and requests for additional copies, book club rates and author speaking appearances may be addressed to Marcus McGee or Pegasus Books c/o Ms. McGhee, P.O. Box 235, Neptune, New Jersey, 07754, or you can send your comments and requests via e-mail to marcus.media@yahoo.com

This is a work of fiction. The events described are imaginary, and the characters are fictitious and are not intended to represent specific living persons. Even when the settings are referred to by their true names, the incidents taking place there are entirely fictitious; the reader should not infer that the events set there ever happened.

For Guinevere

As she fled fast thro' sun and shade,
The happy winds upon her play'd,
Blowing the ringlet from the braid:
The rein with dainty fingertips,
A man had given all other bliss,
And all his worldly worth for this,
To waste his whole heart in one kiss
Upon her perfect lips.

"By and by they came to the beautiful palace in which lived the wise King, and upon being brought before him, they all shouted at once, 'Good and wise King, we have come to warn you that the sky is falling!'

'How do you know the sky is falling?' asked the King.

'Because a piece of it fell on my head!' said Chicken Little.

'Come nearer, Chicken Little,' said the King, and leaning from his velvet throne, he picked the pebble from the feathers of Chicken Little's head.

'You see it was only a little pebble and not part of the sky at all,' said the King. 'Go home in peace and do not fear because the sky cannot fall. Only rain falls from the sky.'"

Shadow In The Sky
by
Marcus McGee

CHAPTER 1

An act of Almighty God or a matter of sheer coincidence? Divine judgment or pure science? For years it had been drawing closer, the overwhelming gravitational force of the giant dragging at it for over one hundred thousand miles of an elliptical orbit that stretched 16.3 million miles. It had never been classified as a *PHA*, or a potentially hazardous asteroid, because it had always been too far away to represent a real threat to Earth. Yet if the universe is truly mechanical, then the event was ordained from the moment of creation or the Big Bang or both.

Elements of the equation had occurred many times before. Many times before, the orbits of Ganymede and Callisto had positioned the two moons directly in line during their closest approach, causing a momentary eclipse on the planet, seen as a double circle on the planet's surface. Many times before, the oblong object's orbit had eroded as it passed the planet. Many times before, Earth had reached aphelion and the longitude of the sun was beyond 95º, in the zodiacal sign of Cancer.

But from the beginning of time, the cosmic clock had been set so that at exactly 11:58 a.m. GMT, the object passed directly *between* the two planet-sized moons. It first encountered Callisto's gravity, causing it to wobble. Then it was shaken violently by Ganymede so that when at last it had cleared the moons, the huge star-like planet tried to capture it. The object's extreme velocity made capture impossible, but the grip of the planet visibly altered its trajectory for all time. The event went unnoticed on Earth hundreds of millions of miles away, a mere glitch in the infinite calculus of the universe.

Three weeks later, a mistake by a first-day trainee at a Starbucks in Maui resulted in a restless night for Dr. Helen Engstrom, chief director at the Near-Earth Asteroid Tracking observatory site at the Haleakala Crater. She had noticed the object two days earlier and had been casually concerned, but on July 23, having little else to do on a sleepless night, she did the math.

****

"So neither the FBI nor all those expert detectives you hired can figure it out?"

Davis Franklin glanced up from the screen, trying to disguise mild irritation, which tugged the top right corner of his upper lip into a subtle sneer. He sighed.

"Whoever he is, he's got to be one of the most computer-savvy people in the world. He's gotten past every security protocol and broken some of our highest-level encryptions, but we still can't figure out what he's after. If I didn't know any better, I'd say he's toying with us."

Asia smiled as she studied her husband's fascination with whatever he was reading. He was probably unaware that she was even in the room. Davis was like that. When he was working, he was absorbed in the screen before him. If he answered an inquiry, he responded from some autonomic area of his brain that enabled him to reply without breaking his concentration or even considering the question. Taking into account the indifferent nature of many of his non-responsive replies, Asia was content that this one *sounded* conversational.

Davis Franklin was the CEO and founder of Tomorrow Systems, a San Francisco based computer software company, which had become the symbol for innovation in design and application technology since the mid-1990s. Tomorrow Systems had been one of the early pioneers of human/computer interface technology. Its product line included voice recognition programs, touch screen applications, CATS (computer-assisted technology systems), dictation/translation programs and robotics. In addition, Davis was one of the world's foremost experts on computer hacking.

Years earlier, Davis left his parents, brother and a failed business in Seattle and ventured to San Jose, where he launched Tomorrow Systems. His earliest contracts were with the Department of Defense, but he quickly found custom engineering opportunities with many private colleges and university systems in the U.S. and abroad.

His huge estate in Sausalito, which he called *Cupid's Palace*, sat on the eastern coast of the peninsula, with a virtual postcard of the San Francisco skyline looming surrealistically just across the water.

Owing to his special area of expertise, his home was an interactive environment, responding to dozens of spoken commands. Robotic devices drew the drapes, opened and shut windows and doors, flushed toilets and controlled music, temperature and lighting. When Davis spoke the words "martini, dry, up," the drink would arrive fifty-five to one hundred and twenty seconds later, depending on where he was in the home.

A transport robot named Spartacus, consisting of a small board, a battery, six wheels and a storage compartment, followed a metal strip, attached to the floor under the carpet or tile, to its destination. For locations on the second and third floor, the robot used the lift. Spartacus also fetched beers, sandwiches, snacks and reading materials. If a closed door stood between the robot and its purpose, Spartacus was equipped to issue the "door, open" command remotely.

The invisible and robot servants at Cupid's Palace were part of Home Servant 6.1, a pioneering operating system developed and improved by Davis and Tomorrow Systems over ten years. The system, integrated into the home's computer circuitry, would be the prototype for a less expensive model the company planned to mass-produce and sell to middle-class households.

Home Servant was composed of five major programs and numerous ancillary sub-programs. These included Home Server, Home Bartender, Home Librarian, Home DJ/VJ and Home Host, in addition to other programs that directed the robots and robotic devices.

Perhaps the greatest innovation of Home Servant was its cassette system. The bartender cassette could be loaded with up to one hundred and fifty pre-determined, perfectly pre-mixed, pre-measured drinks. Davis plugged the cassette into the back of a console hidden in a wall. Chilled drinks and beer passed through a refrigerated coil system before filling track-fed martini and pilsner glasses in the 24x24-inch service station opening in the wall. Mixed drinks poured into ice-filled highball glasses, wine flowed from a separate cassette into wine glasses and neat drinks went into snifters.

Refrigerated dinner cassettes contained elaborate meals, with selections such as fettuccini Alfredo, bouillabaisse, sweet and sour pork and fried chicken, along with dozens of possible side orders and desserts. Hot food required forty-five minutes from confirmation of order to delivery.

Home Librarian cassettes, filled with books, periodicals and newspapers, and Home DJ/VJ, containing hundreds of CDs and DVDs, were responsive to voice commands.

The robots, robotic devices and atmosphere and censorship programs were all part of Home Host. Thus interfacing with Home Host, Davis's favorite robot, Aunt Bea, brought him piping hot gourmet meals, blackberry pie among other desserts, coffee, brandy and cigars. Still other devices ran baths, mopped or vacuumed floors and dusted the furniture.

Every room in the house held microphones, cameras, speakers and huge touch screens. Davis designed the house so that it was infinitely upgradeable, and thus with every new month, there was another robotic invention or innovation.

Cupid's Palace was operational even before Davis married Asia almost six years earlier, so Asia was as uneasy with the house as many of the people who visited. In fact, Asia usually chose manual operation over voice commands. Users spoke all verbal commands directly to Calypso, a massive mainframe computer locked in a secret, protected location outside the house. Asia didn't remember many of the commands and feared that one day Calypso would develop artificial intelligence and take over everything.

Asia glanced at one of the cameras and then at her husband who still stared into the screen.

"If I didn't know any better, I'd say you almost admire whoever it is. You seem so fascinated by him."

Not even a twitch.

"You think he's gotten to Calypso?"

Davis snapped away from the screen, turning toward his wife, fear and anger actuating his voice.

"No! Never! He could never get to Calypso. She'd never let him!"

****

"*For as the lightning cometh out of the east, and shineth even unto the west; so shall also the coming of the Son of man be.*"

Reverend Jonah Williams scanned the faces in the first two rows as he always did, hoping to gauge the degree to which the congregation was following the message.

"And verse 29. *Immediately after the tribulation of those days shall the sun be darkened, and the moon shall not give her light, and the stars shall fall from the heaven, and the powers of the heavens shall be shaken.* These are signs of his presence, Brothers and Sisters. These are the signs he said we would see."

He looked to the far left of the auditorium, spying on his fifteen-year-old son, content the boy was following in the text.

"And 30. *And then shall appear the sign of the Son of man in heaven: and then shall all the tribes of the earth mourn, and they shall see the Son of man coming in the clouds of heaven with power and great glory.* And won't that be a glorious day indeed, Brothers and Sisters? To have the privilege of seeing our Lord Jesus return!"

The great crowd responded with a medley of "Amens," "Yeses" and "Praise the Lords."

"So we have to be prepared for that day, Brothers and Sisters, because that day could come at any time. In fact, he said it would come like a thief in the night. So we have to get ourselves right, Brothers and Sisters. We have to get ourselves on the right track because we don't know when that day will come. It could be tomorrow and it could be next year. So we have to get it right. We have to live each day and each year just like they might be our last. What are we waiting for?"

Reverend Williams paused for effect.

"I'll conclude with verses 38 and 39: *For as in the days that were before the flood they were eating and drinking, marrying and being giving in marriage, until the day that Noe entered the ark, and knew not until the flood came, and took them all away. So shall also the coming of the Son of man be.* If we're on the right track, Brothers and Sisters, if we're doing the right thing, we don't have to fret his coming. We'll welcome it with open arms."

The choir rose simultaneously with the organ's upbeat introduction to *What A Friend We Have in Jesus*. Jonah Williams watched as the eighty-member chorus rocked back and forth, singing and clapping. He sighed, scanning the spacious interior of the church and the sea of over two thousand inspired faces watching the choir and swaying with the music. His eyes moved to the video control booth, where the director held his thumb up, indicating that the taping for live broadcast had gone well. Jonah inhaled, his chest struggling to contain his uplifted and overwhelmed heart.

He nodded toward Aaliyah, his pretty, young wife, who on rare occasions sang in the front row of the choir. At breakfast that morning, he had told her about a disturbing dream he had had three nights in a row, a horrific dream that involved the fiery destruction of his church. Still worse, he saw yet another son dead in the incident.

****

When the maitre d' asked Reggie if he had a preference, Reggie opted for a seat near the bar, where he could see the television. Fortunately, his wife liked football. Otherwise, he would have left her at home. Sure it was a pre-season game, but this was all Jersey. It was the Jets versus the Giants at the Meadowlands.

Layla wasn't one of those wives who merely tolerated sports to humor her husband. She was usually the loudest in the bar, and she was a fiercely competitive, obnoxious Giants fan.

Layla Reed was America's best hope for the women's pentathlon at the upcoming Olympics. At five-foot-eleven-inches, she played one season for the WNBA Sacramento Monarchs before deciding to focus on her Olympic ambitions. She was muscular and well coordinated, owing to the rigorous physical discipline enforced by husband/trainer Reggie. Her face was pretty and her shoulder-length reddish-black hair hung a little past her bare shoulders.

She and Reggie had been married for exactly one year that night, so though she looked like a walking New York Giants merchandizing display, she and Reggie were celebrating their very first anniversary at this popular Newark sports bar.

The game proved close. The Giants had just intercepted and had the ball on the Jets 38-yard-line when all the screens in the restaurant went blank. Groans and the profanity filled the sound void.

The nervous shift manager rushed to the largest screen and worked at manual adjustments when a loud, dissonant tone began from each set. After the tone, there appeared a bright blue screen with the white image of an eagle right in the middle. Within seconds, there was another series of groans as patrons recognized the presidential seal.

A non-modulated, computerized woman's voice interrupted the cacophony.

"Please stand by for an emergency message from the President of the United States."

Layla sighed.

"Aww! Couldn't this have waited till after the game?"

She raised her hands to her ears as the tone pierced the air again, and then it stopped.

"Please stand by for an emergency message from the President of the United States."

The screens flickered, making the cut to the President's face seem more like a dissolve. President Whitmore's expression was severe and strained. His eyes belied grave concern, underscored by dark half circles that defied the fastidiously applied make-up. He sat at his desk in the Oval Office, a flag and a window in the background. Reluctant to begin, he sipped from the coffee cup on his desk and spoke.

"My fellow Americans, my fellow citizens of planet Earth, I come before you today under the most dire and most extraordinary of all circumstances in human history. With a sense of deep sadness and profound frustration, I find it my duty to inform you of a cataclysmic event that occurred in the heavens over two hundred million miles away exactly eleven days ago."

Layla stood with her palm cupped to her breast in the silent bar, bracing for some horrible revelation by the President. Behind her, a nervous woman announced her own fears.

"Oh my God! What is it? What's goin on? Terrorists?"

An irritated man across the room was quick to respond.

"If you shut up, we'll all be able to find out."

The President continued.

"Over the past twelve years, scientists with NASA's Jet Propulsion Laboratory and the United States Air Force have been monitoring the sky for asteroids and comets at a Near-Earth Asteroid Tracking observatory site at the Haleakala Crater in Maui, Hawaii. It's been their job to watch the sky, identify potentially hazardous asteroids, known as PHAs, and to inform us of any danger."

In an estate just across the water from San Francisco, Asia Franklin sat with her arms crossed on the warm leather sofa, withdrawn as she stared at the large screen. The room was half-dark. Davis stood in the doorway thirty feet away, his concerned eyes glancing from his wife to the President. She called out his name when the emergency screen came up, and he had rushed from his lab. Recognizing the presidential seal, he stopped at the door, calling a command.

"VCR, gamma, record, analyze feed, seek source code."

He walked toward his wife as President Whitmore continued.

"Seven days ago, Dr. Helen Engstrom called to inform me about a major threat to Earth."

The President bowed his head and continued.

"She said that while she and colleagues have monitored many of the asteroids and other near-Earth objects in orbits that could potentially impact our planet, it was impossible to predict the consequences and influence other planets might have on these objects and their trajectories as they traveled through space."

Another labored pause.

"Thus despite all the resources we've dedicated to an early detection system and the energy invested by Dr. Engstrom and her colleagues around the world, we've all known that while the odds were long, the Earth could be faced with a disastrous event that could destroy all life on the planet."

In Los Angeles, Reverend Jonah Williams held hands with his wife and his son while they watched the broadcast. Aaliyah had served dinner minutes earlier, though no one had touched the food.

"Eleven days ago, a previously undiscovered, largely metallic object of approximately thirteen kilometers, or about eight miles wide, crossed paths with the planet Jupiter, passing between Callisto and Ganymede, two of its moons. The pass by Jupiter was recorded by cameras aboard NASA's *Galileo* spacecraft and confirmed by astronomers using NASA's Hubbell Space Telescope, as well as by Dr. Engstrom and colleagues at the Electro-Optical Deep Space Surveillance site in Maui."

President Whitmore had memorized the next portion of the text so that he could look directly into the camera.

"As a result of Jupiter's huge gravitational field, the near miss resulted in a shift in the asteroid's trajectory, which if nothing changes, puts the object on a direct collision course with Earth. According to estimates based on the projected intersect course, this object, named Nostradamus by Dr. Engstrom, will collide with our planet on August 7th next year, exactly one year from today."

The President batted his eyes, struggled to swallow from his nervous, dry mouth and continued.

"Over the past seven days, I have conferred with world leaders and scientists alike to determine if and what we, as a planet, could do to avoid such a severe, far-reaching disaster, or at least to minimize its effects. To our utter regret, we came to the conclusion that there is little we can do except maintain peace and order on Earth, provide leadership and examples of strength for our respective nations and wait."

In Times Square, the giant screen displayed the President's face and a PA system carried his voice as thousands stood watching.

"Some of you may have watched the Hollywood movies where Earth sent up a team of experts or heroes to blow the asteroid apart or to alter its trajectory. Unfortunately, this is reality. What worked in the movies can't work for us for two reasons. One, the asteroids in the movies were made of rock and ice, something that *could* be blown apart. But Nostradamus is metallic, made of nickel and iron—two heavy metals that could withstand anything we could send up there. The second factor involves the enormous velocity at which Nostradamus is traveling, roughly sixty thousand miles per hour. For that reason, the asteroid will not come into the range of our farthest-reaching weapons systems until early August. By then, it'll be too close. Any attempt to change the trajectory at that point would be futile."

Nearby in the room, just out of the line of the cameras, the President's wife, Jean, sat huddled with their two daughters. All three sobbed.

"The sad truth, my fellow Americans and citizens of the world, is that as of August 7th, or shortly thereafter, all life on Earth, or certainly all life as we know it, will cease to exist."

On the streets of New York City, the military transports began to arrive, and the men and women of the National Guard began piling out of the trucks and lining up along the street, rifles at the ready. The uniformed sergeants within the ranks called orders to soldiers who assembled and stood at attention, a few flicking their eyes toward the screen as the President spoke.

"This will be a trying year for America as a nation and indeed for each of us as individuals as we begin to consider our predicament and all the implications that come with it. But as your leader, I call on all Americans to be examples of quality and bravery as we face this ultimate test of our character and courage as the greatest nation in the history of the Earth."

Earl Krebbs flicked from one station to another, yet the image was the same: President Joe Whitmore's face was ubiquitous, the strain in his voice evident.

"At this very moment, the National Guard is setting up bases in every major city across our great nation in order to achieve a smooth transition of government. I have issued an executive order declaring martial law. Thus as of this moment, the governments of every state, city and county jurisdiction in America shall defer to federal government directives as they are issued and executed by duly appointed officers of the National Guard, by officers of the American military and by me."

Earl spat the thick, black liquid over his quid-distorted bottom lip into a stained coffee cup.

"Ultimate government takeover! Ah *knew* it!"

Earl's voice was uncharacteristically nervous as he called over his shoulder.

"Bobby! Ah'm tellin ya, ya *gatta* get in here ta hear this!"

A careful, controlled voice spoke from the other room.

"Already watchin it, Earl."

Bobby's chiseled features were barely recognizable under the green paint and black grease pencil markings. He sat at a table, his M-16 before him in pieces. Bullets were scattered on the surface to his right.

"Just like I told y'all. It was gonna happen. Just a matter of time. Let's get ready!"

Bobby aimed the remote, raising the volume of the broadcast as Whitmore continued.

"For those persons in America and abroad who might see this impending catastrophe as an opportunity for plunder and mayhem, for those who might think to exploit perceived American vulnerabilities in this time of crisis, let me issue this warning: America will answer any threat or action against her with immediate and brutal vengeance. The National Guard commanders in your respective cities have shoot-to-kill orders for rioters, looters and others who might seek to disrupt order and domestic security."

His eyes narrowed.

"The American military is on standby status to strike, with the purpose of obliterating any country or group linked to threats or actions carried out against America and Americans. There are no doubt persons and groups, domestic and abroad, who will be audacious or foolish enough to challenge America's resolve to preserve security and order. Thus, America will demonstrate her commitment to her safety and stability by making earliest reprisals swift and extremely severe. Order will be preserved."

Bobby, known formally as Robert E. Lee, sneered as he listened to the broadcast. With amazing speed and dexterity, he reassembled the M-16 and took aim at the President's image on the television set.

"He's been tryin ta do this since the beginnin of his administration. He's talkin right at us!"

He flicked the weapon's selector switch to semi-automatic mode.

"You're a liar! There ain't no asteroid out there. It's gonna be war."

Joe Whitmore looked away, signaling a transition in thought.

"Here in America, I am working on a daily basis with Federal Emergency Management Agency Director Jerrod Freech, with your respective governors and with an executive joint congressional committee consisting of twenty of your representatives and twenty of your senators to enact measures that ensure domestic security for all Americans through next August 7th."

"So much for the fuckin United States of America!"

The television exploded as the staccato shots rang out. Outside the isolated fortress, located near Mount Isabel, standing between the Salt River Range and Absaroka Ridge in the middle Rocky Mountains of Wyoming, other uniformed men stood under warm summer skies, whooping and discharging M-16s into the air.

For Reverend Jonah Williams and his family, still seated at the dinner table, the shock of the President's announcement was just beginning to register. Jonah closed his eyes and whispered a prayer.

"Lord Jesus, if thou be willing, remove this cup from me, remove this cup from me."

He stopped, took a deep breath and refocused on the television.

"First and foremost: No American family shall lose its home for its inability to make mortgage payments. You'll notice as early as tomorrow that thousands of businesses will go bust and will no longer exist. Millions of other jobs will simply become irrelevant. Analysts predict that unemployment in the next two months will be higher than fifty percent. Many of you will not have jobs through no fault of your own. Two days ago, I met with Congress in a specially convened joint session to create specific measures that will preserve domestic order. So, as of this moment, and with the unanimous support of Congress, I am issuing an executive order that will suspend all debt. You will no longer be obligated to make mortgage or car payments or pay for any other credit transaction you have made until this moment. My order ensures that there will be no foreclosures, no repossessions or other consequences that have typically resulted from your inability or unwillingness to pay."

On a split screen, television coverage displayed Whitmore's image, the scene at Times Square in New York and the scene along the steps outside the Capitol in Washington, D.C. as the President continued.

"On the other end, Congress has also authorized me to issue an executive order that will in effect suspend all credit. As of this moment, traditional credit as you know it—your American Express cards, your Visas, your MasterCards—they are no longer good for purchase transactions. Most of America will operate on a cash exchange basis only. There very well may be *some* private businesses that might establish non-traditional credit for customers, but as a rule, you'll have to buy what you want with actual cash."

The camera backed, revealing Jean Whitmore and daughters, twenty-two-year-old Beth and eighteen-year-old Susan, sitting just to the President's right.

"And where will Americans get this cash? Well, while millions of jobs will be lost, many more will be created. Millions of American workers will be needed to assist in the orderly distribution of food, fuel and other necessities. We'll need workers to build housing for many rural Americans who will have to relocate to the larger cities for provisions and protection. We'll need social workers, counselors, psychologists, administrators and security personnel. We'll need artists who'll assist in the erection of a national monument. We'll need people to assist our scientists and researchers. There will be guaranteed cash available for those who are willing and able to work for it. And for the unwilling and unable, there will be guaranteed food, shelter and security."

The scenes in New York and Washington dissolved, enlarging the shot from the Oval Office. Joe Whitmore stopped, glanced toward his wife, forced a strained smile and continued.

"Just this morning, Jean asked me why I had to go before the American people with this unsettling and devastating news today, so soon after even I had heard about it. She wondered if it would have been a better thing if the government just sort of sat on this information for a while. She asked me if it would have been a better thing for the government to either deny the asteroid's existence or at least hold off telling the American people about it until the last possible moment. My answer to her was the same answer I make to many of you out there who are probably upset, if not angry, with me for coming to you with this alarming news. Let me ask you these questions:"

He glanced over at Jean.

"What if I *hadn't* come before you today? What if tomorrow you started hearing about Nostradamus on the Internet from scientists and astronomers in other countries around the world who knew about it? What if millions of Americans could confirm independently the asteroid's existence in spite of the fact that their president and top government officials were either lying to them or refusing to verify its existence? How long would it be before mistrust, chaos and anarchy would ensue?"

On a split screen, the other side displayed live coverage of a large riot. The subtitles identified the scene as Paris, France. Armed forces were firing into the crowd. Coverage ended after a woman was shot in the face. The left side of her face had exploded onto two horrified children. Unaware of events in Europe, Whitmore concluded.

"The truth, my fellow Americans, is that I had no choice but to be honest with you. I had no choice but to put the truth before you, to put the government's proposals before you and to put my faith in you as Americans. The truth is I had no choice but to *lead* America in this time of crisis. As Americans, it is incumbent on us to lead the world through this last year as we grapple with destiny. We must not waste this year in sadness, regret or misery, but we must find joy, fascination and peace in every moment we live from here on. A great American writer, Steven Vincent Benet, spoke volumes when he wrote, 'Life is not lost by dying; life is lost minute by minute, day by day, in all the thousand small, uncaring ways.'"

Whitmore stood, came around the desk and approached the camera.

"After having met extensively with FEMA Director Freech, I strongly urge all Americans to remain in their homes for the next few days to allow for the smooth transition of government and to allow FEMA and other agencies to set up distribution facilities. The National Guard will strictly enforce a seven p.m. to seven a.m. curfew. If you absolutely must go out, keep your excursions brief, direct and within the curfew parameters."

He smiled and sat on the desk.

"From here on, every evening at eight p.m. Eastern Standard Time, I will come before you, the American people, to apprise you of the status of this emergency, to strengthen you and to bring us all together as a nation in this time of crisis. So until tomorrow at eight o'clock, I'm asking all Americans to draw on their reserves of patience, composure and, above all, character. God help us all. Good night."

Chapter 2

Asia cried herself to sleep where she sat on the couch during the broadcast. A half-full bottle of Ketel One vodka stood on the table at her left. Spartacus had brought the first two martinis, but he took too long and Asia grew impatient. It took some doing, but she managed to bypass Calypso's insistent requests for a spoken password and access the liquor room by using a code key. Right after the President's announcement, Davis disappeared behind the locked door of his computer room.

"This is great!" she shouted, pounding on the door as she went by, vodka bottle in her hand.

"On a night like tonight, on a night you should be out here *comforting* me, you're in there with that bitch!"

Calypso's pleasant voice responded from speakers in the hallway.

"*Asia—profanity is unacceptable.*"

Asia's nostrils flared and her eyes narrowed to slits as she glared toward the speaker.

"Oh fuck you, Calypso. If I could trash you, I'd crash you, bitch."

"*Asia, profanity is unacceptable. Asia, profanity is unacceptable.*"

Asia kicked the door one last time as she headed back to the couch.

"Censorship, disable. Gamma, camera, disable. Gamma, microphone, disable! Gamma, music, Hendrix, Purple Haze, repeat mode, very loud."

Huge television on mute, she sank onto the couch and drifted off to sleep as she watched disturbing images of chaos and mayhem from around the world.

The phone rang at five a.m., startling her from troubled slumber.

"Phone, answer," Asia shouted, forgetting she had turned off the microphone.

"Phone, answer!"

The phone continued to ring until she stumbled around the room and found it next to a pillow on the love seat.

"Hullo?"

Suddenly she was awake, though nervous.

"Oh, oh sure! It's no problem, Sir. I'll get him."

She looked toward the speaker.

"Gamma, microphone, camera, on. Pi, intercom, open."

Cupping the mouthpiece of the phone, she spoke toward the microphone array on the ceiling.

"Davis? Davis, I know you can hear me. Are you there?"

The huge image of Davis appeared on screen. His giant face seemed tired and annoyed as he peered toward his wife. He had been up all night.

"Asia? Asia, you all right?"

She sighed, forcing a smile.

"No, the world's gonna blow up and I spent the night all by myself, again. I'm just fine."

It was a chronic problem. Davis was a compulsive worker, addicted to his latest project, whatever it might be. Yet he insisted Asia knew about his obsession with work when she agreed to become his wife. Hoping to avoid an argument, he ignored the sarcasm.

"I'm, I'm sorry Asia. Now you did call me to tell me something?"

She raked her hair away from her face with stiffened fingers.

"Yes, I did. You have a phone call."

He seemed incredulous. He never took phone calls at home.

"Direct whomever it is to the office. I can't talk right now."

She paused, hoping to gauge his reaction.

"Not even to the President of the United States?"

****

"How many did they kill?"

"Twenty-three in all today. Over fifty citywide yesterday."

Aaliyah sighed.

"At this rate, there won't be *any* black boys left when it's all over. Then again, does it matter? We're all supposed to be dead in a year anyway."

Jonah carefully hung his hat on the rack. He closed his eyes as he sank onto the couch, wagging his head.

"On the one hand, it's martial law out there. The military has to keep order."

He clenched his teeth, drawing in a deep breath.

"I watched it. They lined those kids up, forced them to lie down on their stomachs, and then, one by one, they went down the line. Rifle right in the back of the head. Pow! After they shot the first boy, the rest went to panicking, but they forced them back down, and one by one, they shot them."

He looked over at his wife, blinking back tears.

"Last boy they shot, Reverend Curtis's son, Zachary. Think he was maybe fourteen? He cried like a little baby. I remember the night that boy was born."

He stood, searched for the remote and aimed it at the television.

"It's a tragedy, and if I had a solution, I'd be the first to speak up. But those kids are going crazy out there. It's got to be done, otherwise gangs would run everything. Folks like us wouldn't stand a chance."

News footage on the set was a graphic montage of violence and panic from around the world. A mass riot had erupted in Pakistan, resulting in the military spraying the crowds with rounds from automatic weapons, two hundred and eighty-nine dead. A similar incident in Liverpool left forty-four dead and many more wounded after a second day of looting and burning in the troubled city. A horrific explosion had obliterated one entire wall of a synagogue in Jerusalem, leaving one hundred and twelve dead and hundreds injured.

The government of Brazil had collapsed, and the country's major metropolitan areas were under the control of feuding military leaders who exercised imperial powers with horrendous cruelty. In South America, there was no apt way to measure the death and human suffering.

Bloated bodies choked up tributaries to the Amazon, and the stench of burning flesh rose twice a day in many cities, a sacrifice to Tezcatlipoca, the god of night, the god of sorcery, confusion and chaos, and to Mictlantecuhtli, Lord of Mictlan, the god who consumed human sacrifice. Civil war had erupted in Bosnia-Herzegovina, threatening the stability of Greece, Lithuania and the Czech Republic.

In the United States, the government of Wyoming had yielded to demands from a group called MAPS, or Militias of the American Plains States, allowing them to establish a separate government in the western state.

Los Angeles was a war zone with U.S. forces encamped downtown. Heavy artillery had been used to shell an office complex at 7th and Figueroa, the alleged headquarters of the West Side Crips, a notorious gang that had claimed responsibility for assassinating two city councilmen and the governor's spokesperson. Gang members killed eleven police officers and five soldiers in the standoff. A reporter detailed the execution of fourteen captured gang members by the Army, and among those, young Zachary.

Jonah bowed his head as he listened to the story.

"It was a black Army officer who gave the order. You would think he would have thought to give Zachary a break. He was just a baby."

He looked toward the hallway, thinking of his own son.

"Where's Dexter?"

Aaliyah cringed and closed her eyes, preparing for the disagreement that was certain to follow.

"He's over at the Brown's. He'll be back in the morning."

Jonah stared at his wife in disbelief, his countenance distorted by anger and irritation.

"Liyah, didn't I tell you?"

He stopped, taking a deep breath.

"Didn't I ask you not to let him go over there? I was very specific about that. Why would you disrespect me by doing the exact opposite of what I asked?"

She turned away, crossing her arms.

"You had it right the first time. You didn't ask. You *told* me like you always do, like you were some dictator and I was your lowly subject."

She caught his eyes.

"I mean, do you ever consider what I want? Have you ever thought about what Dexter might want?"

"He doesn't know what he wants. He's fifteen years old."

He felt a dense cloud of resentment, which lingered even after she brushed past him on her way to the bedroom. She stopped at the door, calling back.

"And I don't know what I want because I'm a woman, right?"

The door slammed behind her, leaving a brief silence in its wake. Then a voice on the television set became audible.

The running story focused on the steady stream of people migrating from rural areas to the big cities. The streets of Chicago were full of homeless refugees from small cities and communities in La Salle and Kendall counties in Illinois and from Jasper and Warren counties in Indiana. Frightened families came from as far away as Chickasaw County in Iowa and Freeborn County in Minnesota. The Army had set up a huge camp by Lake Michigan, but in three days it became filled to capacity.

Hospital officials warned of potential epidemics and disease associated with the overcrowding and poor sanitation. There had been more than two-dozen cases of *E. coli* infection, caused by human fecal solids in the lake, on the streets and in parks throughout the city. New York, Philadelphia, Washington, D.C., Miami, Salt Lake City and Los Angeles were experiencing similar hazards.

Reluctant at first, Jonah had allowed fifty families to occupy space at his church, with the stipulation that they vacate the church an hour before all services. His congregation had grown threefold, as had his influence in the city. By circumstance, he was emerging as the pastor of Los Angeles, the father of the city.

As one of the city's most prominent leaders, he felt the weight of thousands of troubled refugees and parishioners who sought his guidance daily. His television audience, which had spread across the nation, would mushroom from ten thousand to three million within the next few weeks.

On Sunday, his anxious audience awaited a message that would deal with the asteroid that threatened to end all life on Earth. In earnest, he had prayed to his God for direction. Yet, for the first time in his life, he couldn't "feel" God listening. It was as if God wasn't there anymore. It worried him. He walked toward the television and turned it off. Then he yanked down his tie and unfastened the top two buttons of his shirt.

Solemn, humble, he eased down onto a chair in his adjacent study. Closing his eyes, he drew his palms together, touching his nose with both index fingers. Rocking, Jonah prayed again.

****

"Welcome to the Lazarus Project. I take it you've been briefed?"

Davis scanned the three-story ceiling of the cavernous Cheyenne Mountain underground enclosure, considering possibilities for and signs of interface technology. The place needed Calypso.

"I know nothing. No one's told me anything about it. What is it?"

The officious beadle of a man, who was striding at least three paces ahead of Davis, spoke without looking back, though he did not answer the question.

"Then we'll schedule a briefing in thirty minutes. Certainly, you've received, read, signed, notarized and submitted the non-disclosure contract. You do realize that you won't be able to discuss anything you learn at this facility with anyone, and that includes your wife and parents, don't you?"

Davis stopped as the irksome man continued walking and talking.

"Why am I talking to you?"

The man stopped, never turning as Davis continued.

"I mean, who the hell are you? And where are your manners?"

The man turned back toward Davis abruptly, his matter-of-fact voice conveying arrogance and efficiency.

"Dr. Don Smock, and I distinctly remember saying 'welcome' to you when you arrived. Here—you'll obviously need one of *these*."

He handed Davis a small, wooden lacquered box. It was three inches long, 1½ inches wide and 1½ inches tall. It seemed like a miniature coffin. Indeed, it was a small casket. Davis examined it and finally opened it, only to find that it was empty.

"What is it?"

"It's a place for you to put your ego until we've accomplished our mission. We've got a lot of work to do, Mr. Franklin. Your ego would only get in the way."

Davis sneered toward the irritating man who turned and led him down a long hallway with glossy floors. They walked on in the hollow, echoing corridor until they reached a door near the end of the hall. The doctor punched a seven-digit code to open a large door, calling back to Davis as he entered.

"But don't feel too bad about needing that box, Mr. Franklin. Just wait till you see mine."

Davis saw it the instant he entered Smock's office. It was sitting on a desk in full view. He understood as he looked back toward Dr. Smock's uncharacteristic grinning face.

"Have I made my point?"

There behind the desk, against the wall on the left, stood a lacquered box that looked like the one he gave Davis in every way, except it was six feet long, three feet wide and three feet high.

Chapter 3

"Well, is there a possibility that the government could expand the *space station* and keep a small group up there?"

Don Smock, the project's unflappable director, paused a moment, massaged the bridge of his nose in the place where his glasses usually sat, and answered.

"Let's not get ahead of ourselves, Davis. It was one of our early considerations, but then event projections began to come in from science contingency teams in Washington. They're predicting that, while Nostradamus will not destroy the Earth, it will bring on a cosmic winter that could last over three hundred and fifty years. Right now, we don't have the logistics in place on the station to sustain human life for that long, let alone the animal and plant species that humans would have to depend on if we were ever to repopulate the planet."

Davis looked from Don Smock's face to the expressions of the four other men and two women at the table. It was apparent that all six had resigned themselves to the conclusion that all life on Earth was destined for destruction.

Until that moment, Davis held onto the faith that somewhere on Earth there would be survivors. He was certain that the United States government had some miraculous technology at its disposal that would save the planet at the last possible moment, but it seemed the government's top scientists knew better.

Taking a deep breath, he resigned the last of his hope, directing his question toward the director.

"Okay, so what is Life Ark?"

Smock, director of the Lazarus Project, slid a huge notebook across the table toward Davis.

"Back in 1986, at about the same time that scientists and astronomers began to acknowledge and explore the reality of potentially hazardous asteroids, or *PHAs*, the government assembled a think tank to deal with various impact contingencies, many involving asteroids of the same general proportions and composition as Nostradamus."

Scanning one of the introductory pages of the notebook, Davis saw the image of Nostradamus for the first time. It seemed like a bumpy, elongated potato, sprayed with splotchy gray paint. He glanced back up as Dr. Smock continued.

"After analyzing the group's findings and recommendations, the Pentagon and the National Security Council created special committees to draft a series of plans dealing with a wide range of asteroid impact possibilities. The potential hazards of these predictable Earth impacts were placed on a chart called the Engstrom scale, ranging from .01, which could be a barely noticeable meteor shower, to 9.99, which would include impacts with objects as large as, if not larger than, Earth. The smaller numbers indicate the potential damage of objects that would have little effect on the planet, while the larger numbers represent objects that would cause varying degrees of damage to the planet, ranging from the temporary eradication of life on Earth to the complete obliteration of the planet. Lights."

On that cue, the room went dark and the image of a chart was flashed onto a large screen in front of Davis. It was obvious Smock had done this presentation many times before.

"On the Engstrom scale, slightly more accurate than the Torino scale, the threshold size for an asteroid that would end all human life is 3.15, while the threshold for the destruction of all life on the planet is 5.69. On that scale, Nostradamus comes in at 4.26. At thirteen kilometers wide, Nostradamus will cause plate tectonic instability, resulting in earthquakes that will be off the Richter scale and volcanic fissures and eruptions on every major continent. In turn, many of the more pronounced maritime earthquakes will result in super tsunamis, huge tidal waves that will surge seven hundred miles inland on some continents."

The screen displayed the fiery destruction of New York City. Panicked people ran about like ants during a breach of their nest.

"Most of the human population of Earth will be lost within minutes of the impact on August 7th, with the rest lost in the cold, dark days that will follow. The majority of plant life will suffer the same fate, though many seeds and spores could be expected to survive in dormancy."

The next image that flashed on the screen was a dark portrait of a barren landscape. Everything, the rocks and the dead trees that still stood, was covered with heavy, black soot. Portions of ice peeked through the charcoal blanket covering a frozen lake. Two cockroaches met on a dead branch in the foreground, communicating with extended antennae. In the black sky, a slightly brighter area suggested the position of the hidden sun.

"This is an artist's depiction of nuclear winter, based on Carl Sagan's theory of events following a nuclear war. The same basic concept holds true for a *PHA* impact, which would bring about cosmic winter, only the effects of cosmic winter would be much more dramatic. Some scientists believe that after the last major meteor strike sixty-five million years ago at Chicxulub on the Yucatan peninsula, cosmic winter endured for over seventy years. According to present projections, which are subject to adjustment, Nostradamus will strike the planet on August 7th at approximately 5:33 p.m. GMT somewhere in northern Romania."

At Davis's left sat Dr. Helen Engstrom, chief director at the Near-Earth Asteroid Tracking observatory site at the Haleakala Crater. She had introduced herself to Davis a few minutes before the briefing, commenting that she admired him for the innovation he had brought to the computer industry. She was attractive for an older woman who wore glasses. While it was obvious her blonde hair should have been gray, her body was shapely and tan.

Davis had also met Dr. Thomas Ross, chief director of the Air Force Research Laboratory Space Vehicles Directorate. Davis thought Thomas seemed young for the unwieldy title vested upon him. Davis was just about sure he himself was the only non-doctor in the group.

Dr. Smock responded to the next image on screen.

"The resultant cloud of dust and ash will rise to obscure the sun within a matter of days. Within a week of the impact, the plankton bloom, the basis of life within the seas, will disappear, causing a chain reaction that will cause mass extinction in Earth's oceans. Terrestrial life will disappear just as suddenly. Mammals, birds, reptiles, amphibians and fish—all the various species of these major divisions of life will experience a sudden and massive extinction, like the dinosaurs, and like the biblical flood."

The red-filtered image on the screen depicted a *Tyrannosaurus rex* ripping at a triceratops' viscera, while in the background, a huge asteroid streaked toward the Earth.

"This may very well be a repetition of a similar event that happened on Earth hundreds of millions of years ago and possibly as recently as four or five thousand of years ago in the case of the ancient flood. Some insects will survive and many worms will survive. In the deep seas, perhaps some species of photogenic fishes, sponges and mollusks will survive."

A split screen depicted a wintering grapevine on the left and an encysted worm on the right.

"Certainly many plants and microorganisms have the ability to go dormant until the sun returns. But for all intents and purposes, all flesh on Earth will perish, and the Earth will be uninhabitable for nearly four hundred years."

Next came the image of a man, mummified, frozen in a cryocooler. Sealed in a silver colored cryosuit, he looked similar to the aliens depicted in Hollywood movies.

"This ability to go dormant, or stasis, is the key for species' survival on earth. Thus if a group of humans, like some plants, insects and microorganisms, could in effect 'go dormant' for the period of darkness and cold on Earth, then it is possible for that group to survive Nostradamus and restore a human population on the planet. Lights."

Don Smock looked toward Davis matter-of-factly.

"You wanted to know what Life Ark is, Davis. It's a super shuttle, equipped with cryocoolers, that will eventually attach itself to the space station. It will contain forty-four humans. At a separate facility on Earth, there will be preserved samples of many plant and animal species as well as complete history, science, technology, religion and humanities databases encompassing all that man has ever known and accomplished on Earth."

Dr. Smock smiled as his eyes scanned the faces in the room.

"In four hundred years, when the Earth is again inhabitable, Life Ark will disengage from the station and return to the planet, where we as humans get to start all over again. Maybe we'll get it right the next time."

By this time, Davis's mind was reeling. He was well ahead of the doctor, already plotting a way to save Calypso. From the moment of the President's announcement about Nostradamus, his first concern had been protecting Calypso. Under normal circumstances, he would have never considered working with the federal government, but this offer presented with the possibility of saving her. He needed to know how much authority he would be given.

"And what will I be doing?"

"You'll oversee the writing of all computer programs and integrate the robotic systems aboard the Ark. Lazarus, our Earth-based computer for this project, is located in the Crypt, a subterranean fortress here in Colorado. We've made arrangements for you and your family to live there from here on."

Davis nodded, struggling to disguise his eagerness to access the closely guarded Department of Defense military computer system. Dr. Smock stood, triggering others at the table to rise.

"I'm not sure if you've met the rest of our elite team, Davis. You've got Dr. Helen Engstrom on your left. She and her team will be tracking Nostradamus from several locations on Earth as it approaches. They've already launched a probe equipped with cameras that will intersect with it and follow the asteroid into Earth's atmosphere. And you've met Dr. Ross? He and Dr. Matsumata of the Space Technology Advanced Research Center will oversee the engineering, construction, implementation and initial operations of the super shuttle."

The Japanese scientist bowed toward Davis and extended his hand as Smock continued.

"Across from you is Dr. Isabel Benoit, certainly one of the world's most prominent geneticists. The gene separation processes she pioneered in the 90s proved indispensable to scientists working on the Human Genome Project. She will be responsible for screening potential Ark candidates for defect and disease, and she'll oversee collection and testing of all genetic materials to be stored in the Ark."

Dr. Benoit smiled and coolly looked away.

"And the two gentlemen on your right, Chief Engineer Charles Wright and Colonel Ryan Brainbeck, are from the NASA Space Shuttle Program. With the assistance of the United States Air Force, they will be responsible for flying top-secret missions to and from the space station."

He handed Davis a golden zip drive, encased in plastic.

"Everything you'll need to know about this project and your colleagues is right here. We meet every morning at 0600."

He checked his watch, tapping it.

"Well Ladies and Gentlemen, let's get back to work."

As the men and women filed out the room, Don Smock lingered, signaling for Davis to approach. He spoke in a whisper.

"Quid pro quo, Davis. I invited you in. Now there's a good chance you and your family will be spared on Judgment Day. We needed someone with your expertise, and I chose you for what you bring to the project. While you actually owe me nothing, perhaps you could satisfy my professional curiosity about something."

Davis's eyes narrowed, signaling suspicion.

"What's that?"

"Calypso. Calypso *intrigues* me. I'd like to get to know Calypso. I want you to bring her to the Crypt."

Chapter 4

The huge tanker roared as its driver struggled to match the gear with the grade. Most drivers experienced a brief period of adjustment in the moment right after delivering loads. As the truck exited the gate, another truck, just like it, pulled up to the entrance gate. A uniformed guard carrying an M-16 came out of the booth and approached its driver.

"State your name."

"Jake Stanton."

"I'll need to see your ID, registration and clearance papers."

The driver lit a cigarette and sighed as he blew over his right shoulder. He had seen this nervous kid before, and it was the exact same routine. The guard would study the papers and punch a code into a hand-held computer. Then he would climb onto the truck and open the tank to check its contents. Finally, he would appear at the window, return the ID and registration, and recite the following,

"Please be informed that you are leaving the former United States of America and you are entering the New Republic, a new and sovereign nation under God, a nation loyal to the Constitution of the former United States of America and to the ideals of America's Founding Fathers. We are committed to protecting the lives and rights of our citizens and will fight to the death for freedom and liberty."

"Yeah, yeah."

As Jake watched the guard grow smaller and smaller in the side rear-view mirror, he felt bad for being rude. It wasn't that he disagreed with Robert E. Lee and the MAPS (Militias of the American Plains States) council. It just bothered him that so many young people, especially young boys, had left their homes and families to join Lee's ranks. The guard with the rifle had to be sixteen or seventeen years old at best. What did he know about freedom and liberty?

It was sad really, Jake thought. But then, with the asteroid coming and all, these young people needed something to believe in, right? What bothered Jake most was these kids in uniform reminded him of another troubled era in human history, complete with overzealous, idealistic kids with big guns and fancy uniforms. He couldn't put his finger on why, but it was unnerving. Something wasn't right about Robert E. Lee and his New Republic.

****

For Robert Edward Lee, what started in November six years earlier as an angry protest against the government and the IRS, who had closed his father's business and impounded family property, had grown into a major movement.

Indeed, less than two months after Whitmore's announcement, Lee and seven hundred and fifty thousand followers, over half of these under twenty years of age, had declared their independence and secession from the United States of America. They called their new nation the New Republic of America and elected Robert E. Lee as its first president.

Although the majority of the nearly five hundred new citizens per day were young people, many others were refugees and defectors from the United States military. According to Lee through a spokesperson, a retired U.S. Army general, two defected Marine colonels and many others from the "former American" armed forces were acting as military commanders and advisors for the newly formed country.

Lee was born in Monroe County in Alabama, near a town called Burnt Corn. He was the illegitimate son of the popular mayor, Leland Lee, and Trudy Culpepper, a sixteen-year-old servant working in the Lee household.

Carrying little Robert Edward under one arm and a brown paper bag stuffed with a clean pair of panties, a jar of peanut butter and a small framed picture of the mayor under the other, Trudy got on a Greyhound bus and headed down south to Mobile. The baby was sick again.

They slept at the station the first night and at a homeless shelter for two weeks before pretty Trudy met Billy Dare, the owner of a busy hardware store in town. Billy was forty and divorced, but he fell in love with Trudy and her youth. He had only known her for six days when he married her at the church. Childless in his first union, Billy took to Robert Edward and formally adopted him, though Trudy insisted that the baby should keep "his real daddy's" last name.

Thus Robert Edward grew up with a degree of privilege since Billy Dare, though not wealthy, made a good living in the hardware business. Billy taught the boy to love his country, to love his God and to be gallant at all times.

Good-looking and athletic, Robert Edward, or Bobby as friends and family called him, got a football scholarship to the University of Alabama at Tuscaloosa, where he started as quarterback during his sophomore year. After an injury during his junior year, he left both the team and the school and joined the Army.

As a member of an elite Army Rangers team, he went to Saudi Arabia in early August 1990 to stop the Iraqi invasion of Kuwait. Ironically, he was more like his mayoral father than he would have ever imagined. In November, the Kuwaiti Emir personally visited the Special Forces commander, carrying with him purported "evidence" and punishment demands for the rape of the Emir's sixteen-year-old niece.

During the brief trial, Robert Edward insisted that he hadn't had sex with the girl and then, after he realized she was pregnant, that the sex was consensual. To Robert Edward's surprise, instead of defending one of its own, the government "was totally kissing up to those Arab bastards!"

When the trial ended, Robert Edward was court-martialed and shipped back to the United States to face his mother and grief-stricken, disappointed Billy Dare. He spent a year imprisoned at Fort Leavenworth after he returned.

If that wasn't disgraceful enough, the government launched an assault on Billy Dare next, accusing him of tax evasion and fraud. When Bobby left for the military, his parents seemed young, healthy and vibrant. However, on the day he arrived home, both seemed broken, eyes glazed over, devoid of spirit. They were staying at a filthy hotel because the government had shut down the business and impounded their house, their car and most of their earthly possessions.

It wasn't right. Billy was nothing but a gentleman. He always paid his taxes. The problem turned out to be a mistake by the accounting firm that processed his returns, but the government didn't care. Billy loved his country, but the "compromised" government of the United States kept "beatin up on him and pesterin him till one day he just sat down and had a stroke. He didn't live to see the IRS admit that he hadn't done nothin wrong, that it was their mistake. He just died of grief." Doctors diagnosed Trudy, Bobby's mother, with vaginal cancer a year later.

Disillusioned and angry, Robert Edward began drinking to excess. People figured he got drunk so easily because his paternal grandmother was a full-blooded Shoshone Indian. He got a job, miles up north in Fountain, where his mother had family.

He worked as a deputy for High Sheriff Earl Krebbs, his cousin by his mother's sister. Living out in the country in the dilapidated old family home with his mother and a crazy, thieving uncle, Robert drank himself senseless every night on Jack Daniel's Tennessee whiskey.

One night when he was drunk, Robert shot a man for speeding, only to find out that the man had ignored the siren because he was rushing his wife to the hospital. When the deputy's gun discharged in the man's face, she went instantly into delivery and had the baby on the spot. Robert Edward swore many times the gun went off by accident and promised to take care of the woman and her child, but everyone knew the truth: Bobby Lee was a drunken Indian who had no business carrying a gun. Yet the incident changed him.

He never took a drink after that November night. He quit cold turkey. In sobriety he realized that his family's problems and his drinking were not the result of some defect within his own person.

A large part of the problem was the United States government. The government had capitulated at the trial in Kuwait, refusing in any way to support an American soldier risking his life overseas. The government had cost him disgrace and incarceration.

The government had attacked Billy Dare, the only father Bobby had ever known, and the most decent and honest man in the world. The government had, without cause or evidence, gone in and impounded Billy's life savings. The government raped and shut down his business. They took Billy's rental properties and broke his heart and spirit.

And finally, the government had forced Bobby's mother, Trudy, to spend her middle age in poverty, pain and squalor, condemning her to suffer from vaginal cancer in a broken-down shack.

The government was the problem. Yet the Founding Fathers never meant for it to be that way. According to the U.S. Constitution, the government made a guarantee that the American people are guaranteed freedom and liberty, not the brutal mob-style treatment his family had received from the IRS. Like the mob, the government leaned on his family and took everything without considering the consequences.

The government was leaning on many white families in the South and in the American Plains states, but they didn't lean on the rich and the minorities. No, instead the government sent young men to their deaths in places like Saudi Arabia and Kuwait to protect the interests of rich friends.

That's why the government hadn't supported him at his trial. They were in bed with the Kuwaiti government and all the rich American and multinational companies making money over there. What the *god-damned* Emir wanted, the *god-damned* Emir got.

Bobby, along with friends, had read about the Trilateral Commission, a group of rich Americans, Europeans and Japanese who wanted to rule the world. Many of the rich Americans from the Commission were heavily involved in government. Thus these rich Americans, the Rockefellers, the Volckers and such, didn't care about the American people or the aims of America's Founding Fathers. They only wanted more money and consolidate power.

According to powerful evidence that Bobby observed with his own eyes, these rich Americans were willing to sacrifice America and her ideals to rich foreigners in order to achieve a one-world government run by the Commission. That's why the government had gone to hell. The interests and rights of decent Americans had become secondary to some underhanded globalization plan.

That's why Robert Edward, along with cousin Earl Krebbs, formed the White Knights of the American Constitution, a militia group dedicated to preserving the intent of the Founding Fathers on that day when the government of America was officially given over to foreign interests. Robert had the military experience, the good looks, the charisma and the leadership ability, while Earl had big money and an armory stocked with weapons in a remote complex near Fountain.

Thus with Colonel Earl Krebbs beside him, Robert began training a group of young men that would form the major division of an army. This army would launch the second American Revolution for freedom, life and liberty.

Robert married Rebecca Lee Scott, the same woman whose husband he fatally wounded in the drunken accident. He raised, as his own, the child born that night and another boy from Rebecca's first marriage.

When President Whitmore spoke to the nation and world in August, affirming that a massive asteroid named Nostradamus would slam into the Earth, Robert Edward denounced the notion. He called the warning and plan "a cruel government hoax, crafted in Hollywood," a government takeover and "the final capitulation of the American government to foreigners and the shadowy Trilateral Commission." He warned the American people to do whatever was necessary to protect their liberty and their possessions.

He called on all the militias in the Plains states of Colorado, Oklahoma, Wyoming, Utah, Kansas, Arkansas, Tennessee and Missouri to unite at New Lexington, his fortress near Mount Isabel in the mountains of western Wyoming. He also invited conservative, anti-government militias from Idaho, Montana, Mississippi and Alabama.

At a conference in late August, the newly formed MAPS, or Militias of the American Plains States, under new Articles of Confederation, elected Robert E. Lee as its first president. By mid-September, the New Republic of America announced its formal secession from the "former United States of America," publishing the following words in the nation's largest surviving newspapers:

> *Governments are instituted among Men, deriving their just powers from the consent of the governed. That whenever any Form of Government becomes destructive of these ends, it is the Right of the People to alter or to abolish it, and to institute a new Government, laying its foundation on such principles and organizing its powers in such form, as to them shall seem most likely to effect their Safety and Happiness. But when a long train of abuses and usurpations, pursuing invariably to the same object, evinces a design to reduce them under absolute Despotism, it is their right, it is their duty, to throw off such Government, and to provide new Guards for their future security.*
>
> *The New Republic of America—Welcoming new citizens at New Lexington*

http://www.newlexington.nra.com

In the weeks that followed, a slow trickle of disaffected people began to arrive at New Lexington. One of these new citizens was Anton Bunch, the billionaire owner of a national supermarket chain who, in anonymity, offered to finance "an appeal to former-America's youth," who would be the future of the new nation. Through an involved series of Internet ads and websites, the campaign was so effective that, by mid-September, the migration of America's youth to New Lexington had become a national phenomenon.

****

At the road division, another teenager with an M-16 waved Jake Stanton's truck in the direction of two other people at a docking station, along the edge of a forested area. An older man in a white lab jacket sat at a table next to a teen in military clothing. There were a few testing kits on the table before them.

After pulling into the makeshift dock, Jake cut the engine and waited. Through the side mirror, he watched the teen open the valve on the tank to obtain a sample, which he delivered to the man at the table.

The test was performed and approved, and a suction hose was attached to the truck's tank. Within twenty minutes, the tank was empty and Jake was cleared to go. He glanced around at the surroundings, sketching the last details of a boulder and a fallen tree as landmarks.

This was the fourth separate location he had delivered to in two weeks. Wherever they were storing it had to be within that perimeter. They certainly were careful if nothing else. The teen with the M-16 peered into the window and saw him drawing.

"Open your window, now!"

Jake shut his eyes, sighed rolled down the window.

"Yes?"

"What's that you're drawing?"

"I'm an artist. I get bored sitting here waiting. I draw."

The young man reached into the cab and grabbed the sketch.

"Give me that!"

Jake thought to start the truck and make a run for it, but he knew he would never make it to the gate.

"What's your name?"

"Jake Stanton."

"Give me your keys and your ID."

Jake pulled the keys from the ignition and his ID from the visor and relinquished them.

"Wait here."

The young man returned a few minutes later with the older man and another guard. He yanked the door open.

"Mr. Stanton, under martial law, you are now under arrest for the crime of high treason against the New Republic of America. You have the right to a defense after we've had the chance to investigate your actions and background. If you don't come out clean, you will be executed immediately."

The guard shifted the firing switch.

"Get out of the truck. Now!"

Chapter 5

There were six news vans parked along the street, just outside the designated parking area. Five had satellite dishes attached to their roofs. There was no space available in parking lots and at curbsides for ten blocks away on that sunny Sunday morning in Los Angeles.

Inside one of the vans, a gray-haired, bearded technician was engaged in a hardware check with a cameraman located inside the church. He slammed the door to mute the loud, sensationalized lead-in in progress outside the vehicle.

In her typical exaggerated style, the easily recognizable blonde KNBC reporter described the standing-room-only scene inside the vast church and the seven hundred or more people outside who would watch and hear the address on remote monitors and speakers placed high on scaffolds.

As her voice yielded way, another reporter, an older black male, described the expected objectives of the address. He was speaking live to news commentators located at his home studio in Atlanta, commenting about what Reverend Jonah Williams needed to accomplish with the speech if he was going to maintain and build his following.

A third reporter interviewed one of the church officials about Reverend Williams' community involvement and his charity toward the city's youth, many of whom were struggling with the reality of their imminent destruction.

In a private room on the left side of the stage, Aaliyah Williams stood against the wall with her arms crossed, her neck stiffly holding her face in opposition to her husband. Her fifteen-year-old son, Dexter, sat at a table with an attractive young woman, Brenda Brown, his sixteen-year-old girlfriend.

"Look Jonah, we're not getting anywhere here. I think we need table this discussion until after you've done your speaking out there. You're obviously upset. You've got a big job to do today."

Jonah's shoulders slumped as he closed his eyes and drew a deep breath. He nodded, looking at his wife.

"You're right, Lee."

Then he spoke toward the children.

"Like I was saying, you kids need to pick up your Bibles and reread First Corinthians, chapter 7, verses 29-35. In the meantime, Dexter, I don't want you going back over to the Browns. You understand?"

Dexter looked toward his mother, never answering or viewing his father. Jonah wagged his head, casting a reproachful glare toward his wife. He sighed.

"Are you going to *support* me on this one?"

She unfolded her arms and looked at her son.

"Dexter, answer your father."

The boy said nothing. His head remained bowed. Aaliyah, easing up behind him, answered in his stead.

"He'll be here."

She clutched Dexter's left shoulder while stroking the right side of Brenda's face with her fingers.

"In fact, we'll all be here. We're going to talk this thing through. You better get on out there."

****

"So... so, does that mean we're not going to *die* when it hits?"

"I don't know, Asia. There's a lot they haven't told me about this project. I'm not sure *what's* going to happen to us. I only know that they asked me to help develop the operating system and write software for the government."

Asia sipped a martini. Davis was certain she must have had a few earlier because she always gulped the first and second. Besides that, her pronunciation had begun to falter, each sip washing more and more soil from normally well-hidden southern roots.

"And, and who's going to be in this, this government facility?"

"According to the information they gave me, one hundred people."

She opened the binder on the desk and flipped through it, scanning the pages.

"What's this about putting people to sleep? Thirty-nine women and five men? To repopulate the planet?"

He took the binder from her hands.

"It's classified. You can't even be in this room with this in here."

She swallowed a big mouthful as he escorted her out.

"Well, ain't that nice! That means each man will have what, eight wives? Perverts! Wonder what sick man thought that one up?"

Davis smirked as he reprogrammed the entry locking code on the keypad next to the door.

"It was actually a woman. You'll meet her. Her name is Dr. Isabel Benoit, and if she had it her way, there'd be no men. She thinks they're irrelevant because they don't have wombs. She wants to nix them and take an encyclopedia of select sperm samples instead."

Asia laughed aloud, from her stomach, and then she stifled a belch.

"*That* doctor! I like her already."

Davis snatched the bottle from the table, found the metal cap and screwed it on. He held the bottle as he continued.

"There will be men. Five men. If they want to repopulate the Earth with humans, they'll need men for protection. Who knows *what*'ll be waiting on the other side!"

Asia glanced at the bottle in her husband's grasp. Her little happy hour was over. All the pleading and seduction in the world wouldn't get her another drink.

"So will you be one of these five men, Davis?"

"No."

To Asia's surprise, Davis opened the bottle, reached over and poured her another shot of vodka. She nearly spilled the precious elixir when he grabbed a glass and poured one for himself.

"Since I'll be monitoring and testing programs until the moment this asteroid hits, you, Blake and I'll have to be in Colorado at the Crypt."

The sudden flood of euphoria from having a drink with her husband ebbed as she considered the implications of moving to Colorado.

"So what's going to happen to us in this Crypt? I mean, what happens to us when it hits?"

Davis shrugged, making a face as he swigged from the glass.

"I don't know, but for some reason, I'm not really worried."

"Why?"

"Because President Joe Whitmore will be staying right down the hall from us. I don't know, but I'm sure they have a plan. They just haven't told anyone yet."

Chapter 6

What surprised Jake Stanton even more than the youth of the soldiers was the degree of organization, at all levels, in the secluded military facility. The thirteen-year-old who conducted him to the interrogation room answered questions curtly and efficiently, citing military code twice. The kid wore a wedding ring on the fourth finger of his left hand, affirming rumors Jake and the rest of the country had been hearing about twelve- and thirteen-year-olds being allowed to marry in the self-declared nation.

As they sat awaiting the arrival of Colonel Earl Krebbs, Jake was able to engage the boy in reluctant conversation. The boy had been married only recently, and his wife was fourteen.

He was a good-looking boy. His tender face probably didn't need shaving, yet the red, swollen gash on his chin indicated he had nicked himself that morning. His hair was short and brown; his teeth were clean and disturbingly crooked.

Although at five-feet-ten-inches, this guard had the height of a man, Jake saw a vulnerable boy, a frightened and troubled boy, clinging to the desperate hope that just maybe this asteroid thing really *was* a great big government hoax as part of a complete takeover.

Jake felt sorry for him and thought it was probably better to let the boy keep on hoping right to the end. Hope was a powerful thing. Jake smiled. He envied the boy's faith and hope, and yet he felt profoundly sad for him as he watched him tear off a fingernail.

"You got parents?"

"I got a mama back home in Memphis, and two little sisters. I swore to em I was gonna go back and get em after the former American government falls."

"You talk to them?"

"Not since I been here. They don't even know I got married yet."

Jake glanced down at his own wedding ring. He, his wife and their two children had grown closer since the President's announcement. Never had he given and received so much love in his life! He couldn't imagine having a child stranded away in that last moment. It was a horrible thought.

From the first minute he heard about Nostradamus, he knew how he would spend his last moment: he, his wife and children would be together; they would be holding hands after praying together. They'd be wearing their best clothes after having eaten a gourmet last meal. Their minds and lives would be totally at peace.

Weeks earlier, they sat down and planned it in extreme detail. They made promises to each other. However it happened, they would be together. It couldn't happen any other way.

"Look kid, I don't know you, but would you do me a favor?"

"Probably not."

"I just want you to call your mother and sisters. Now maybe Robert E. Lee is right. Maybe there is no asteroid out there, but just in case there is, you have to call your mother and sisters before August 7th. You're a man now and they need you. Just in case it *is* out there, you wouldn't want them to have to face it alone, would you? They need you to be there for them."

The boy listened and bowed his head. Jake turned away because he knew the teenager would be embarrassed for breaking, but the tears were there. After a few minutes, someone knocked on the door.

The young soldier stood, holding his stiff body at attention. He batted his eyes, nervous, wiping the corners with the thumb and index finger of his right hand.

"Enter!"

Jake had only seen pictures of the rebel they called Colonel Krebbs, so he had always imagined a much taller, better-looking man. On the other hand, all of America had an accurate understanding of Krebbs' reputation for being nasty and vicious. During one interview at the complex, he shot a reporter in the knee for misrepresenting a statement issued by General Lee.

Another time, when Krebbs captured a group of Alcohol, Tobacco and Firearms agents after a border skirmish, he hung their tortured, mutilated bodies out under the hot Wyoming sun in a swarming cloud of flies for two days before dragging them behind a jeep to the border.

He allowed soldiers from the U.S. military to retrieve portions of the bodies strewn out along a mile on the road leading to the gate. Earl Krebbs was a killer who inspired fear and awe in his largely teenaged militia army.

In the wake of the incident, President Whitmore's advisors and the governor of Wyoming called for a surgical military strike against Lee, Krebbs and the New Republic, with the intent to destroy the pseudo-government and its growing influence and appeal. The problem with any such retaliatory attack, however, was the sheer number of American teenagers living on the base and in the camps surrounding the area.

According to intelligence, an estimated eight hundred fifty thousand American teens had immigrated to the New Republic since August 7, the day the President announced the coming of Nostradamus. In an effort to stop the flow of young people to the area, the Army erected perimeter fencing in early October, but the fences and guards had merely *slowed* the migration.

The key appeal for many of these teens was General Lee's flat refusal to believe the government's story about the asteroid, an idea he promulgated on teen-oriented sites on the Internet. He called President Whitmore's announcement a hoax and "the capitulation of America to foreign interests."

He called for renewed American patriotism, for renewed faith in America and God. Thus Lee offered hope to hundreds of thousands of American teenagers who were unwilling to accept the reality that there was no hope, that the Earth and all its creatures could not escape the imminent destruction.

While leaders condemned the cruelty and savagery of Colonel Krebbs and the Knights of the American Constitution, the strained yet patient American public objected to any military attack on the New Republic. Many American families had missing teenagers, and many of these suspected their children were in the mountains of Wyoming. Lee and Krebbs knew from the beginning that if the New Republic could attract great numbers of American teens, the government would never be able to launch any offensive against the movement.

The young guard still stood at rigid attention, his eyes darting left every few seconds to observe the Colonel. Jake sat on the cot, concerned that the Colonel might perceive his standing as a challenge. In contrast to the guard, who wore a tan and brown camouflage uniform, Colonel Krebbs wore a dark green officer's uniform, a beret and dark sunglasses. He had a Glock 45-caliber pistol holstered at his waist and a black lacquered stick in his right hand.

Krebbs spoke to the boy without looking at him.

"What's yer name, Soldier?"

"Shaw, Sir!" the boy shouted in the small room. "Private Bobby Shaw, Sir!"

"At ease, Son."

Krebbs went to the prisoner, raised the stick and slammed it down hard on Jake's shoulder blade. Jake doubled over from the pain, clutching his right shoulder with his left hand. He groaned aloud. The next blow of the stick landed in the small of his back, sending him sprawling to the floor, where the Colonel stomped the side of his face with a steel-toed boot.

"God-damned government spy!"

Krebbs kicked Jake twice in the stomach and again in the mouth, which sprayed teeth, blood and saliva across the floor.

"We found yer little drawins, and we found yer camera."

Jake's shoulder burned like fire. He was sure the shoulder blade was cracked. Grabbing the back of Jake's shirt, Krebbs dragged Jake back up to the cot and used Jake's hair to yank his head back.

"My first thought was to come in here and put a bullet in yer head, but I'm not gonna shoot ya. Now, I'm gonna let ya help us out here and help yerself in the meantime."

Krebbs spoke to the guard.

"Open the door, Boy. Tell em to come on in."

After fifteen more minutes of violence and instruction, a cameraman sat prepared to record the brief interview, which would be sent to national news agencies and Internet websites after taping.

A reporter with a microphone sat at a table across from a bloodied Jake Stanton.

"What is your name?"

"My name is Jake Stanton."

The camera closed on Jake's face as the reporter continued.

"And Mr. Stanton, why are you a prisoner here?"

Jake flicked a nervous glance toward Krebbs and answered.

"Because I, because I'm a government spy."

"A spy? And what did the government of the former United States of America send you in here to find out?"

Jake thought of his wife's face just then. He loved it from the first moment he saw it. They had a few problems over the years. There was a girlfriend once and again, but no one in the world could compare to Cherie.

"What did the former American government order you to come in here and find out?"

"Where you people have been hiding all the water you've been buying. They're looking to take you out first chance they get, and they want to poison your water supply and take out your generators early to shut you down."

Earl interrupted.

"Cut!"

He stomped on Jake's foot and jammed the nightstick into his stomach.

"Don't play fer the sympathy. Get it right, Spy!"

Earl backed away, turning to the reporter.

"I'm sorry. Carry on."

The reporter was unnerved by the violence, though she tried not to show it. Her hands trembled as she tried to find her place on the question sheet.

"And why would they want to poison our drinking water? Why would they want to wipe us out? Why would *we* be a threat to them?"

He was thinking about his son, about fishing on Dawson Lake in early summer, *catchin a bucketful of crappies*. By then, he was afraid to look at Earl Krebbs.

"Because, because General Lee knows the truth. Because General Lee knows there is no asteroid out there. Because he knows the government and Hollywood made the whole story up to take control of the people."

The reporter removed her glasses.

"So let me get this straight. All those images of Nostradamus that we've been seeing on TV these last few weeks, all that so-called proof? They were all created in some secret Hollywood studio by the government of the United States?

Jake bowed his head.

"Yes, that's right."

"Amazing! So if there is no asteroid out there, and no asteroid is going to hit Earth to create this so-called global Armageddon, then what's going to happen on August 7th, on the day they've told us all it's going to hit?"

He was thinking about his twenty-one-year-old daughter, about how frightened she would be on that last day, about how she cried in fear when she first found out about Nostradamus, about how he had promised her they would all be together.

Jake struggled against everything he had ever believed in and held sacred to speak the extorted words, words that stuck and lodged themselves in his dry throat. Thus with tears streaming down his bloody face, he answered.

"On August 7th, the government of the United States and the governments of every other country in the world will all fall under the dominion of the New World Order and the world will be ruled by the Trilateral Commission and the multinational corporations."

****

The interview over and the reporter and camera gone, Earl Krebbs stood over Jake Stanton, his stick back in its holster.

"I'm a man of my word, Mr. Stanton. I said *I* wouldn't kill ya, and I won't. But yer a spy, so ya gotta die."

Earl turned toward the guard, unstrapping his revolver.

"Private Shaw? Private, isn't it?"

"Yes, Sir!"

"I'm promotin ya ta sergeant, an yer first official duty in that capacity right here and now is the execution of this enemy of the state."

Krebbs held the gun out to the thirteen-year-old, who hesitated.

"Here. Take it, Sergeant."

Bobby Shaw lipped the word "no," though he took the gun in shivering hands.

"Ya ever *kill* a man, Sergeant Shaw?"

Bobby looked into Jake Stanton's fearful, apprehensive eyes, half-answering/half-declaring.

"No! No, I haven't, Sir."

"Well Boy, today's the day we all get ta see what yer made of. Now ya can distinguish yerself in the New Republic by executing this goddamned, piece-a-shit traitor and spy, or ya can go on back home ta ya mama in Memphis. Now's the time ta decide if yer gonna keep on bein a boy, or if yer gonna step on up and be a man."

Bobby gripped the gun, and still shivering, approached Jake.

"No!" Jake pleaded. "Don't let him make you a monster like he—"

Earl punched Jake in the face, grabbed a handful of his hair and yanked his head down, speaking to the frightened thirteen-year-old.

"If ya shoot im right there, right in the center of the skull back here, he won't even *feel* it."

He helped guide the gun so that the barrel rested on the back of Jake's skull.

"All ya gotta do is pull the trigger, Shaw."

In this penitent position, head bowed and eyes closed, Jake made a final appeal to higher justice, a desperate plea for divine intervention.

"Lord God in heaven, how could you let this happen to—?"

Jake's forehead exploded forward, spraying gore and blood onto Earl's uniform pants and boots. The body tensed and fell limp.

Wobbly, Shaw almost threw up when he realized he could see clear through Jake's dripping, partially hollow head. Looking through the hole in the back, he saw the floor and one of Earl's boots on the other side.

Earl released Jake's hair and let the body slump to the ground. One of Jake's eyeballs had been blown out of his head and hung by a strand of veins or nerves, stuck to his cheek. Earl kicked the inert body out of the way and took the gun from Bobby's hands.

"Congratulations Sergeant Shaw. You've proved yer loyalty to the New Republic and ta all we stand fer. This oughta be the proudest day of yer life! Ya ain't a little boy no more, Shaw. Yer one of us now. Now yer a man!"

Chapter 7

"This know also, that in the last days perilous times shall come. For men shall be lovers of their own selves, covetous, boasters, proud, blasphemers, disobedient to parents, unthankful, unholy, without natural affection, trucebreakers, false accusers, incontinent, fierce, despisers of those that are good."

In the huge Los Angeles church, banners of varying sizes displaying the expression "The Power of Faith" were ubiquitous. It was the theme of Reverend Jonah Williams' important Sunday morning address.

During the week before, he had been part of an international interfaith conference in Jerusalem convened to address the asteroid as it related to aspects of Christian, Muslim, Jewish, Hindu, and Buddhist faith issues. He returned from the conference with a sense of ebullience concerning Man's future in spite of its uncertainty. Man's salvation, Jonah advocated, would depend on *the Power of Faith, that whosoever believeth in him should not perish, but have everlasting life.*

The Reverend continued.

"Traitors, heady, high-minded, lovers of pleasures more than lovers of God; having a form of godliness, but denying the power thereof, and I'm going to stop right there. Having a *form* of godliness, but denying the power thereof. Now just what does that mean, 'In the last days, men will have a form of godliness, but deny the power thereof'?"

He raised the Bible to read it.

"Steven Byington, in his translation, calls it 'a formulation of piety but denying its efficacy,' referring to those who *say* they believe in the power of the Lord, but who do not put their faith in the power of the Lord to secure their future, whatever that future may be. They tell us they believe in the power of the Lord, but they are unwilling to exercise that faith by putting their lives in his hands. They are unwilling to *demonstrate* that faith by saying like David, 'Salvation belongeth unto the Lord;' like Isaiah, 'Here I am, God,' like Jesus at the moment he faced death, 'Not my will, but thine, be done.'"

Jonah closed the Bible.

"Now Brothers and Sisters, I am not about to stand here and tell you *I* know what's going to happen next year on August 7th. I don't presume to know. True believers accept that *as the heavens are higher than the earth, so the Lord's ways are higher than our ways, and his thoughts are higher than our thoughts.*"

He removed his glasses.

"Whether or not this asteroid is going to hit the Earth shouldn't *matter* to us. And I'm going to say it again. Whether or not this asteroid is going to hit the Earth shouldn't matter to us. The faithful know that whatever happens, it will be the Lord's will, not man's, but the Lord's will, that prevails. And in the end in some way we might have never imagined, in some divine way that we as lowly humans don't have the ability to imagine, the Lord will make his purpose known and the Lord will accomplish that purpose."

He replaced the glasses, scanning the huge multi-racial audience.

"I see many of you out there nodding your heads, giving some indication that you agree with me that, in these last days, we have to put our faith in the Lord. When I finish today, some of you will come up and tell me the same. But head nods and words really mean nothing.

"This church is filled with the Holy Spirit, so all the head nodding and the 'amenin' and 'praisin the Lord' out there, that's the Holy Spirit acting on you. But the reality is, you have to go *home* when the service is over. You have to go back to places where there isn't so much Holy Spirit around. In fact, some of you have to go to places filled with the wicked spirit of these last days.

"So the true test of our faith in these last days is not what we do and say in the Church, but how we live our lives when we go *home*. For if we truly have faith, the Holy Spirit we feel right now will be with us wherever we may go."

Jonah held up his left hand, palm forward.

"If a man says he has faith in the Lord in the morning and then goes out to the bar at night and gets drunk to escape dealing with the thought of this asteroid, is he demonstrating the faith we need in these last days?"

The congregation answered with a medley of "noes."

"If a widow or single mother proclaims her faith in the morning and takes up a secret life of fornication at night because events of late have made her scared, lonely and searching, is she demonstrating the faith we all need in these last days?"

More "noes" and energetic head shaking.

"If our young teenagers confess their faith in the Lord before the congregation this morning, and later take up the practice of the world by seeking to marry at fourteen and fifteen years old, are they demonstrating their faith in the Lord to see to their future?"

He spotted his son seated with the Browns, next to Brenda. Dexter's head was bowed as all around him the congregation responded to the question.

"But Brothers and Sisters, just what exactly *is* faith? According to man's definition in Webster's Dictionary, faith is 'belief in the value, truth, or trustworthiness of someone or something, belief or trust in God.' In light of that definition, we have to ask ourselves, in these last days, where are we going to put our belief and trust? In God and his word, the Holy Bible? Or in man and science?"

Jonah lifted the Bible and read.

"The Holy Bible gives us the Lord's definition for faith at Hebrews 11, verse 1, where it says, 'Faith is the substance of things hoped for, the evidence of things not seen.'"

He paused, nodding his head.

"Let me ask you all this. Have any of you actually *seen* this asteroid that man and science have told us will collide with the Earth on August 7th? When you go out at night and look into the skies, can you see it?"

Caught up in the dialogue, the spirited audience answered in the negative.

"But you have faith that it's out there. You believe it's out there because you trust in what man and science are telling you. What's more, you don't just believe it's out there, you believe that from millions of miles away in this vast universe, it's going to somehow collide with Earth on a specific day next year. Believing all that takes faith, doesn't it, brothers and sisters?"

The congregation signaled agreement with comments and vigorous head nods.

"Can we say we have the same faith in our Lord God and the things he's told us in his word, the Holy Bible? For what has he promised us there? Didn't he tell us that the righteous would not be forsaken? Didn't he promise that *he that endureth to the end shall be saved*? Didn't he promise that the meek shall inherit the Earth?"

Crescendo building throughout the series of questions, the audience erupted in spontaneous applause and "praise the Lords." Jonah waited for the clapping and shouting to end and continued.

"So when we look at what man and science promise us related to the destiny of the Earth and at what the Lord promises us, where are we going to put our faith? Who are we going to believe?"

Jonah sipped water from the glass at his left and cleared his throat.

"Now I told you earlier that I don't presume to know anything about this asteroid. I don't have any evidence to offer one way or another about whether it's going to hit us or not, and I don't worry about that. Because as I've always said from this pulpit, if you're living your life righteously, it doesn't matter when He comes, because you'll be ready for him."

He glanced toward the booth, where the director signaled that the taping was proceeding as planned.

"If this asteroid just flies right on past Earth and nothing happens, I'm fine with *that*. I imagine the rest of you'd be fine with that too?"

The audience agreed.

"But if man and science are right, and it hits us, I'm fine with that *too*. Because I put my faith in the Lord God! I have faith that no matter what happens, his will must be done, and if I'm a righteous person, I have a place in his bosom. I have faith in his plan for me, whatever that might be."

Jonah paused and removed his glasses again, examining them before replacing them.

"For you scientific-minded people out there, you have to ask yourselves: Does Almighty God have the power to control even the heavens, the sun and the stars? Sure you believe he caused the Flood to come about. Scientists and historians have written many books and advanced various theories about how that could have happened. Of course you believe he brought ten plagues on Egypt. Scientists, like the magic-practicing priests in Egypt on Moses' day have been able to explain and, in some cases, duplicate those events."

He stopped, nodding.

"But this is the *universe* we're talking about here, Newton's Universe, Einstein's Universe, a very mechanical, mathematical, scientific system of matter, forces, opposing forces and things working together in ways even the world's best scientists don't yet understand. Man can stop up a river and *create* a flood down here on Earth— doesn't take an act of God to do that. Through genetic engineering, man can bring about not only a plague of frogs, but a plague of frogs all with the exact same DNA—doesn't take an act of God to do that."

Jonah stared toward the heavens, extending his hand toward the sky.

"But to stop or change the course of an asteroid headed toward us, one that measures some eight miles across? An asteroid that renders man powerless to engineer his own deliverance, despite all his scientific brilliance? An asteroid that science tells us will definitely wipe out all life on Earth? Now that, Brothers and Sisters, requires an act of God. It requires action on God's part, and it requires faith on our part."

He found his wife's eyes in the audience, seeking and receiving her approval.

"Almighty God gave us his word, the Bible, so that we might know his ways, so when I first heard about this asteroid, and I heard what all the great scientists were saying, I immediately looked to the Bible to see what my great God was saying.

"In a moment of weakened faith, I wondered, 'Do you, O God, have the power to alter events even in the heavens?' And he answered me from his Word. He first directed me to the Bible book of Job, the 26th chapter, where he says at verse 7, *He stretcheth out the north over the empty place, and hangeth the earth upon nothing.*

"So I realized that he was telling me that *He* put this earth here, in this place in this universe. Thus Almighty God, as the engineer of the mechanical universe, if he placed the physical earth where he did, then everything that followed from that moment on would be part of his divine plan. I trust him in that."

For an instant, he felt the spirit of God, the spirit he always felt when he preached. But it was a fleeting moment. In the past month, he had felt an odd disconnect with God, and he couldn't understand why. Until that moment, he was had doubts and a feeling that God had forsaken him, but now there was hope. Heartened by the feeling, he took up his Bible.

"Then I was directed to the book of Joshua, chapter 10. I'll begin reading at verse 12: *Then spake Joshua to the Lord in the day when the Lord delivered up the Amorites before the children of Israel, and he said in the sight of Israel, Sun, stand thou still upon Gibeon; and thou, Moon, in the valley of Ajalon. And the sun stood still, and the moon stayed, until the people had avenged themselves upon their enemies. Is not this written in the book of Jasher? So the sun stood still in the midst of heaven, and hasted not to go down about a whole day. And there was no day like that before it or after it, that the Lord hearkened unto the voice of a man: for the Lord fought for Israel."*

Pausing, Jonah put the question to the congregation.

"Based on what we just read, I ask you Brothers and Sisters: *Does* Almighty God have dominion over the sun, the moon and the skies?"

The crowd answered with yeses and applause.

"Will Almighty God hearken to the earnest voices of men?"

More applause.

"Will our Lord fight for us?"

The entire audience was on its feet, cheering and calling comments of agreement. Jonah held up a hand, signaling for and setting a more somber tone.

"While I don't presume to know what will happen on August 7th, I have faith that in these last days, that all over the Earth, man will be forced to look to the heavens, *and every eye shall see him, and they also which pierced him; and all kindreds of the earth shall wail because of him. Even so, Amen."*

The congregation responded with "amens."

"Our Lord Christ Jesus, when explaining to his disciples how they would recognize his glorious return to Earth, said, *There shall be signs in the sun, and in the moon, and in the stars; and upon the earth distress of nations, with perplexity; the sea and the waves roaring; men's hearts failing them for fear, and for looking after those things which are coming on the earth: for the powers of the heaven shall be shaken. And then shall they see the Son of man coming in a great cloud with power and great glory. And when these things begin to come to pass, then look up, and lift up your heads; for your redemption draweth nigh."*

Jonah stopped for a moment, his voice assuming a serious mien.

"Brothers and sisters, man and science have named this phenomenon Nostradamus, after a 16th century astrologer, conjurer and mystic, but I refuse to use that name. I refuse to use that name because I believe using it would be nothing short of blasphemy. I believe that on August 7th, the *coming* the world is going to witness won't be anything that man and science have ever seen before.

"The coming that every eye will see, the coming that will cause men's hearts to fail them in fear, the coming that will shake the powers of heaven—go to your Bibles and consider the specific language he used when describing the manner of his return to his disciples. Yes, Brothers and Sisters, I believe that whatever is going to happen, on August 7th, all eyes on Earth will be forced to look up to the heavens to witness the coming of our Lord Jesus Christ. It will be the Second Coming of the Son of man!"

Chapter 8

In Semarang on the island of Java, an indigent Sundanese mother of eight stood weeping before a firing squad. Nabylla had given "the pink pill" to her four oldest. Soldiers found their decomposed bodies in a grove of trees next to a large pond in the community. The eldest, barely fifteen, was a pretty girl who would have fetched a high price on the black market, perhaps as much as two thousand U.S. dollars.

In Java and in many other Third World places, it had become common practice to sell off pretty, young daughters for cash. In fact, in places like Semarang, the junta government *required* each family to sell off its oldest daughter in order to pay an emergency government tax. Families could negotiate the sale of other daughters on a split percentage basis. Occasionally, families sold handsome boys as well, and some of these went for higher prices than the girls.

What happened to these children after they left these Third World countries remained a mystery. The Javanese government told the people they sold the girls to wealthy Americans to work as domestics in big houses, but many people like Nabylla believed otherwise. They had heard rumors that the girls more often went to places like Saudi Arabia, Thailand and Japan, where flesh brokers exploited them in the sex slave trade. A tribe elder reported been seeing others dismembered in "snuff" films through secret, expensive Internet websites.

****

In the months since the President announced the impending destruction of all life on Earth, the most affluent societies around the globe had become profligate, desperate and sexually deviant. In America, prostitution had become so commonplace that local governments erected pleasure camps where women could exchange sex for cash within the protection of a military facility. Purveyors established separate rooms where voyeurs could pay to watch various activities through openings in screens. In many places, twelve years old became the legal age for consent and prostitution.

Across the nation, various cities developed distinct sexual proclivities. San Francisco became a magnet for homosexuals from all over the world. In converted and restored bathhouses, gay men would congregate by the thousands like snakes in a pit, where they became a writhing, squirming mass of arms, legs, gyrating torsos and buttocks.

In the shadow that Nostradamus was already casting upon Earth, AIDS was no longer a threat or reason for pause. Safe sex was inconvenient and passé. News agencies marveled over the sheer number of so-called straight men who had deserted their families and relocated to engage in the carnal indulgences of that sparkling city by the bay.

Los Angeles and New York City were the sex and drug capitals of the West Coast and East Coast, respectively. On Friday and Saturday nights, promoters staged huge concerts at the Coliseum in Los Angeles, followed by wild sex festivities with live features on stage and on huge screens all around the stadium. The Hollywood Bowl hosted the New Eleusinian Mysteries, presided over by "gods" Demeter and Persephone, where the privileged few participated in the most secretive and most closely guarded ceremonies.

During pagan rites, other cultists slashed their own arms and legs, immolated unwitting pledges, drank hot blood and howled at the moon. Sex, in all its varied forms, was encouraged and sometimes extorted. A group of men called the Rapists carried whips and descended on groups of idle young men and women to keep the orgy in motion.

Opium circles were ubiquitous. Yet the most popular drug at ceremonies and rave parties was Ecstasy IV, typically called "four" by users. It was a super potent form of the original drug Ecstasy. Each morning, dozens of dead bodies were collected from the Bowl, loaded onto trucks and shipped to disposal sites outside the city. The majority of the casualties were "four" users, though as weeks went by and the body count doubled, tripled and then quadrupled, authorities blamed the pink pill for the difference.

The pink pill was, after all, the most desirable method for suicide. It was painless. It was even pleasant. Fifteen minutes after taking the small tablet, users experienced a sense of euphoria or well-being. In interviews with reporters, many called it "a oneness with the universe."

There was no fear of death. There was no sadness, no anxiety, and most importantly, no pain or discomfort. Forty-five minutes after taking the pill, users became pleasantly sleepy. Some reported sensing a "brightness" that called to them, which encouraged them to become a part of the light, which encouraged them to let go and sleep. One hour after taking the pink pill, the user was dead, often with a smile on his or her face.

Compared to Los Angeles, New York City seemed even more debauched, due to the population's obsession with sex acts that ended in heinous murder and suicide. Revelers there, like those in Los Angeles, circumvented military curfews by having private all-night parties at enclaves in and around the Garden and other secluded places.

When morning came, dozens of butchered victims, decapitated heads and dismembered limbs were collected and burned in the street. In fact, the grotesqueness of the hacked up pile of corpses on fire drew huge crowds.

On some days, the stench of burning human flesh filled Manhattan from dawn until noon, causing the *Times* to refer to the place as New Nuremberg City. A well-armed coalition of street gangs had driven the military out and had taken over Queens, which became the hub for the huge metropolis and its main supplier of drugs and prostitution.

Yet the most bloodthirsty cities in America were Atlanta and Miami, where they played an arena game called Ultimate Survivor. Similar to the gladiatorial shows of ancient Rome, the games pitted teams against each other, fighting to the death.

Planners filled the stadium with animal hazards. There were pools of hungry crocodiles, injured grizzly bears tethered to chains and pits filled with tiger snakes from Australia, the most venomous of all vipers. In the beginning, officials loosed a baited Siberian tiger into the game. Thirty minutes later, others released a vicious wild boar.

Initially, teams would fight together against other teams. When members on all other teams were dead, then remaining teammates fought each other until only one person survived. The winner received on an all-expense-paid pleasure cruise that constantly circumnavigated the Earth and would continue to do so through August 7.

Outside the Ultimate Survivor stadiums, human life held no greater value. Miami was the murder capital of the world, followed by Atlanta. Across the South going westward, cities played similar games of mortality, though none with the passion of the games in Atlanta and Miami. Nowhere in America were people so bloodthirsty.

****

The military commander called out the staccato order in a stentorian voice, causing the soldiers to raise their rifles to the vertical plane. Before the soldiers stood the frightened village woman, Nabylla, arms extended and fingers spread out wide, as if she might stop the bullets with her shivering hands. She turned her face up to the heavens, where she made one last entreaty to Allah.

"Eiyeh!"

In unison, the soldiers raised and leveled the rifles, taking aim at Nabylla. The poor mother of eight was before this firing squad as an example to the rest of the community. The government had ordered her to deliver her eldest daughter and her set of twin girls to authorities in order to sell them on the black market. The eldest was fifteen and the twins were twelve. Desperate to save her daughters from lives of prostitution, torture and murder, Nabylla gave each a pink pill and urged the girls to swallow them.

Earlier in the month, she traded her grandmother's pearl necklace with a friend from Jakarta for four of the pink pills. After hearing news of soldiers raping young boys in the village, she gave the final pill she had reserved for herself to her fourten-year-old son.

She initially told local authorities the older children had run away a week earlier, but then a fisherman found the bodies by the pond. After a six-hour beating by soldiers, Nabylla confessed to complicity.

Standing there, she gazed over at her four youngest, huddled together between her sister and brother-in-law. She knew her sister would care for her babies. She didn't regret for one moment what she had done. By killing her four eldest, she had saved them.

"Fire!"

The commander's final order was muted by the hollow, popping sound of the rifles exploding. The soldiers had aimed for her heart, and most of the bullets plowed into her chest and stomach, except one, which tore into her throat. Eyes wide open and glazed, Nabylla dropped to her knees clutching her neck, coughed up a mouthful of blood and fell on her face into the sand.

Chapter 9

Dr. Isabel Benoit's fingers worked as she inputted the final set of database factors into the supercomputer. After two months of searching, collection, analysis, narrowing parameters and triple cross-referencing, she was a little over thirty minutes away from the answer to a question that had intrigued her from the very beginning of her career. In fact, she chose to pursue advanced studies and research in human genetics because she had always sought an answer to the question.

She took off her glasses and watched the screen, nervous, anxious, sipping every few moments from a tiny cup of steaming Darjeeling. Thirty minutes, she thought, a lifetime of research and she was only thirty minutes away from an answer!

In her professional life, Isabel Hong Benoit was an ordinary-looking woman. She was of an average height at 5'5". She was born at Andrews Air Force Base outside Washington, D.C., and although her face didn't look thirty-five years old, her hair was as gray as it was jet black.

At work, she always wore that hair pulled straight back and fastened in a bun on the back of her head. She wore over-large glasses without rims, which distorted her eyes and broke up the outline of her well-composed face. She also wore baggy men's clothing that obscured any hint of her femininity. Thus her plainness was by design.

She wanted to project her image as a serious scientist, and the scientific community agreed with and supported this self-definition. She was chosen to chair the Specimen Selection Committee for Life Ark because many considered her the best geneticist in the nation.

Her personal life was another story. Very few of her colleagues ever saw her outside the laboratory environment, though those who did either failed to recognize her or were amazed at the disparity between the conflicting personas, ego and alter ego.

Dr. Isabel Benoit was two separate women. Those who recognized her outside work told stories about meeting a worldly, sophisticated and very sexy woman with exotic eyes who wore her wavy hair down and radiated sensuality. Yet she was careful to keep her two lives separate. She did not want rumors and gossip that might evolve from her personal life ever to affect her professional life. Such separation was her mantra, and it worked for her, though she couldn't escape rumors involving her unmistakable animus toward men and sexism.

She did her undergrad work and her post-graduate studies under the tutelage of the world-renowned Dr. Sabra Goldstein at the University of California at Berkeley. Dr. Goldstein had won a Nobel Prize for Science for her work in genetics as one of the pioneers on the Human Genome Project.

Protégée Isabel, whom Goldstein ordained as her successor, took up the work Sabra became too old to continue. Ironically, Dr. Goldstein died a mere month before the announcement of the completion of the Human Genome Project, though her spunk and determination had survived in her student, Isabel.

Isabel compared the clock on the computer to the watch on her wrist, as if any difference in the times would affect the wait. Only ten minutes left! After what seemed like an interminable wait, someone tapped on the door, and then the knob turned. The door eased open.

"I knocked. Isabel? You in here? Isabel?"

She checked her watch again.

"Come on in."

Dr. Smock's face appeared in the opening.

"Got over as soon as I could. You find her?"

"Two minutes."

He entered the office, took the seat next to her and studied the computer screen.

"Are you excited?"

"Are you crazy?"

She laughed to herself.

"No. Actually, with a minute and a half to go, I keep thinking something'll go wrong. I'm expecting the computers to crash any second now."

He eased closer to the screen, undoing his tie.

"That's not happening."

He thought to take her hand, but he stopped himself. He turned away instead.

"How do you feel? Think you got it right?"

She nodded, suppressing a smile.

"Yes. I think so."

A minute later, the words, *DATABASE SEARCH COMPLETE*, appeared on the monitor in a highlighted box, causing Isabel to snap to attention. Her hand pounced on the mouse.

"It's done. This is it!"

She clicked the box and waited as the screen changed. When the list appeared, she clicked on the name at the top.

"Here she is."

"Your Eve?"

"The world's most perfect woman, from a genetic point of view."

She read as she scanned the screen.

"Five-eleven, one hundred and thirty-five pounds, twenty-two years old, athlete, vision 20-15!"

She paused as she read, and then she continued.

"Genetically resistant to ovarian cancer, breast cancer, diabetes. Resistant to osteoporosis, heart disease, tooth decay, HIV—the list goes on. Genetically superior immune system."

Don Smock listened, fascinated by Isabel's level of excitement.

"Her fertility window is twelve days a month—that's *double* most women. Eight percent body fat. Genetically prone to multiple births. 36D cup. Hips a little heavy, but within specs. I'm wondering why she doesn't already have children."

Smock interrupted.

"Is she married?"

"Don't know."

She read for another minute before restarting the narration.

"Let's see. Personal history. Never broken a bone, straight teeth, luxuriant hair, no cavities. Disease-free, no hospitalizations. No family history of cancer or hypertension. Great-grandmother still alive at one hundred and five—IQ—140. Maintained a solid three-point-eight throughout high school and college. She's incredible!"

Smock nodded.

"Looks like you found your Matrix, your Eve."

"She's a goddess."

"Well, congratulations. You found her. Does your goddess have a name?"

Isabel laughed.

"You know, in all the excitement I forgot to check! Her name?"

She scrolled back up the screen.

"Yes, it's Reed. Her name is Layla Renee Reed."

****

"So when will *Helios* intercept Nostradamus?"

"Not until early March, but we should have continuous imaging from the probe's cameras as early as February 5th."

President Joe Whitmore sat at a conference table with Jettson Turner, his National Security Advisor. Across the mahogany expanse sat Dr. Helen Engstrom of the Near-Earth Asteroid Tracking observatory site and Dr. Thomas Ross, chief director of the Air Force Research Laboratory Space Vehicles Directorate. The scientists were there as part of a weekly science and technology briefing intended to keep the President updated on the approach of the asteroid.

"And then it will fly *with* the asteroid?"

Dr. Ross answered.

"After intercepting Nostradamus, the satellite will sweep around it in order to send back data that will help NASA scientists map its entire surface and better determine its composition. Then it will take up a parallel course approximately two kilometers away, and it will fly alongside the asteroid until it enters our atmosphere."

Although NASA was handling the satellite's guidance system and telemetry, *Helios* was a joint project involving United States and British corporations along with businesses from Israel, Syria, Russia and Turkey. The project would benefit the entire world, as the governments of all nations would have access to the information and images sent back to Earth.

President Whitmore massaged his right earlobe as he thought.

"I know this is going to sound silly, but is there any chance that once we get this more detailed view, we might discover a weakness or anything that might... change things?

Helen Engstrom answered.

"Unlikely. We already know Nostradamus is mostly nickel and iron. Even if there were a weak point and we could break it up so we would have two four-mile-wide rocks instead of one eight-mile-wide rock, the impact would be basically the same."

Whitmore sighed, frustrated. He started to speak but stopped. Sighing, he started up again.

"Look I, I realize I'm not a scientist, but what if you could, what if you could hypothetically break this eight-mile-wide rock into sixty-four two hundred yard-wide rocks? And then when it got in the range of our weapon systems, we dealt with as many of the pieces as we could and hoped some of the others burned up as they entered the atmosphere? Would that lessen the effect of, say cosmic winter or the earthquakes and tidal waves?"

Dr. Engstrom wagged her head, removing her glasses.

"It's like belling the cat, Mr. President. Great idea, but how do you blow a huge chunk of solid metal into sixty-four little pieces? Metal is malleable. It's just not going to happen."

Her hand was steady as she sipped her coffee.

"Nostradamus is coming. The fate of the Earth is sealed, and no last minute twist or novel little idea is going to change that. The purpose for having *Helios* up there is purely scientific."

Thomas Ross checked his watch for the third time.

"Anything else, Mr. President?"

"No. I think that's all for now. We'll see you next week."

After thanking the President for lunch, the doctors gave him a huge packet of material from various scientific journals and left the room.

Jett Turner, the President's National Security Advisor, who had been silent throughout the briefing, offered an opinion.

"She's right, and the world knows it. That's why I say we take Iran out right now. Don't give him a chance to do it. He'll do it because he's got nothing to lose."

Turner referred to a recent intelligence report referring to the president of Iran. According to agents operating in Tehran and confirmed by agents in Bagdad, Iran's president had been talking of planning one last strike, an all-out assault translated as "the mother of all holy wars."

In this war against "murderous America and her little dog, Israel," the Iranian leader had called for an all-out assault on the United States and on American citizens all over the world on August 5.

Several rumors in the intelligence community involved thousands of suicide squads, some in well armed bands, others rigged to explosive devices, launching against America from within and from without its borders. In fact, there was a confirmed report that one Sunni leader was declaring August 5 a holy day, the great day of retribution. He said that Moslems all over the world had a duty to God to carry out the war.

Thus in the end, as the sun rose on August 6, America would know "the judgment of Allah." America would recognize the arrogant, lying and murderous ways of her leaders and their anti-Islam policies.

America would understand that, despite her formidable military power and technical expertise, she would not escape justice in her last days. In her final hours that, as she in fear looked to the skies to face the vengeance of Allah, she would still be stinging with the pain of retribution delivered in the holy war the Iranian president and others had waged against her.

President Whitmore pondered Jett's comment in silence, reflecting on the meeting he had had earlier in the morning with Lucas Draco, Chairman of the Joint Chiefs of Staff, and three other military leaders.

"If we took out Iran, there's no guarantee we'd get him. If he survived, our destroying his people and his homeland would make him an even more powerful figure in the Islamic world. He'd have the support of many otherwise neutral leaders in his holy war."

Whitmore lit a cigarette and blew smoke before continuing.

"If somehow we *were* lucky enough to go in there and take him out, he'd be replaced the next day, probably by some extremist with a worse agenda and even less to lose. Besides that, we've got a half dozen bin Ladens out there just looking for a cause."

He hadn't smoked for going on twenty years. In late September, he had casually borrowed a few cigarettes from Jett's stash and smoked them in the security of the Oval Office bathroom. Then in October, when a united Korea expelled U.S. military forces, attacked Japan and invaded as far north as Hiroshima, he began smoking in Jett's presence. No one else, including his wife and daughters, had any idea he had resumed the unhealthy habit.

"We have to find a way to discredit him, make him a traitor to Allah, and the Islamic world. We have to de-legitimize his so-called war. That's why we have to shore up our support from our Arab friends in the region, not take action to alienate ourselves."

Jett mashed out a cigarette in an overfull ashtray and blew the gray and black ashes across the slick table.

"That's why we wait till late July, provoke him to start this war early and have ourselves prepared to wipe his ass completely off the map. There won't be enough time for new leadership. Anyone else who wants to support him, we wipe their asses out too. We've got all these nukes and untested special weapons stockpiled for what? To just sit there while that piece of shit defies us before the whole world? If we're going to maintain any sense of credibility and security in the end, we have to make the world know that we will kick ass at the slightest provocation. We've gotta take em all out."

Throughout twenty years of craving and reminiscence, Joe remembered cigarettes tasting *better* before. Perhaps manufacturers were making them differently. Perhaps it was the additives, but cigarettes just tasted better before.

Perhaps he should have never started again. That way, his wonderful, smoke-trailed memories of the great-tasting cigarettes he enjoyed as a youth would have never been tainted. He felt a greater degree of disappointment with the experience every time he put one out.

"And Wyoming?"

"Take em all out. Screw the teenagers. If they're old enough to drink, marry, carry guns and shoot ATF agents, they're old enough to die."

At five-feet-five inches, Jett was short, a feature that made him unusually aggressive and praetorian. His dark eyes were set in deep sockets, surrounded by permanent black circles. He hardly ever smiled and never laughed. He referred to a wife on occasion, but no one had ever seen her or his gay son.

He had three obvious obsessions: cigarettes, chess and winning. To him, everything in life was symbolic of a huge cosmic chess match, and he played to win at all costs.

"Joe, when are you going to realize that might makes right, and we've got all the might. Right now, we have the power to do whatever we want. There is no next year, and there is no history to judge us."

Jett stood, and lighting yet another cigarette, spoke in an undertone.

"We're all going ta Hell anyway, the whole world. What difference does it make if we do a little well-deserved ass kicking on the way out? Call together the Joint Chiefs. Order the strikes. We'll all sleep better at night."

Dragging his heavy overcoat from the rack, Jett stood silent for a moment. Pulling the scarf around his neck, he sighed.

"It's only October, but it's cold as fuck out there."

The President only nodded, his face blank, his mind lost to deep, distressing thoughts.

Jett clutched his shoulder.

"You think about what I said. If there was any real justice in the universe, none of this would be happening in the first place."

Joseph Whitmore did not react to the sound of the door closing. Stoic, he walked to the conference table and sat.

Fifteen minutes later, Jean Whitmore entered the room and sat beside her husband. She did not speak. Her gentle hand atop his brought him around. He smiled.

"I love you so much, Jean. You do know that?"

Her eyes watered as she nodded. Her smile trembled.

"Yes."

He stiffened his jaw in a gesture of resolve.

"Yes. That's why it's so difficult for me to tell you what I'm going to tell you."

Her eyes flashed with growing fear. No sound came from her throat. She only mouthed the word.

"What?"

"Jean, you and the girls are going to die next week in a fiery plane crash, your bodies burned beyond recognition. You will be identified through dental records."

She was both stunned and confused.

"Joe?"

"There will be a memorial service for the three of you on the White House lawn one week from Saturday. On Wednesday night, you and I will be together for the last time for a while."

"What are you saying?"

"Your actual bodies will be transported by special agents to a private airport, and you'll be flown to Colorado. There you'll briefed and installed in the Crypt."

Wagging her head, she reached up and turned her husband's face toward hers.

"And the Crypt is?"

He removed her hand from his cheek, turned his body to his wife and spoke.

"It's a huge, subterranean classified government complex expanded from natural caves in the Sangre de Cristo Mountains in south central Colorado. It's a sealed enclosure measuring over eleven square miles, under two thousand feet of pink granite, though it is still four thousand feet above sea level. It will be the safest place on Earth on August 7th. That's where you and the girls will be."

She interrupted.

"And what about *you*?"

He closed his eyes, sighed and responded.

"I'm not sure. You know how unpredictable things have been over the past few months. They can only get crazier. I have a duty to lead the nation during this time of crisis. I have to be at the helm to the end."

Jean was standing, her hand at her brow.

"So you're saying the girls and I might never *see* you again?"

He closed his eyes and bowed his head.

"I'm just saying it's a possibility. I just don't want to get the girls' expectations up in case I don't make it. We have to tell them I won't be coming."

She crossed her arms.

"You know Beth—she's Daddy's girl. She won't go without you. And I don't think Susan will either."

"That's why we don't tell them about what's going on until they've already been installed in the complex."

"So your daughters won't be able to say goodbye to you?"

"I'll call in."

She wiped a tear that trailed down her cheek.

"Will you be able to visit us?"

"I don't think so, but I'll try to get there."

He stood and embraced her, speaking to reassure her.

"I wish it could be some other way. I just want to make sure that you and the girls are safe."

She struggled from his arms.

"What if I don't *want* to be safe, Joe? What makes you think you should make that decision for me?"

"Jean, you—"

"It's not your decision to make. It's mine. I'm staying here."

"At this point you don't have a choice, Jean. You and the girls are going. I've already made that decision."

There was something in his voice. It was a sense of resolve that Jean only heard on rare occasions. After twenty-five years of marriage, she realized there were times when her strong-willed husband's decisions were unassailable. This was one of those times.

"And what if we refuse to go?"

He grabbed her shoulders, looking into her eyes.

"I don't need to say it, Jean. This is a matter of national security, so don't fight me on it. And you're better off not saying anything to the girls. These are critical times, and we both know how rash Susan can be. If she did anything to jeopardize this project, I'm not sure what they would do to her."

He released her and concluded as he went to his desk and sat.

"As heartless as we all think Jett Turner is, he's a softie compared to the guys on this detail."

Jean sank into a chocolate brown leather chair next to the wall.

"So we might as well be dead. Why don't you just crash the plane for real?"

"No, the rest of Earth will die. You'll live."

Her face was nonresponsive though she answered.

"Live for what? For the sake of being alive? In some cold, dark hellhole prison in a mountain without my husband for the rest of my life?"

"A prison? I've heard it's more like a resort. It's got a shopping mall, swimming pools, bowling, restaurants, you name it. Besides, you'll have the girls with you."

She rose and was staring out the window at the scarlet-, orange- and yellow-dappled trees across the lawn, at the fire-colored fluorescence of a gossamer sheet of sunlit clouds, at the bottom edge of a yellow autumnal moon that dared to intrude on the sun's blue-gray skies.

"But it's only October in the last year of life on Earth. Right now, it doesn't matter how nice that complex is. If we go away now, we'll miss the last Christmas on Earth, the last New Year's Eve, the last snowfall, the last spring, the last sunrise and sunset, the last everything!"

"But then August 7th will come."

"So let it come. I'd much rather enjoy ten months of joy on Earth than twenty-five years of life in that damn prison in a mountain, and so would the girls!"

Joe Whitmore batted tears back and clenched the bulging muscles of his lower jaws. He strained to speak because his throat felt sore and tight.

"It won't be easy on any of us. Let's not make this any harder than it already is. You have to go."

Throwing her arms around him, she hugged his torso, sobbing.

"But we want to be with you! Please, Joe, please! Please don't send us away! Call it off!"

He pulled her close, and staring into her face, he kissed her weeping eyes.

"Wait for me Jean. Wait for me there. I promise I'll get there."

"No you won't, Joe. I know you. You'll never come! It's *duty before all else* with you. You won't come. That's why I want to stay out here with you. I'll die if you make me go. I'll die."

She stopped crying, sniffed a few times and dabbed her eyes with a pink handkerchief.

"The girls and I aren't going along with this plan, Joe. We're not going to sacrifice the last year of our lives for you, our country or anybody. And if that means Jett Turner and company are going to send their goons after us, then that's on you, because I know they won't hurt us, unless you let them.

Chapter 10

"Ladies and Gentlemen, Gentlemen and Ladies. Now I ain't no kinda public speaker. I'm just a regular ol boy from Alabama. I ain't even sure why CNN, ABC and Fox News came to me and told me they were gonna give me this chance ta talk to you. I don't necessarily trust none of em. CNN's Time Warner and ABC's Disney—both big corporations, and believe me they don't have me on here for my benefit or yours. Fox News I trust a little, but they're still the media."

Robert E. Lee sat in the makeshift studio in the New Republic's Wyoming complex at New Lexington, near the base of Mt. Isabel. He reluctantly allowed the camera crews and reporters access to the camp, to select areas of the base and limited access to the lives and lifestyles of carefully selected young soldiers in exchange for five minutes of national broadcast time.

Lee's gray cap featured a prominent confederate emblem worn by rebels during America's Civil War. Likewise, the old-fashioned officer's uniform he wore resembled General Lee's. A black ribbon bowtie decorated the neck of his crisp white shirt.

According to a woman reporter who had followed the story of the movement since secession in September, Lee was "a tall, handsome man with an almost irresistible personality." When he removed his hat, a thick, braided black ponytail hung down his back. His dark sideburns and beard were neatly trimmed.

"Inasmuch as I'm here, I'm gonna say my piece. As ya watch it, look at your screen carefully. If you see any cuts, then ya know what I said has been edited, and you shouldn't trust it. I've asked these television people to use one camera only, and ta tape what I say non-stop, so there shouldn't be no cuts unless someone's playin games here."

He glanced down at the desk, referring to his notes.

"First of all, for those of you who don't know who I am, my name's Robert E. Lee. I am the president of the New Republic of America. On September 17th, the New Republic announced its formal secession from the United States of America as well as the reasons for that secession, and that's what I wanna talk ta ya about taday."

He paused, studying the notes. He read verbatim.

"It's not that we're *against* America. The folks here at the New Republic are the most patriotic and dedicated of all Americans. We believe in the ideals of America and everything the Founding Fathers and generations of decent Americans worked so hard to achieve. We revere all the men and boys who, over the years, gave their very lives for our country."

He stopped again. He had lost his place as he glanced up. Frustrated, he raised the sheet and squinted to continue where he had left off.

"It is because we love our country so much that we found it necessary—no, we found it mandatory, to declare our independence from a government that has lost its soul, a government that has forgotten what America is about. It's all right before our eyes.

"We got a few super-rich, anti-American families runnin the whole show, and these people got money invested in countries all over the world. They elect your president and congress and send your boys all over the world ta die in battles that got nothin ta do with America. What's worse, alotta these rich folks out there runnin America ain't even American. That's the problem. And they don't give a shit about you or me."

Irritated with the note sheets, he crumpled the papers, tossing them over his shoulder.

"Yeah, yeah. So now we got this story about this asteroid, this Nostradamus thing. They say it's out there. They say it's gonna hit an there ain't nothin no one can do about it. Now that don't even make sense.

"Do any of ya out there really believe that the government of the goddamn United States of America is just gonna sit there and do fuckin absolutely nothin if it was true? Ya think they wouldn't be makin top secret plans if there was a rock out there? But what do ya see em doin? Nothin! Your president is sittin there on his ass on TV every night smilin, wife and gals at his side, tellin all y'all out there to be calm and show that good ol American class and character."

He laughed to himself.

"If there is an asteroid comin, he's lyin through his teeth. Else, someone needs ta ask him and follow him to see where *he's* gonna be on August 7th if he believes it's out there. Ya think he'll still be there givin speeches? No, he'll be in some secret bunker watchin it all on TV. An all these rich assholes runnin this country behind the scenes—

where do ya think they're gonna be if they think there's an asteroid out there? If it is out there, they're gonna save themselves and let the rest of us die, cuz they don't give a fuck about any of us. And that brings me ta ma main point."

He smiled with a new confidence. He never needed the notes in the first place.

"It ain't out there, Ladies and Gentlemen. There *is* no asteroid. It ain't out there. The government of former America is once again playin into our deepest an darkest fears: the apocalypse, Armageddon, God's final judgment on man. And why are they doin this? Cuz they're changin the rules of the game.

"Ya've all seen it happenin before your very eyes from the election of this president, but you're too naïve and trustin ta understand it. Meltdown of the economy. Merger after merger. Huge banks buyin other huge banks. The big insurance companies. Oil companies buyin up each other. Airlines, television, computers, power companies, all that consolidation. By the beginning of the year, it was just a few multinational companies at the top runnin the whole world. The name they go by is the Trilateral Commission."

He nodded, pointing a finger toward the camera.

"Yeah, bingo, the Trilateral Commission. *Now* some of y'all already know what I'm talkin bout! The year 1998 marked a turnin point. That was the year the former American government got in the way of the inevitable. That was the year the government filed its antitrust suit against one of the biggest of these giant multinational companies, Microsoft and that Bill Gates who's one of the worst assholes of em all.

"Microsoft fought back by electin their own U.S. presidents. They got Whitmore, a man completely owned by the world's big corporations. They've been electin their own people. That's when all these big companies realized they had the power ta take over. Not just America, but the whole world."

The cameraman gave a sign to let Robert Lee know that he only had two minutes left. Lee nodded in acknowledgement and began speaking more urgently.

"So they used all their high tech computers and science networks and PR firms and invented this Nostradamus asteroid and said the world was doomed. Said there was no hope. And what happens next? Chaos. Governments fallin all over the world. Thousands of folks committin suicide every week. Financial panic. The destruction of the family unit. Folks sellin homes and property for next ta nothing ta get cash. But let me ask ya somethin: who do ya think is buyin up all the property you're out there sellin? Yeah, look it up. It's the big multinational companies, America's greatest enemies."

He stood.

"So on August 7th, when the asteroid *don't* hit, where are y'all gonna be? Dead? Hungover? Drug addicted? On coke? On meth? Sick? Pregnant with AIDS? Outa money? Outa property? Ain't took care of yourselves? Pissed off at God and the world that you're still alive? Well, that's when you're gonna remember me.

"That's when you're gonna remember that nut Robert E. Lee in Wyoming who refused ta buy inta the government scam, this takeover by the government. And hopefully I'll be here for you, but I can't make no promises. Ya see, the government don't *want* me here. I'm a threat to their New World Order. I'm out here tellin folks the truth. Very soon, I guarantee they'll come over an try'n take me out. It's gonna be a war, and whether you're with us or not, we soldiers of the New Republic of America will be out here fightin for you. We welcome alla y'all ta come and join us."

When a member of the crew indicated that five minutes was up, Robert's wife, Becky, held up a cardboard placard with red letters. Robert understood.

"Oh! If ya wanna learn more on what the New Republic of America is all about, please visit us on the Internet at www.newlexington.nra.com. Or ya can call 1-800-4NEWLEX, an we'll be glad ta do whatever we can to show ya how ya can help America reclaim her soul. God bless you all."

Robert Lee was finished speaking, but the cameras continued rolling. Growing suspicious, he studied the actions of the crew at first, and then he spotted the red light, which indicated the camera was on.

"What's this?"

The production manager/negotiator was a slight, shaky man who answered.

"President Lee, as I, as I think I mentioned to you, at least I *think* I did—we have reporters from Fox News, CNN and ABC here who would, who really would like to ask a couple questions if you'd care to, care to hear them."

By this time, Bubba Barnes, a very large, muscular black man standing next to Colonel Earl Krebbs drew his revolver and approached the production manager.

"Didn't I tell you you'd die if you started playin games up in here?"

Robert reached out, stopping the six-foot-eleven-inch guard before he could reach the cringing man.

"No. It's alright, Bubba."

Robert looked toward the manager.

"They can axe questions, but tell em they do it at their own risk. Wrong question and I think ol Bubba here might be sendin one or two of em home in bags."

"Under, understood."

The former evening news anchor from CBS posed the first question. He was at the complex on assignment with Fox News. CBS and MSNBC were the first media casualties since August, when the industry experienced a sudden shortage of production personnel and huge shortfalls in anticipated revenues from advertisers. By late August, almost forty percent of the workforce in the television news media had either taken early retirement or simply walked off the job. News producers panicked, offering substantial cash incentives to keep key people in place.

By mid-September, the industry became cannibalistic. Sensing vulnerability at MSNBC, CNN launched a campaign to convince dedicated employees to move over to Atlanta. ABC followed, so that by the end of September, MSNBC announced its withdrawal from the news media scene. With MSNBC gone, desperate producers turned on CBS, employing bribery and treachery to steal away all the talent that remained at the struggling company. In early October, as CBS News closed its doors, industry experts predicted that by late July, there would be only one news agency left, though no one was sure which company would survive.

CNN had set up the deal with President Lee for two reasons. The first of those reasons involved the newsworthy nature of the New Republic of America. Since the announcement of Nostradamus in August, American television-viewing proclivities leaned toward the sensational, with bloody, violent shows like *Cutthroat* and *One-Minute Death* capturing the greatest share of prime time ratings.

Both shows capitalized on the public's obsession with death and dying. *Cutthroat* involved three nude men or women on a jungle-like one-acre lot, each armed with razor-sharp machetes. During the show, contestants faced the challenge of either eliminating the other opponents or being put to death with them at the end of one hour. The winner received two hundred thousand dollars in cash.

One-Minute Death was another hour-long show. It featured forty-five one-minute home videos of suicides and executions, each with a parting message to the world. The sensationalism of bloody, violent deaths in arenas and images of gross dismemberment dominated television programming, and the major entertainment companies had to either find a glitzy way to package it or get out of the business.

The other big sellers were conspiracies and conspiracy theories, advanced on many of the political talk shows on cable. Cynicism was on the rise as stories surfaced about officials from Third World governments neglecting and essentially murdering massive numbers of commoners in attempts to save themselves.

The people of Ibadan and Ogbomosho in Nigeria were facing starvation, outbreaks of disease and daily burnings of the dead, while the ruling general and other government officials overstocked tons of rice, wheat and soybeans in massive warehouses that stretched miles wide underground. The government of Nigeria, like those of Ecuador, Laos, Azerbaijan and others, had contracted with the New Millennium Construction Corporation to build huge subterranean shelters.

A prevalent rumor in America was the existence of two of these shelters in Colorado and West Virginia, respectively. Reporters discovered the West Virginia facility in the 1980s and opened to the public in the 1990s.

Newspapers and television newsmagazines ran daily features about persons who claimed to have seen or helped the government construct the Crypt in Colorado years earlier. There was an equal amount of speculation about how many people these facilities would hold and who would receive the temporary salvation government shelters could offer.

Polls taken by CNN and Fox News indicated that the public did not trust most of the things that the government was telling them about the asteroid. Many believed the government was intentionally exaggerating the size of Nostradamus to make the situation seem more severe and hopeless.

Still others believed the government wanted the majority of people in the world to perish in the impact. Even some scientists disputed the government's claims about the endurance of the cosmic winter that was supposed to follow.

If the public believed the government's claims, fewer people would undertake the time and expense to protect and shelter themselves. Many would simply give up or give out. In the end, by having fewer survivors, there would be less competition and fewer complications when the President and chosen friends emerged from shelters a few years in the future.

Conspiracy theories abounded. There was even a suggestion that the pink pill was a government invention cooked up in a government lab, purposed to decimate America's population and to wipe out "all the weak-minded, the poor, the minorities and the druggies."

But the main reason for CNN, ABC and Fox News being at New Lexington in Wyoming was a poll that indicated a growing number of Americans were beginning to look credibly toward Robert E. Lee and his New Republic of America. While audiences for the President's nightly addresses to the nation remained steady, national audiences for Lee's weekly address had grown one hundredfold and more. People were listening to him. During that same week, his favorability rating had surged to a mark higher than those of the President.

Robert Lee was unprepared for his role as a head of state. He had no set of policies in place for dealing with foreign governments, though the nation's constitution had only recently been ratified. Thus he had to decline the offer for a meeting at New Lexington by Germany's prime minister. He declined another by the head of state from Belarus.

Eyes flicking back and forth between the former CBS news anchor and the camera, Lee waited for the question.

After first gauging Bubba's proximity and the position of his gun, the aging newsman began.

"President Lee, you allege that there is no asteroid, that Nostradamus is a big hoax perpetrated by the government and big business, but can you offer viewers in America and all over the world one shred of credible evidence to back up that allegation?"

Robert smiled.

"Sure can. We got a top government agent on tape, fella by the name of Jake Stanton, who tells us all it's a hoax. Says Washington, D.C. and Hollywood got together and cooked the whole thing up."

"And where is Mr. Stanton today?"

Bobby hesitated a moment before answering.

"He's, he's here at the complex. Changed his name. Wants nothing else ta do with the government of the United States of America. Doesn't wanna be found."

The anchor considered a follow-up, but he sensed a threat in Lee's final words.

"President Lee, aside from what the President and the government are telling us, we have confirmation from the world's leading astronomers and scientists that Nostradamus is indeed headed our way. How do you respond when scientists, not just in America, but scientists the world over are predicting this impending collision?"

"That's what I been tryin ta tell ya! Look, maybe there *is* an asteroid out there. There're tons of asteroids out there. All over the universe. An maybe one of em is gonna fly by the Earth pretty close. Happens all the time. But is one gonna hit the Earth? No.

"What I think is the government knows a big one is gonna fly by us real close, and that still means maybe millions a miles away, an they capitalized on that. They said, 'Let's tell the world it's gonna hit, an in all the confusion, we can get our one world government. Screw all the folks we gotta kill an destroy! Screw Robert E. Lee!'"

He paused, realizing he got carried away.

"All y'all out there must notice that it was mainly the American government that was sayin we ain't got a chance, and everyone else just sorta followed along. We at the New Republic don't trust the government of the former United States of America and we pity the fools who do, but we welcome alla y'all ta come join us."

A young soldier approached Lee and whispered something into his ear. Apparently, it disturbed the President.

"Now if y'all'll excuse me, I got somethin very important ta take care of."

Chapter 11

"So I don't understand what you're telling me here. Are you saying I'm some kind of a freak?"

"That's not at all what I'm saying. I'm saying that, genetically speaking, you are the best the human race has to offer at this time."

Layla's face was blank as she sat stunned, confused. After a moment, she reached for the water glass and sipped. Dr. Isabel Benoit reached over and grasped Layla's hand where it rested on the crisp white tablecloth.

"It's actually a compliment."

Layla sighed and smiled, showing flawless, perfectly straight white teeth.

"I guess it is, but... how did you arrive at that conclusion?"

She shrugged and continued.

"I'm just curious."

Isabel Benoit was in her worldly, sophisticated persona. She wore her black hair down over tan bare shoulders. Both women wore colorful dresses, as the décor of the posh little mid-Manhattan restaurant suggested a degree of formality.

Isabel smiled.

"It *was* a very complicated process. I've worked non-stop at it for over five years, but you *do* remember meeting me four years ago in Sacramento when you gave blood, tissue and hair samples to me and technicians, don't you?"

Layla was embarrassed.

"Well, I remember consenting to the screening, yes, and I remember giving the samples, but I just don't remember meeting you personally. I'm sorry. I meet so many people."

The doctor nodded.

"It's okay. I understand. So do I."

She sat back.

"Our initial prescreening involved sixty thousand women from places all over the world. All these women fit preset parameters determined to include the most promising and healthy women on the planet. After examining medical records and personal histories, we narrowed the number to a little under twenty thousand. Narrowing parameters still further, we arrived at ten thousand, and that's when we began collecting genetic samples from the candidates remaining in our databases. To make a long story short, it took seventeen months to collect samples and another eighteen to set up and run the analysis."

Taken aback, Layla wagged her head.

"*Now* I remember reading a couple of stories about you in the *Times*! So *you're* the Dr. Benoit from the Genome Project? I always thought you were a man."

Twenty minutes later, after the appetizer, Isabel began her appeal.

"I imagine your lawyers let you know in no uncertain terms that this is a top-secret project involving the United States government?"

"Yes."

"And you realize that you cannot discuss any aspect of this project with anyone?"

Layla nodded.

"Yes, I do."

The doctor withdrew a set of documents from her lap and placed them on the table.

"I'll get right to the point. On August 7th, when Nostradamus collides with Earth, it will wipe out just about every form of animal life on the planet. The only hope for the continuance of the human species involves placing select persons in cryogenic stasis for a period that will exceed the time it will take for the Earth to recover. These persons will be removed from Earth during that period and returned to re-establish a human population on the planet."

Eyes fixed, Layla was intent on listening to everything before responding, and yet she interrupted.

"Waitaminute! Removed from the planet? What's *that* about?"

Isabel's voice remained steady.

"NASA and the United States Air Force are in the process of constructing a super shuttle to house forty-four individual cryocoolers in space. Once launched, it will attach to the space station, where it will tap into the station for power generated from solar panels. The station itself is being refitted and reprogrammed to maintain orbit for the next five hundred years."

She handed Layla an illustration of the space station with the super shuttle attached.

"The shuttle will be equipped to house forty-four humans for four hundred years in individual cryopods. Upon the appointed time for a return to the planet, two pilots will be first awakened in their cryopods. The pilots will be Life Ark surrogates with shuttle flight experience, but the shuttle has already been programmed for its return flight. The women at the helm will merely monitor the computer system as it flies the shuttle back to Earth."

"Good Lord! Sounds like a plot right out of science fiction! You mean the government can do all that?"

Isabel smirked.

"You'd be surprised. Once humans return to Earth, it will become necessary to determine the genetic make-up of the next population of humans. That's why we have been so dedicated to finding a best genetic prototype for the next population."

The waitress arrived with the hot plates and entrees for the family-style dinner. Within a minute, a dish of black-eyed peas, a bowl of collard greens, a side order of okra and a platter of garlic-baked chicken sat in the center of the table.

"Enjoy ladies. And if you need anything else, my name's Emilie."

Neither woman touched the food. They paid little attention to the server or food presentation. Yet both had gone silent, anticipating the resumption of the discussion. Isabel watched the server walk toward the bar, removed her glasses and spoke again.

"We were looking for an Eve of sorts, a Matrix, someone to be the mother of the next human population. And naturally, this Eve would have to be virtually free of recurrent genetic flaws in the natural human population, she would have to be young and fertile, she would have to be an almost perfect physical specimen and she would have to possess remarkable intelligence."

Layla laughed.

"And as evidence of my remarkable intelligence, I guess I'm supposed to realize you're talking about me, right?

The doctor smiled.

"I knew I wouldn't be disappointed. We'll finish this after dinner."

****

Asia swung the large, glossy shopping bags over the back of the bench seat of the restaurant booth and let them plop down on the other side. She sighed and then smiled.

"Mind if I leave those there?"

"No problem. Don't expect much of a crowd tonight."

She slid onto the bar stool across from the middle-aged bartender.

"Great. Then I'll have a double vodka martini, up—no fruit. Only takes up space."

The bartender nodded and walked away. A minute later, he placed the drink on the bar before her.

"You're Asia Franklin, right?"

"Yes. How'd you know?"

"They said you'd be a regular."

She nodded and shot the entire drink to be flippant.

"Just goes to show you shouldn't listen to gossip. You'll probably never see me again."

She tapped the glass with a shiny, polished fingernail.

"I'm empty."

She shot the second drink and ordered a third.

"How many bars are there down here?"

"Two, and I work at the other one as well. So if you ain't comin to either one or the other, you'll hafta drink at home."

"How many restaurants?"

"Three."

She sighed.

"Three? That'll never work."

She flicked the glass again.

"What's your name?"

"JR."

"Well JR, looks like I'm stuck with you, or you're stuck with me. Why only three?"

He held up a bottle of Jack Daniels.

"Mind?"

"A drinkin buddy? Please do."

He poured an ample shot and threw it back.

"I'm not sure how much you know about this place down here, but when it's all done, there will only be one hundred people. No more, no less. And that includes people like me whose only purpose down here is to serve people like you."

Her slurring and amplified voice let on that she was feeling the alcohol.

"And how many people like you are down here?"

JR shot another drink.

"Twenty-three, I think. Seven people between the three restaurants. Four in four boutiques. There's another two in a beauty salon. Then there's one biographer, a doctor, two nurses, a librarian, a cinema operator I think, two maids, a handyman and I think an event planner. Rest are VIPs and people like you."

"People like me?"

"Wives or husbands of VIPs. I suppose it won't matter after a while. We'll all die down here."

She stopped with the glass to her lips. Her mind lost in thought, she sat it on the bar.

"Then it's true? We'll never be able to *leave*?"

He laughed.

"And you're complainin? Hey, we're the lucky ones. The rest of em'll die out there when that goddamn asteroid hits. We'll be able to live out the rest of our lives down here."

"The rest of our lives? I'm only thirty-four and my grandmother's still alive at ninety-two. That could be another sixty years for me."

"Yeah, but at least you'll be alive. Where's your problem?"

She finished the drink and signaled surrender.

"No problem here. *You're* the one who might have a problem. For your sake, for your sanity and for your own safety, I just hope you brought along a *shitload* of booze."

****

"What about Reggie?"

Isabel pulled the cup of coffee front and center and answered.

"Ah yes, Reginald Reed, your husband. What about him?"

"Is? Will he be able to go?"

Isabel reached across and clutched Layla's hand.

"Look, he's your husband and I'm certain you love him very much, but everyone on the Life Ark is required to pass genetic screening and fit established parameters. I tried to include him, Layla, but the truth is he has the recessive gene for sickle cell. He's genetically prone to diabetes and hypertension and his father was an alcoholic. Those are just a few among many of the genetic flaws we are hoping to eliminate in the next population of humans. I'm sorry, but the government's invitation is specifically for you and does not include him."

Layla sat back in the leather armchair and took a deep breath, contemplating. She thought in silence for a couple of minutes before clearing her throat and responding.

"I, I really appreciate what you guys are trying to do with this Life Ark thing. It gives me hope for the future, something I think I had lost. It's not so dark and bleak now. Now I can hope humans will survive."

A tear ran down her right cheek.

"I'm also flattered to be chosen as the mother of your next human population, as you say. And you're giving me an opportunity to live past this thing."

She clenched her teeth and shut her eyes.

"But it's Reggie. He's my husband. I can't leave him to save myself at a time like this. We've been together through this so far. In a way, it's made us closer than ever. I love him. I've promised him and he's promised me that whatever goes down, we're going to be together in everything, right to the end."

She dragged her right palm down her face, smearing away the tears.

"I feel bad enough about lying to him about where I was going tonight."

Isabel was unaffected by the younger woman's unrestrained emotion.

"Fine, you love Reggie and he loves you. But this isn't about Reggie, Layla. It's about the future of the human race. You do realize what's going to happen on August 7th, don't you?"

"Yes."

"If there was some way Reggie could be saved, but he had to leave you behind, would you want him to be saved?"

Layla sniffed, wiping away the last of the tears.

"Yes."

"If you two really love each other like you say you do, then he would be happy that you are first among the 44 humans on Earth chosen to survive this asteroid. He would be glad that you will be the mother to the next human race."

Layla glanced over at the illustration of the cryochambers.

"But he'd never know it."

"No, he'd never know."

"Now that's what I have a problem with. I mean, how would this work?"

Isabel was silent as the server poured coffee refills. Then she leaned over and spoke in a hushed tone.

"Layla Reed will die in an automobile accident next February, and while friends and loved ones celebrate her life at her funeral, you will be transported to a government facility in Colorado where you will receive a final briefing on the project and you'll be prepped for cold sleep and life thereafter."

She sipped the steaming coffee.

"The shuttle that will serve as Life Ark is set to depart for a deep space orbit on March 15th. Prior to that, it will take three days for doctors at a separate facility to put us under."

"Put us under? I take it that means you're planning on going?"

The doctor shrugged.

"Not by choice. In addition to acting as a surrogate myself, it will be necessary for me to go to oversee the *in vitro* fertilizations, embryo analysis and selection, as well as implantation in the surrogates."

"So you'll be in effect *breeding* humans for this next population?"

"That's what some of my critics and the raging moralists have called it, but in reality, it's not terribly different from what individuals do naturally. In selecting a mate, most humans, either consciously or subconsciously, consider factors relating to the genetic make-up of the potential offspring from a successful coupling, or breeding. We're just helping that process along, on a purely genetic and much more efficient level."

Layla enunciated her next words.

"You *will* be breeding humans?"

Isabel sighed.

"I'll be... pairing combinations of genes over three generations in order to achieve a diverse and deep gene pool that will ensure the survival, prosperity and dominance of the human race."

Layla nodded in silence as Isabel continued.

"I'll also be assisting Dr. Meyer, another surrogate who will be working to reintroduce and re-establish animal populations on the planet."

"Animal populations? So your scientists plan on going completely around this thing? You want to re-create Earth?"

"We *will* re-create Earth, and it will be a better Earth. We'll eliminate many of the diseases and defects that have plagued man for millions of years. Ovarian cancer—gone. Alzheimer's disease—history. Birth defects, venereal disease, mental illness—all eliminated within three generations. We'll expand the average human life span to one hundred and twenty or even one hundred and fifty years. We'll create the utopian society. We'll do away with the insanity of war. We'll wipe out prejudice and injustice. We'll perpetuate all the good in humanity and eliminate defect."

Layla sat back in the seat, crossing her arms.

"And that's why you eliminated Reggie, isn't it?"

"Excuse me?"

"That's why you eliminated Reggie? Because you've determined that he's defective?"

Isabel seemed insulted that Layla did not appreciate her excitement.

"I'm really sorry, Layla. But when you're starting all over, you don't exactly want to use a genetic sample with diabetes and sickle cell as one of your primary building blocks. It's nothing personal, really."

Layla wagged her head, stiffened her neck and pointed her index finger.

"Not for you. It's nothing personal to you, but this is very personal to me. We're talking about my husband here, not some—"

Isabel interrupted.

"What we're talking about is the future of the human race. We'd like you to be a critical part of that future, but if you decide for whatever reason you don't want to be, this discussion ends here. We didn't leave ourselves without other options."

The cold directness of the doctor's reply stunned Layla. Her jaw slackened, leaving her speechless mouth open. Sensing her own advantage, Isabel pressed to close the deal.

"Answer me now. Are you saying you don't want to be a part of the Life Ark project? Are you saying you'd rather die here on this doomed planet next August rather than become the mother to the next human population on a new and improved Earth?"

"No. No, I'm not, not saying that."

"Then you *are* planning on being a part of the project?"

Layla held her palm toward the doctor in a defensive gesture.

"Now hold on! We don't even need to go there. I'm not saying I don't want to go, but I'm not about ready to commit to going under pressure either. This is all new to me, and I'm still struggling here just trying to take it all in. I'll need some time to think about this, and then I'll let you know for sure."

Isabel Benoit was already entering the deadline on her Palm Pilot.

"Fair enough. I understand. You have until November 1st to arrive at a decision. That's a little more than two weeks. It should be more than enough time."

She placed a one hundred doller bill in the restaurant bill folder and stood.

"Just remember, even if you do go, you won't have to leave the scene until February 15th. That's three and a half months plus Valentine's Day. Reggie will have you all that time."

The doctor smiled.

"And after that, you'll be mine."

Chapter 12

The room was dark and warm. The air was still, save the labored breathing coming from a place farthest away from the door. Gato Barbieri's heated, liquid, electrically-charged saxophone glided along and filled every wrinkle in the sheets, its breath tickling between her toes, its lips kissing the back of her left ear, its tongue tracing circles on the insides of her thighs, its fingers dancing on aroused nipples. She sighed aloud.

The slow, writhing art form that danced beneath the white sheets could barely be discerned in the windowless room. A tiny wisp of light from the artificial fireplace twenty feet away cast an exaggerated flickering shadow across the room, which played at times on the bed.

At times, it played on a woman's smooth ankle, her manicured foot extended into the air, swaying gently back and forth. Her breathy groan was followed by a man's muffled moan. A second ankle and foot extended from the sheets, swaying in unison with the other. She panted and cooed for three minutes. The intensity grew.

"No, no. Stop. That's enough."

The ankles came down as the shape under the sheets morphed once more.

"Come up here.

Another transition in the *pas de deux*.

"Yes, come up here. I'm ready. Yes, right there."

He grunted and then she sighed long and loud.

"Oh, yes!"

The shape under the glistening satiny expanse became more animated as his head and shoulders breached the white surface.

"Yes! Yes! You know I've wanted it. You know how bad I need it!"

In an instant, she ripped the sheet away, exposing the contorted juxtaposition of the rocking, tangled bodies on the bed.

"Yes! Fuck me, Davis! Oh! You know I need it! You know I need you to—"

A female voice interrupted in the darkness.

"Asia, profanity is unacceptable."

All motion on the bed came to a sudden and complete stop.

"Oh shit!"

"Davis, profanity is unacceptable."

"Get off me!"

Only the sound of silence.

"Goddammit Davis! I said get the fuck off me!"

"Asia, profanity is unacceptable."

The bodies fell apart as Davis called the commands.

"Censorship, disable. Lights on."

Asia was already tying her robe.

"Davis, how *could* you?"

"What?"

"You brought that bitch with us! You said you left her behind!"

He sighed and sat.

"I did. Calypso is a software system on a mainframe computer thousands of miles away. I can access her from anywhere. You know that."

She lit a cigarette, dragged and exhaled.

"I don't care where her fuckin mainframe ass is. You didn't have to bring any part of her here. I'm pissed, I'm really pissed."

"Once again, you're being irrational about this. She's a software system."

She sighed.

"I mean what if I brought some man in here to fuck me while you were out working all those late hours you work. What if I told you we were just interfacing? How would you feel?"

She could tell by the look in his eyes that he perceived the veiled threat. Blowing a cloud of smoke, she cocked her head and crossed her arms.

"Exactly!"

He stared at her for a moment.

"You don't understand."

He went over to the computer terminal in the corner of the room.

"I had to know."

"You had to know what?"

"If he had gotten to her. I had to know if he had found a way in."

She was amused.

"Oh really? Who's he?"

"This, this person. He calls himself *Misanthrope*. I told you about him. He's that hacker who's been trying to get inside her for the past two years. He's a very dangerous, very crazy person. I had to make sure he hadn't gotten in."

She swirled the glass to help the ice cool the vodka.

"So you brought her here, to a top-secret government facility?"

"It was the only way."

"They allowed that? I mean, once he gets into Calypso and she's here, won't he then be able to hack into the government's system?"

Davis spun the seat around to confront his wife.

"I've told you a hundred times, Asia! He's not getting in. Why don't you just pour yourself another drink and leave me alone."

"Does Smock know?"

She knew even before she asked the question that it wouldn't be answered.

"Does he know that you just compromised his whole project and the future so you could have your little bitch with you down here, you freak?"

Davis spoke without turning.

"Music, pop 60s, *You Talk Too Much*, loud."

The crystal tumbler just missed the back of Davis' head on its way toward the monitor, which was ruined.

"Music, off."

She was crying aloud.

"You're a very cruel man, Davis Franklin! I've never given you any reason to be so mean to me! But you're gonna pay. You're gonna pay for how mean you treat me!"

She screamed.

"You hear me?"

She went to the closet and began pulling on a pair of pants.

"You know, there's an old saying that you of all people need to think about, especially when I've got so much on you."

She opened the door and stepped out into the hallway, looking back.

"It goes, 'Hell hath no fury like a woman scorned.'"

****

"Would you care for perhaps a little more tea, Reverend?"

"I'm fine, Rabbi. Any more tea and I'll wind up floating out of here."

Reverend Jonah Williams and Rabbi David Blum had been friends for years. Their sons were the same age and had attended the same private schools for eight years. Over that time, the Reverend and the Rabbi had attended special school ceremonies and events, concerts and debates. They always seemed to find themselves standing side by side or sitting next to each other at functions.

Three years earlier, during an incident involving an alleged drug problem at the school, concerned parents looked to the team of Jonah Williams and David Blum for leadership. They considered themselves good friends since that time.

They often discussed which teachers were better and which administrators needed to go back to school. They debated the merits of the private high schools in the area. The Reverend loved the Rabbi's jokes, while the Rabbi was always up for the Reverend's down-home, kosher-style barbeque. Three times, the Reverend attended services at the synagogue, and the Reverend's congregation would never forget the day the Reverend had gotten a rabbi to "come go ta church."

A month earlier, the two went together to an interfaith conference in Israel, and when they returned, each faced the same set of challenges: a wife who was frightened and felt neglected, a bewildered, desperate and shrunken congregation looking for answers, and a resentful, angry fifteen-year-old son who wanted to marry.

A portion of the boys' anger was partially at God for the threat of the asteroid's existence, forcing fifteen-year-olds and other young people to try to live their entire lives in just one year. It wasn't fair.

Yet the sons directed a degree of the anger and resentment at their two fathers, Jonah Williams and David Blum. The boys thought their fathers often put the needs of their congregations before the needs of their sons and their wives. They resented their fathers, who never listened to or even considered the fears and concerns of the family, who assumed their faith in God was hereditary.

The situation was easier for the fathers, who had lived full lives, complete with independence, experience, adventure and years of sex. They had already lived the greater portion of their earthly lives. They were ready either for salvation or make to peace with God.

The prospects were different for classmates Dexter Williams and Stephen Blum, sons of these two influential men of faith. At fifteen, they had just begun to understand the prosperity that had surrounded them since birth. During their short lives, America was the most prosperous earthly environment of all time, while among all Americans, Dexter and Stephen were in positions of privilege.

They already attended one of the best high schools in the nation. In time, they would date the prettiest girls, attend the country's finest universities, land the best jobs, attract the most beautiful wives, acquire elegant homes in the best neighborhoods and enjoy long and prosperous lives. Thus the announcement of the impending collision with Nostradamus was especially difficult for them to accept.

Ironically, the boys got into an argument with another group of boys at the mall on August 7, just hours before President Whitmore made the announcement about the asteroid. During verbal sparring with boys from Compton, Dexter, acutely aware of class differences, sneered at the other boys and hurled a hubristic remark that silenced the other side.

In a moment of rash anger, he called them "lowlife niggers who'll never amount to anything," daring them to come see him in ten years to see who is better off then. Ten years. Yet four hours after that, the President informed him that he and Stephen had but one. Fate was the great equalizer.

In school, Dexter's favorite subject was science, while Stephen liked astronomy. Both were honors science students at Palos Verdes Peninsula High School, and both were enrolled in the high school outreach *Partnership in Science* program at Occidental College. So when the President and Dr. Engstrom described the series of events in the heavens that would lead to calamity on Earth, both boys followed with rapt attention.

Dexter believed in the Lord and believed he had adequate faith, but he considered himself a realist. God could change a person's heart, a person's actions or a person's spirit. God could protect Israel, God could part the sea, God could cause prophets to prophesy and God could raise the dead. He believed all that that happened back in ancient times.

But next year, could God stop a massive, eight-mile-wide chunk of solid metal hurtling through space on a direct collision course with Earth? The very thought of it defied all the physical laws of the universe. *Would* God do it? Why would God let such a situation exist in the first place? Was it just to test the faith of people on Earth?

Since August, the boys traded theories about God's purpose in this asteroid business. They discussed faith issues and questioned the nature of God and the overall scheme of the universe. While the public schools would shutdown on December 16, the private academy Dexter and Stephen attended was set to continue with classes through early June.

After school, the boys usually sat in the library together and proposed a hundred "what-ifs." Occasionally, girlfriends Brenda Brown and Joyce Heller joined them. Both girls were 16-year-old juniors, while the boys were sophomores.

September was a difficult month for all the kids at the school, especially for Joyce, whose father was shot by a group of wild teenagers on a random killing spree. The tragedy panicked Joyce, who became increasingly reliant on Stephen for love, understanding and support.

By September 17, she was urging marriage, not just for Stephen and herself, but also for Dexter and Brenda, who had become intrigued by the freedom and independence marriage offered. By month's end, both couples determined they would marry, with or without the blessing and goodwill of their parents.

Aaliyah Williams and Lynda Blum, the boys' mothers, were shocked by announcements from the boys and blamed the older girlfriends for using the enticement of marital sex to lure the boys away from their families. Lynda continued to be antagonistic toward Joyce, but Aaliyah gradually warmed to Brenda.

Brenda was a member of the church, and her mother grew up three doors down from Aaliyah. Thus, short of showing her tacit support, Aaliyah suggested that the children should receive counseling, that they should be encouraged to "keep the faith and trust in Almighty God." However, she thought the final decision should be left to them.

Jonah took Aaliyah's refusal to condemn the idea as a sign of disrespect to her husband and to God. Aaliyah stood her ground, quiet and courteous, though she knew it was damaging her marriage in such stressful circumstances. Dexter was, after all, "her baby boy, her pride and joy."

"What's this? Turn it back. Turn it back!"

Reverend Jonah Williams, his eyes wide, gestured as he pointed the remote, snapping his wrist each time he clicked. He stopped.

The image on the screen seemed like a horrible scene from a movie, though it was really happening. This was Fox News. Gray and black smoke rose from the tangled, twisted black body of some fallen aircraft as fires burned in trees surrounding the wreckage.

The loud, choppy whirl of helicopter blades overhead obscured much of what the reporter was saying. The reporter stood, facing the camera, his right hand covering his ear while he spoke into the microphone in his left hand.

"Yes, and the truly tragic thing... we have as of this moment an unconfirmed report that..."

Rabbi David Blum squinted as he stared at the television screen.

"Turn it up. I can't understand a word he's saying."

"...were on that small private jet—a sad thing for all of us indeed if the earlier report we got this afternoon is true. Lou?"

The Rabbi was on his feet, his head cocked, as he leaned toward the television.

"Did you hear that, Rev? Who did he say it was?"

"I, I couldn't—I didn't hear it. You're in the way."

Television coverage cut to the desk of the news anchor, where a gray-haired man spoke in a concerned voice.

"Once again, we have an unconfirmed report that the small jet used to transport First Lady Jean Whitmore and First Daughters daughters Beth and Susan Whitmore has gone down. That the jet crashed in the Rocky Mountains in Idaho, we know. Whether or not the First Lady and her daughters were on the jet, we've yet to confirm. If the First Lady and daughters were on that jet, it would be impossible for anyone to have survived the crash. Efforts are being made at contacting the White House and the First Lady's spokesperson in order to confirm what close sources are saying, which is that the First Lady and her daughters did indeed board that jet at 10:00 a.m., just ninety minutes before its pilot reported trouble and the jet suddenly disappeared from radar screens."

Jonah pointed and turned off the television, wagging his head.

"That's too bad, and not just because it might be Jane Whitmore. Certainly *someone* died in that crash. It's almost gotten to the point that I don't want to turn on the television any more. Lord help us all."

David Blum patted Jonah's shoulder as he passed. The rabbi shut his eyes, nodded and sat. Opening his eyes, he smiled.

"And he will, you know."

"What?"

"God will take care of us. We have his word on that."

Jonah smiled, agreeing.

"Yes we do."

The reverend sighed, glancing sidelong at his friend.

"You ever wonder?"

"If maybe this asteroid is part of his plan? I have, but it just doesn't figure."

"You're right. I think, after all these years, I've gotten to know him pretty well. I can't believe he would let it happen. It doesn't matter what physical laws are or what the experts say. He won't let it happen."

Rabbi Blum half-chuckled.

"It's called faith, Jonah."

"And the boys, yours and mine, do you think it's fair for us to expect them to have our faith?"

"Two separate issues. One, should we expect them to have our faith? Yes, because if we didn't insist on it, they'd be lost for sure. And two, this getting *married* to their girlfriends thing. They're fifteen! They're not old enough to make decisions like that. Even the laws of the state disallow it. I compare it to the night God's angel passed over the firstborn of Israel in Egypt. The family heads were responsible for saving their households. It didn't matter what fifteen-year-olds wanted then, just like it doesn't matter now. They only *think* they know what's best for them."

"You're right.

Jonah bowed his head.

"Sometimes I worry that Dex hates me."

"Maybe he does. I'm sure he resents you for being the voice of reason, but in the end he'll respect you for being consistent in a world that's growing more and more chaotic and..."

The rabbi stopped, lost in thought, and after a moment of silence, he sighed.

"Me, I worry about my wife. I worry about Lynda."

"Why?"

"You know, she's always been close to her parents, especially her father. They live in Rhode Island. They're old, and she says she's worried about them. I think she's going to tell me she wants to go stay with them."

Jonah turned toward his friend.

"Why can't you move them out here?"

"Her father's a stubborn old man. He won't come. And her mother, I'd prefer to have at least seven or eight states between us, believe me. But I think Lynda wants to go."

Rabbi Blum wagged his head.

"What's worse, she'll want to take Stephen with her, to protect him from what she calls that little *nafka*, Joyce Heller."

He nodded.

"This I know: If Lynda takes Stephen and she goes to Rhode Island to be with her folks, she won't be coming back until this asteroid scare is over."

David Blum smiled, sarcasm in his expression.

"Wanna rent me a room?"

Chapter 13

The great size of the rosewood bed made Trudy Culpepper seem more like an infant as she lay in a fetal position, alternately wheezing and coughing. On those days when she was strong enough to sit up, she rocked back and forth. A somber Robert E. Lee eased into the room, followed by his wife, Becky, and two stepsons, teenaged Tyler and eight-year-old Dayton. Trudy's eyes brightened when her son entered the room and the rocking came to an instant stop.

"Bobby! Ya came? I knew ya'd come ta me."

He knelt by the bed and took his mother's hand.

"Yeah, Mama, I'm here. Nothin could keep me from you taday."

In that moment, Trudy's body tensed with a violent spasm. She shivered in pain and clutched her son's hand so hard that his fingers turned white. She moaned as tears ran down her face. A dollop of yellow-green snot exploded from her left nostril, dripping over her quivering lips. She gagged, almost vomiting, but nothing issued forth.

Her mouth though, was full of blood and saliva, which trailed from its corners. Nauseated, she swallowed. Robert Lee looked over toward the doctor who clenched his teeth, looked toward Trudy and wagged his head in a resigned manner.

"It's getting worse. Nothing else I can do. That's why I called."

When doctors down in Fountain, Alabama diagnosed Trudy with vaginal cancer, she believed it was a judgment from God. It was a shadow, which had followed her since she was sixteen years old.

When she was young, her parents took her to church. She remembered the preacher's words: "Fornicators will burn in Hell. And adulterers will suffer in the fires of Hades."

It wasn't her fault. She was only sixteen and didn't know any better. She didn't know she could have said no, that she *should* have said no. She was intimidated. Her parents should have never sent her to work at Mayor Leland Lee's house in the first place. Everyone in Burnt Corn, Alabama, knew what a lech he was in the first place. *What the hell were her parents thinkin?*

All that aside, Trudy could have said no. She could have refused to continue working in the home once the Mayor grabbed her that day. He had dragged her into his study and locked the door behind them. She struggled to get away, though only half-heartedly.

She protested when he pinned her to the couch, but not for long. And she relaxed her young, firm legs when he peeled down her panties and began to pleasure her with his mouth and tongue. She had never felt any sensation so incredible in all her life.

At sixteen, she looked like a woman. In fact, she looked better than most women. She completely filled the sexy, lacy 36DD bras and silky panties her mother handed down to her. Her waist was narrow and her hips were shapely. Her stomach and thighs were tight and firm. Her legs were soft and sculpted.

She wore no make-up, but her complexion was smooth and her face was pretty. Grown men began paying unusual attention to her when she was thirteen, and the condition had grown worse over the following three years.

Yet she felt like a woman at thirteen. She had womanly cravings. She craved stimulation. When no one was home, she spent time nude before the mirror looking at herself, touching herself, imagining what a man would do to her body, imagining how a man would enjoy her body.

In the months after the mayor grabbed her and pleasured her *down there*, she imagined Leland Lee as the man in her fantasies. When the Lees weren't home, she sometimes went into their bedroom, found his recently worn shirts and buried her face into the crumpled mass, inhaling.

Leland was handsome and dark, owing to his Shoshone Indian blood. The mixture of man and cologne drove her to near delirium. Once she even crawled naked into the Lee's huge rosewood bed with one of his shirts to her face, imagining he was in that unmade bed with her, pleasuring her again, this time *makin wild, passionate love* to her.

She always felt guilty on Sundays. *Lusting was, after all, one of the seven deadly sins*, at least, that's what the preacher always said. The Bible said it too, she thought. She knew that what she was feeling was wrong, especially when she reminded herself that Mayor Leland Lee was a respected married man with a wife and family.

Every Sunday, she swore to herself she would stop craving him, but ever since that incident in the study, whenever he placed his hand at her waist, whenever he stroked the palm of her hand with his finger, whenever she felt his warm breath as he whispered into her ear, she melted. She forgot those self-imposed promises and burned for him again.

Despite being a lothario, Leland was a handsome man with that same charm and genteel manner that made his son so mesmerizing to women. For the sixteen-year-old, ever since that episode in the mayor's study, it was a foregone conclusion. Impassioned, fertile, Trudy Culpepper would not be satisfied until she had Mayor Leland Lee between her legs, on top of her, his massive, throbbing manhood filling her completely.

Thanksgiving marked the beginning of the Christmas season, complete with all the entertaining and parties, as well as a planned two-week vacation to New York City for the mayor's wife and their children. Already suspicious, Abigail Lee phoned Trudy's mother and told her Trudy wouldn't be needed until mid-January. A day later, she called Trudy and warned Trudy not to come by the house while she was away.

Yet from the moment she learned about the trip, Trudy began scheming a way to get into the mayor's bed. During the second week of December, she went to work braless one day after learning Mrs. Lee would be out of town shopping for the afternoon.

It wasn't difficult to get Leland to notice her large, round, firm breasts under the tight fabric and stressed buttons of her blouse. She sighed encouragement as he undid those buttons with his teeth and tongue. He kissed all over her body that afternoon, but he was nervous about going further than that.

Her insides burning and churning with excitement, Trudy asked him if she could come over when his wife and family were away. Grinning as he imagined the prospect, he agreed.

It was the most exciting two weeks of her life. It was the first time she ever had sex with a man. It was the first time she ever loved a man. It was the singular, memorable moment when she crossed over from being a little girl to becoming a full-blown woman. And it happened right in that huge rosewood bed. Leland was a handsome, worldly man who knew exactly what to do, exactly how to make her body shiver and spasm.

Her parents worried after she had been gone for two days. She hadn't told anyone what she was planning. She just disappeared for two weeks, and she spent the better part of that time in Leland's huge rosewood bed, on her back, on her stomach, on Leland. She didn't care that the community was in an uproar concerning the disappearance of a quiet, demure, once-chaste sixteen-year-old.

She hadn't thought beyond the two weeks that Abigail Lee and the kids would be gone. When she just reappeared on January 3, her parents, relatives and the preacher had questions, but she had sworn to Leland that she would never reveal the relationship. Ignoring condemnation and threats of punishment, she said nothing.

When Abigail returned and heard of the disappearance, she called Trudy's parents and fired their daughter. Yet while Trudy kept her promise to Leland, her young, fertile body did not. No period in all of January. By mid-February, she knew. Her cousin Sandy said there was "a negra woman just outsida town who gots herbs ta cure that kinda thang," and Trudy bought the herbs, but she never took them. She wanted to talk to Leland first.

She hadn't seen him since the afternoon of January 3 and she missed him. On January 10, he had someone pass her a note, thanking her for staying quiet. He promised that someday they would be together again, after he left Abigail. His note was the last communication for almost two months, but now she was pregnant and beginning to show.

She couldn't take the herbs without letting Leland know.

"Kill it!" he said angrily. "Last thang I need! Root it out, gaddamned you! Root out that bastard! You kill it!"

The meeting was short and angry. Leland was changed.

"Do it or I'll kick your ass, ya little whore!"

He probably thought she did it out of spite, but she never took the herbs. She just could never bring herself to kill her own, her own flesh, her own baby. It was un-Christian. Weeks went by. The baby grew inside her and the whispering grew around her. It wasn't long before Abigail Lee called. It was a quiet Saturday afternoon in March. Abigail had been crying. She spoke softly.

"You're just a little girl, Trudy. Ah don't blame you. Ah forgive you."

A day later, to the shock of the entire community came the news that Mayor Leland Lee was dead. As he lay sleeping in the rosewood bed in which he and Trudy first made love, his wife had taken a butcher knife and cut halfway through his penis at the base. He had grabbed her right wrist to keep her from cutting completely through it, but she grasped it with her left hand and tore it the rest of the way through. Once she had the detached penis in her shaking hands, she panicked, threw it and fled from the room.

Leland screamed and groaned in agony as he fell back on the rosewood bed, his fingers desperately trying to pinch the wound closed, blood spurting from the corners of the rugged penilectomy. Micah Edwards, the neighbor from next door, responded to the loud groans and was over in less than two minutes, dragging a terrified Abigail behind him. Micah's curious wife, who neighbors gossiped to be one of Leland's paramours, came as far as the bedroom door.

Micah shouted at Abigail.

"Where is it? We can still save him. A doctor can sew it back on!"

She was hysterical, crying.

"Ah don't know! Ah swear! Ah threw it. It's in here somewhere!"

After searching the room for three minutes, Micah Edwards found it. Apparently, the cat was over behind the bed when Abigail threw the bloody penis. There was a stain where it had hit the wall, but the cat had taken it under the bed and had begun eating it. When Micah held it up, it was obvious to everyone, including Leland, that it was more than half-gone. Leland died an hour later and the sheriff arrested Abigail for first-degree murder.

Thirty-two years later the huge rosewood bed resurfaced at an estate sale after Abigail's death, and Trudy went through great lengths to acquire it. The bed had special significance to her. It was the only object in the world that linked the two great loves of her life: Leland Lee and her son, Bobby.

Many years before, all three had been in that bed together, if only for a brief moment. She and Leland had sinned against God in that bed and Leland had been judged. He died a violent death in it. And now, after all these years, as Trudy looked toward her son and his family, she was prepared to die in it.

She reached out again to grab her son's steady hand.

"They, they said there's a pill you can take, Bobby? They said there's a pink pill!"

Robert Lee sighed and signaled to Becky that it was time for her and the doctor to leave. Becky nodded and escorted the doctor out, leaving Robert, Earl and her two sons in the room with trembling Trudy.

"That's a *government* pill, Mama. It's all part of their plan. We don't take them pills here."

Another coughing spell. More blood, spit and snot. She gasped to catch her breath.

"I, I can't take this anymore. I don't care about the gaddamn government. I want that pink pill!"

He covered her mouth with his hand.

"Don't worry about it, Mama. I'm gonna take care a you."

Earl tapped Robert on the left elbow with the hard object, and Robert reached under his left arm with his right hand, gripping the Glock pistol firmly.

Tyler didn't flinch when Robert inserted the clip into the gun, but 8-year-old Dayton began an immediate protest.

"No! No, Daddy! Please don't! Please don't shoot Granny!"

Earl rebuffed the child.

"Shut up, boy! This is hard enough on all of us already! We don't need ya actin out like a little girl in here!"

Dayton, tears in his eyes, looked toward teenaged brother Tyler.

"No! No, Ty! Tell em! They cain't kill Granny!"

This time Earl grabbed the boy's shoulder and slapped his face with a hand and then a backhand.

"That's enough! Nah ya straighten up and be a man! Yer Granny's in pain. It's a better thang we put her outa her misery. We have a tradition in this family. We kill our own when that time comes. Now you just shut up and watch!"

Tyler was terrified of his Uncle Earl, so he cringed and cried, his head turned and eyes averted away from the bed. Earl had a fistful of Dayton's hair to make sure the younger boy was facing the scene.

Robert Lee looked from the position of the boys around the bed and then into his mother's terrified eyes. He was unnerved by the sight of his mother's frightened face.

This was a face that had comforted him all his life, no matter what. This was a mother who had dedicated her life to her son. She was a woman who had told him many times that she never had another child because, from the moment he was conceived, she selfishly wanted him to have every bit of her motherly love. Yet here he was, aiming a shaking pistol barrel between her eyes.

"No, Bobby, not in this bed. Ya don't know what it means ta me."

She had never told him the full story about his father. She never told him that Leland Lee was the only man she had ever truly loved. She never told him about the time he dragged her into his study, about the flirtation over eleven months, about the two glorious weeks in December she spent with him.

She never told him about the call from Abigail Lee. She never told him the truth about how his father died. She said he died in an accident. She never told him that his father's severed penis had been eaten by the family cat. And she never told him about the huge rosewood bed and its significance in her life.

So Robert Lee had no idea why, as she gasped for life in agony in her final moments, she insisted that he not end her life in that rosewood bed.

"If I hafta die in his bed, let me have that pink pill. Let me die in peace,"

She eyed the gun.

"Not like this."

Robert stiffened his jaw.

"Right now, I don't have no choice, and neither do you."

He batted back tears in his eyes.

"Say your goodbyes, Mama."

"Bobby?"

"I love you, Mama."

"Bobby—"

Everybody in the room jolted the moment the bullet exploded from the pistol, though Trudy's shuddering was the most animated. Robert Lee stepped back from the bed, groaning from his gut as he let the gun tumble to the floor. On the bed lay the corpse of a withered woman, a conspicuous, neat little hole in the center of her forehead, her twisted mouth gaping, her eyes wide open, her pale face bereft of human expression, blood seeping onto the sheets from the shattered remnants of skull behind her head.

"I'm sorry, Mama. We'll all miss you. May your soul find peace in the bosom of God."

Chapter 14

"I don't understand! What happened? What went wrong?"

President Whitmore, frantic and concerned, hurried down the corridor on Level Three toward the control center of the government's Crypt facility beneath the Sangre de Cristo Mountains in south central Colorado. Six Secret Service agents surrounded him and Crypt/Life Ark project director Don Smock.

"Where the hell is Jett?"

Smock answered.

"The Clinton Room. Mr. Turner is finishing debriefing the transportation personnel. Security reported to me that the situation is contained for the most part, but we have one big problem."

"What's that?"

"Your daughter, Susan. She's out there somewhere, God knows where. Somehow she managed to get away."

Whitmore forced a feeble smile as he nodded, acknowledging her escape. Just then, the conference room door flew open and two red-faced Secret Service agents began to exit, walking backward. Whitmore recognized the stentorian, angry, profanity-laced voice scolding them. Nonetheless, he let the agents slink away before addressing his National Security Advisor.

"Jett, what happened? I trusted you with my family. What went wrong?"

Jett Turner lowered his eyes, uneasy and embarrassed, before reaching out and hugging his old friend.

"Joe, I'm sorry."

He reached up with his right hand and clutched one of the President's drooped shoulders.

"Come on in."

The President sat at the table, his expression catatonic. Jett sat across from him, an open folder in his hands.

"Apparently Jean told the girls what was going on. We didn't know. Jean was determined not to come here, and I guess Beth didn't want it either. There's no way they could have known about our plans for bringing them over today, but Jean must have guessed it. Women's intuition!"

Jett placed the file folder on the table.

"All three played along with the plan until the end and then they surprised us. They were supposed to leave Washington aboard the First Lady's private jet at ten a.m. D.C. time for a meeting at noon in Seattle. After they were loaded, we secretly pulled them off and sent the jet on. We told them we were changing their transportation arrangements because we had just received information that their security had been threatened, a routine thing. Then they were reloaded aboard Air Force One and flown over to Peterson in Colorado Springs."

Jett slid the folder across the lacquered table toward the President.

"We had the pilot crash the First Lady's jet with four dead bodies in the Idaho Rockies at eleven o'clock Mountain Time and leaked the story to CNN. By now, they were supposed to be confirmed as dead in the crash, and they should have been comfortable in their quarters here. All this other business just blew me away. I blame myself. I know Jean. I should have anticipated it. I should have had them searched."

Joe Whitmore put on a pair of glasses and pulled the folder in front of him. As he scanned the first page, Jett cleared his throat and continued.

"After Air Force One arrived at Peterson, an agent went back to your family's compartment and found Jean and the girls dead. It seemed they had each taken one of those, those pink pill things. Jean left a suicide note. You have a copy of it right there. It explains just about everything. None of us knew."

Jett studied the President's troubled demeanor.

"Did you know?"

There was no answer. The President held the note in his trembling fingers. He closed his eyes and clenched his teeth on a few occasions while reading, only to resume reading with more resolve. He finished after five minutes, folded the note and put it in his shirt pocket.

"So what happened with Susan?"

Bewildered, Jett shook his head.

"Well, apparently when Secret Service reported the fact that Jean and the girls were dead, they had only checked Jean's body and

Beth's body. The agent just assumed Susan was dead as well, so he hurried away to report it."

Jett paused to contemplate the wording of his next statement.

"When they came back, Susan was gone. They searched the entire jet and couldn't find her."

Whitmore looked down, re-scanning the report as he listened. He interrupted.

"It says here they found her hair in the bathroom. She shaved her head?"

"Probably part of a disguise. She probably did it long before the agent found the bodies. He said he recalled that she was wearing a hat and baggy clothes."

Whitmore smiled.

"Since she was a little girl, she always said she wanted to be a spy. She's read all the books. She knows the game."

He looked back to his advisor.

"They're looking for her?"

Jett lit a cigarette as he answered.

"They think she's still on base somewhere. If she's there, they'll find her, but if she somehow got off and went to Wyoming to hang out with Lee and those wackos out there, we've got real trouble."

The alarm in the President's voice was evident.

"What makes you think she would go to Lee in Wyoming?"

Jett slid another folder toward Whitmore.

"Internet records. She's visited the New Republic's website twenty-five times since August, fifteen times just last month. I told you we should have taken them out a long time ago."

The President was skeptical.

"You obviously don't know Susan like I do. Logging onto the website and then physically going there would be too direct for her. She probably visited the site to lead you guys down a wrong alley. She probably had it planned for at least a month. I'm not a detective, but I know her. Wyoming would be the last place I'd look."

Jett blew a cloud of smoke.

"She's only eighteen. She ain't that smart."

Frustrated, he wagged his head.

"Wherever she is, we'll find her, but I still say we have to take out that complex before Lee and that wacko Krebbs hurt us all. Much as I like bein right, I don't want to have to say *I told you so* about this one."

The President shut the folder and slid it back across the table.

"You won't have to. The blockade's working. They've been allowed to sit out there all through summer and fall, but after the Stanton incident we haven't let any supplies in. Winter's coming, and we've got intelligence that Mr. Lee and New Lexington are unprepared and vulnerable. They'll all freeze out there, and Lee knows it."

Whitmore paused and continued.

"After the first real freeze, the casualties will mount and he'll have chaos. Then, as his people continue to die, he'll have resentment in his ranks. And when he's helpless to do anything to save his people, he'll have their anger and their blame. Without an infrastructure, New Lexington will collapse from within by the end of November."

The President stood.

"We'll drop clemency leaflets on New Lexington for the first two weeks of November. In those, we'll encourage his people to defect and offer a safe passage home. We'll even offer to provide transportation. In the third week, we'll drop warning leaflets, giving them all one last chance to leave before New Lexington is destroyed. Then we'll send in our bombers and fighters to take out the complex on the 23rd."

Jett stood, skeptical and surprised.

"Well, that's good. It's about time."

He still seemed confused.

"Waitaminute, November 23rd? Isn't that Thanksgiving Day?"

The President stood, wiping the moisture from his face with a handkerchief.

"Yes, and with any luck, New Lexington will be a frozen-over ghost town by then. We'll all have something to be thankful about for that. I don't know, but I've had this feeling from the first day I heard about Robert Lee and New Lexington that his New Republic would never amount to much of a threat."

****

Layla awoke at three-thirty a.m., again. It didn't matter what time she went to sleep. When three-thirty came, she just woke up, and she couldn't sleep well for the rest of the night. Usually she would just lie there in the dark, worrying about the months to come and the decision she would have to make. She imagined what the cryocooler chamber would be like, imagined her body being in stasis for four hundred years, imagined being cold to the core, her heart nearly stopped, dead for all intents and purposes.

Dr. Benoit said it would be like a good night's sleep. Layla would go to sleep in March and wake up four hundred years later, and it would feel like she had slept a single night. She worried about something going wrong with the space station or with her cryocooler chamber or suit. Sometimes she had nightmares about being frozen forever in space.

Lately, she had cut her workouts short in order to spend hours at the library and on the Internet, researching cryogenic technology and asteroid impact projections. Since August, the American scientific community had come together and had made significant gains in cold sleep and revival techniques.

The most significant of these involved long-term brain preservation at low sub-zero temperatures. Because intelligence, personality and other sensitive functions exist in the brain, the preservation and resuscitation of that crucial organ dominated the efforts of researchers. According to scientists, when cooling is achieved at slow rates, cellular damage in the brain is greatly reduced.

Individual cells do not burst because the slow cooling causes water to *leave* the cells. Ice, therefore, forms *between* the cells. The slow cooling process, however, caused varying degrees of injury to cell membranes, enzymes and other cell proteins by removing water from them.

Researchers working with the National Institute of General Medical Sciences had conducted experiments on animals using new genetically engineered, sugar-based cryoprotectants in addition to glycerol. In experiments, they had successfully frozen mammalian brains and restored them with minimal damage.

One experiment involved a cat brain treated with a fifteen percent glycerol-based solution and then frozen for a period of five days. Restoring the brain required a detailed thawing process and a perfusion of fresh donor blood, but upon testing, normal brain function had returned.

The same process was repeated on hamsters, dogs, sheep and cows, with relatively the same degree of success. Apparently, researchers were conducting long-term testing on the more complex chimpanzee and porpoise brains, but the results would not be available to the scientific community for months.

"There is always the chance that something might go very wrong, a chance we might not ever wake up," Dr. Benoit warned, "But if that happens, *we'll* never know it."

Layla wasn't even sure that she would want to volunteer to be a part of the Life Ark Project. Sure, the prospect of being the mother of the next human population was flattering, and the idea of seeing a new Earth was intriguing, but it all seemed unreal. An asteroid that would wipe out all life on Earth—unreal. A cryochamber in space where she would be in cold sleep for four hundred years and then restored to life—unreal. Humans returning to the Earth and establishing a new, improved, genetically engineered population—unreal.

Her Internet research confirmed what the television news broadcasts had been predicting for months. The impact would have devastating consequences on the planet. All Earth would feel the shock wave from the collision, and all eyes would be able see Nostradamus in the skies for several nights before August 7.

The materials blasted into space from the impact would rain back on Earth as fiery meteors and cause a global conflagration. The resultant dust and smoke from fires would fill the skies within twelve hours after impact, obscuring the sun for years. There would be rashes of earthquakes, floods, fires, hurricanes, tidal waves and other natural disasters for more than ten years after the collision as the Earth's plates adjusted and began to settle.

Previously existing and new volcanoes would erupt daily for a year, spewing ashes, smoke and sulfur gas into the atmosphere. Carbon dioxide and noxious gas pollutants would quickly rise to toxic levels, extinguishing and suffocating ninety percent of life on Earth within the first four months.

Then would come the great cold. The polar icecaps would double or triple in size. The plankton bloom in the seas would die, rippling starvation and death up the food chain. Even the equatorial environs, after the rainforests had burned to the ground, would be covered with a thin layer of snow and ice for the first hundred years.

Earth would be uninhabitable. For years, it would be a dead planet. After one hundred years, the skies would finally clear and the ice would begin to melt. The Great Thaw, ranging northward and southward from the equator, would take another two hundred years.

Yet, whereas months earlier experts were predicting an Earth void of all animal life, there were recent suggestions that some animal species would survive. During the thaw, plant life on Earth would vigorously begin to re-establish itself.

Several species of insects would emerge from the silt-infested beds of lakes, rivers and streams after the cleansing effect of runoffs. Flies would return. Cockroaches, ants and various other insects would make a comeback. According to some scientists, several aquatic reptilian and amphibian species might re-emerge, but only those that managed to hibernate in time. Some fish would return.

There was even a wild notion that a few species of hibernating rodents and mammals, voles, lemmings and shrews among them, would re-establish populations after the thaw. Life on Earth, scientists were discovering, was much more resilient than anyone previously believed.

The key to surviving the impact for every species, scientists noted, involved the ability to "turn off," "to go to sleep," "to achieve stasis" before the impact. Looking to the future of Earth, scientists were working to induce artificial hibernation, or artificial stasis, in various species of worms, mollusks, insects and animals. Nonetheless, there was no debate about their greatest challenge: sustained artificial stasis in human subjects.

Dr. Benoit said it would be February, sometime after Valentine's Day. There would be "an accident, most likely a car accident," and Layla would be through with this life on Earth, dead to this world by all accounts.

As Layla looked over at Reggie sleeping next to her, her heart ached. She imagined him hearing the news. He would be so devastated! And then he'd be alone. Sometimes she wondered if he'd find someone else to care about, someone else to hold at night in the last days, someone else to make love to on the last night. He always said he couldn't stand being alone. Of course he would! Would he turn to one of her best friends? The thought of it made her angry and her stomach queasy.

She wondered what being the mother to the next human population would involve. There would be five men on the Ark. Would she have to have sex with any of them? All of them? And all for the sake of humanity?

Sometimes the thought of it made her uncomfortable, while at other times it excited her. What would these men look like? Who would they be? What would be her legacy in the New World? Would she be respected and revered? Would she one day be worshipped as a goddess? She hoped not. It was enough to make her want to forgo the Life Ark project altogether.

On two or three occasions, she almost succumbed to the nagging of her conscience and told Reggie about Dr. Benoit and the government's bizarre offer. She hated keeping secrets from him, and yet she knew that if he knew, he'd make major trouble in his typical hotheaded style and the whole world would hear about it. The government might even feel obliged to take measures to silence him. No, it was better he didn't know anything about it, regardless of her decision.

Reggie opened his eyes, reached over and grabbed his wife's wrist.

"What are you doin? What are you lookin at?"

She was startled, unaware of how long he'd been awake.

"No, Noth, Nothing! I, I've just been up. I've been having a hard time sleeping lately. *You* know that."

He sat up in the bed, sighing.

"Conscience finally getting ta ya?"

She turned on her night lamp.

"What are you talking about?"

"Aw, come on! You *know*. You think I haven't noticed all the slippin out you been doin lately. I haven't asked ya about it cuz I trust you. You of all people know that after that New York incident, we agreed that we would tell each other everything. That was *your* idea. Since then, we've had a coupla rough times, but I've always broke it down an told ya the truth. I confessed about that thing I had with Brandy. So now it's your turn. Tell me straight up. Are you havin an affair?"

She was defensive, incredulous.

"No!"

She sighed, disgusted.

"You had to bring her up! Right up in the middle of our bed, you had to bring her name up!"

"I did it to remind you what it felt like, cuz that's how I'm feeling right now."

He could see the tears forming in her eyes. He touched her shoulder.

"I mean, would you really tell me if you were?"

Layla dipped her right shoulder to escape his hand.

"The truth is I would never cheat on you, Reggie. You know me better than that!"

He sat back to avoid her angry eyes.

"Yeah, but these are desperate times. Things happen."

"That's your lame excuse. Nothing happens to us, Reggie. We either make things happen, or we let them happen."

He sat in silence for a moment before speaking.

"So who's the man who's been sendin that black limo for you? The one that picks you up from the library?"

She shut her eyes, wagging her head.

"What? You've been *following* me?"

In the absence of an answer, she continued.

"For your information. The person I've been meeting with is not a man. It's a woman. Her name's Isabel Benoit. She's a government doctor."

"And what does she want with you?"

Layla chose her words carefully.

"She's doing research on the Human Genome Project. She says I have certain unique genetic qualities, and they're, they're just studying me."

"What for?"

Layla shrugged.

"I don't know, but I'm not the only one. I think they're just trying to preserve a record."

Reggie seemed more relaxed.

"And I was worried? I'm sorry, Boo."

"It's okay. See how you are? I oughta be asking *you* some of those questions, but I'll leave it alone."

After another silence, Reggie cleared his throat and spoke.

"Are they, uh, payin you any money for what you're doin?"

She got up, turned on the light and went into the closet. A minute later, she placed a metal box safe on the bed. She retrieved a key from her jewelry case on the dresser and opened the safe.

"I was going to surprise you."

She removed three large stacks of twenty dollar bills and placed them beside Reggie.

"I was saving it up for the anniversary of our first date in February on Valentine's Day two years ago. I guess it'll be our last. I just wanted to do something wonderful with you before it's all over."

Reggie stared in amazement at the money, and then he looked at his wife.

"I had no idea."

A tear ran down his cheek.

"I'm so sorry. I was just bein insecure. I'm sorry. Okay?"

His tears triggered a flood of emotion from her eyes. He pulled her into a tight embrace, his voice breaking.

"I'm all freaked out. I'm havin a hard time with this *dyin* thing. I don't wanna die, Boo. I wanna live! It was never supposed to happen like this."

He was sobbing.

"The only thing that's important to me now is you. If I have to die, I wanna die with you, holdin you like I am right now. I love you so much, Layla. I swear I'll never doubt you again."

"I love you too, Reggie."

He collected the stacks of money from the bed, offering them to his wife.

"Now you just put this money back up where you had it and do whatever you had planned for it. I'll pretend you never showed it to me. And I won't follow you again. I promise."

He embraced her again.

"Will you promise me something, Boo?"

She felt wonderful being wrapped in his strong arms.

"Yes. What is it?"

"Promise me we'll be together in the end, no matter what. I need you to promise me that."

She hesitated and began a reluctant explanation.

"How could either of us promise that? We just don't know what—"

He interrupted, squeezing her tighter.

"We love each other and that's powerful. If we really want to be together at the end, we can make it happen. I know it. Promise me."

"Reggie, I need to tell you something."

"I don't wanna hear it. Promise me."

She closed her teary eyes and squeezed him with all her might.

"I promise. I promise we'll be together in the end, no matter what."

Chapter 15

The two men walked along the narrow dirt road in silence. The only audible sound was the distinctive crunch of the frozen soil under their boots. The air was chilly and thin, stinging the outer edges of their ears and drawing red into their faces.

Great clouds of vapor billowed from their clenched mouths, rising heavenward and dissipating in their wake. One of the men occasionally spat a stream of black tobacco juice off to one side, where it stood in a puddle and froze solid before it could penetrate the frosty, hardened earth.

On their left was a reddish-brown rocky basin, stretching for miles downward until the horizon was lost in a cold, blue, misty haze. At their right were the footings, the subtly enlarged sub-ranges at the foundation of the mountains' eastern edges.

Further right loomed the Middle Rockies, many of the peaks covered with snow. The white cap of Fontenelle Mountain was visible in the southern view, as was the icy peak of Bald Knoll in the southeast. Vegetation was sparse in the immediate area, though further down in the basin were forests of lodgepole pines, cottonwood, spruce, birch, alder, balsam, Douglas fir and aspen.

The men's bundled bodies cast long shadows as they walked northwesterly before the rising sun. Rifles pointed down, they walked in silence for two hours.

Suddenly, they stopped. A flock of seven or eight ptarmigans, a chicken-sized species of mountain grouse, was feeding near a stand of gooseberry bushes. The birds were in their white phase in preparation for an early winter. Both men silently adjusted their feet and weight, lowering shoulder bags and supply straps to the ground.

As if on cue, they raised and leveled their rifles, each holding his breath. One of the men raised his hand, signaling a dog in the distance, frozen in a pointing stance, to rush the birds.

"*Ka—kapow!*"

The sound of the shots sent the already startled birds scrambling upward in all directions. The men held their positions for a moment as the smoke from the rifles cleared.

"I think we got three, Earl!"

New Republic President Robert E. Lee and his cousin Colonel Earl Krebbs were headed up the mountains hunting, but the hunting was just a consequential benefit of the true purpose for exploring the higher terrain.

Captain Clyde, a Shoshone elder and shaman who had lived near Mount Isabel all his life, had come to Lee a week earlier, warning him winter would come "early, suddenly and swiftly this year, probably early in November." The white coloring of the ptarmigans, he advised, clearly portended an early and extended season of cold weather was imminent.

The possibility of an early winter worried Robert Lee. While an instruction page on the New Republic's website went into detail about the severity of winters in Wyoming and directed volunteers and refugees to bring heavy sleeping bags, thermals, extra blankets and heavy-duty tents, many of the youth who arrived came empty-handed.

The New Republic had hoped its Internet campaign would bring about three hundred fifty thousand youth to New Lexington, but the response was overwhelming. Over eight hundred thousand teenagers and young adults had arrived before the government closed the border. The problem was simple: New Lexington had too many people and too few supplies.

The last New Republic Census and Readiness Survey, conducted in late September, revealed that less than half of the 1.4 million residents and settlers at New Lexington and in outlying areas would be prepared for an early winter. One analyst predicted as many as five hundred thousand could freeze to death if temperatures dropped below freezing for an extended period.

Lee had already visited campsites in elevated areas where dozens of teenagers had frozen to death during cold nights. He characterized the deaths as "isolated but horrible accidents due to inexperience at setting up camp," but he saw them as a harbinger of things to come.

This hunting trip up the mountain served to confirm what he already knew. Cold weather was coming and many of his people would freeze. As their leader, he would have to make decisions related to which people or groups of people he would protect and which people and groups he would abandon to the elements.

He had appealed to friendly financier/grocer Anton Bunch for shipments of blankets, fuel, food and supplies, but the government's blockade kept needed provisions from arriving. He was certain the federal government knew of New Lexington's predicament. If the federal government continued to block those supplies, tens of thousands of America's teenagers would freeze in the first week of severe weather alone.

The New Republic's information specialist made several attempts to highlight the federal government's responsibility in the event of massive human losses at New Lexington, but the government had cut their communication lines and shut down their main websites.

United States President Joe Whitmore made several private attempts to meet with Robert Lee "to work together to negotiate an equitable end to the standoff." Lee rejected the offers because the documents contained the word "surrender" in several places.

"Ssssh! Lookee there—"

There were twelve animals in all, five ewes, three yearlings and four lambs. The bighorn sheep seldom came to such low elevations in late October.

Their presence was the second sign that Captain Clyde, the Indian, told them to monitor, as it would indicate "the ancient *demon of cold* was making his way down from his mountaintop home." The wary sheep were still about three miles in the distance, farther up the mountain, so Robert Lee and Earl Krebbs left the dirt road, making their way toward the unsuspecting herd.

One mile off-road, they came upon the carcasses of a female coyote and two of her puppies. The bodies were intact because few carnivorous insects could endure the cold, and larger scavengers were not particularly fond of frozen coyote flesh.

The wind had robbed her body of moisture, causing the skin around her mouth to shrivel and draw back in a hideous death grin. A vulture had ripped a hole in her side and had eaten the better part of her frostbitten liver, kidneys and intestines. One of the pups was similarly ripped open, while the other pup's abdomen was large. The puppies also grinned.

Robert and Earl just stared at the scene in silence for more than five minutes. Both had seen dead animals before, but there was something different, something eerie about this particular omen. Unsettled, Robert was first to turn and walk away.

He hiked about thirty feet toward a huge boulder that offered protection from the bone-piercing wind. He leaned against its huge wall, unharnessed his bags and set his rifle on a rock. He cupped his hands to his ears to warm them. Clouds now covered the sky as the temperature continued to fall.

He could almost smell the impending snowfall. Two sets of stiff bird legs with feathered feet stuck out from the bag on his left, while he withdrew a large thermos and a pack of cigarettes from the other bag.

He poured two cups of coffee and lit a cigarette as he waited for Earl to come up the hill. Both men drank and smoked in silence for about ten minutes, and then Robert harked, spat and began.

"Ya know, Earl, all my life I always imagined Hell was hot. Fire, brimstone, flames jumpin everwhere. Well, now I know better."

"What's that?"

"Hell, it ain't hot at all. Hell's a cold place. Probably looks a lot like winter up here."

Earl shrugged, lighting one of his finger-rolled marijuana cigarettes.

"Cold? Well, I never thoughta that."

Robert continued, staring blankly as he spoke.

"Way I figure it, if I was Satan, I wouldn't burn people up. See, cuz when you burn people they can at least scream to express their pain and agony. They can twist and arch and wallow and react to the fire. I imagine the worst man in the world, a man guilty a the worst crimes since God made the Earth, ya watch im burnin an screamin an cryin an pleadin an beggin long enough, ya start feelin sorry for im. A burnin Hell would give folks an outlet, maybe even redemption. Burn the sin right out. Somehow ya just feel better when you can scream, when you can get it out."

Robert lit another cigarette and drew a long drag, blowing a huge cloud of smoke and vapor.

"A freezin Hell is another story. When it's cold an you're freezin, ya cain't scream, don't even wanna scream. Ya just draw up and hold it in. Ya shiver and ya suffer in silent agony. Insteada reactin like ya might ta flames, you're forced ta cringe up in some dark corner and think about how miserable you are. You're isolated. Ya can't express how you're feelin. All you have is cold. Now that's Hell."

He paused to hit the cigarette again.

"Ever see a man freeze ta death, Earl?"

"Seen em dead, but I ain't never watched it happen."

"Cold takes the fight right out've a man. Slowly sucks out his spirit. Eyes sink in his head, he don't talk, hardly moves, no hope an then he just kinda accepts his death. In the meantime, his brain is workin. He's sufferin right up until the moment he dies."

The wind had changed direction. Earl cringed and clutched his coat as a sharp, icy gust knifed through his body.

"This is Hell alright."

Silence fell and endured for five minutes until the wind changed again, offering a respite for another conversation. Snow began to fall, lightly at first.

Robert poured another cup of steaming coffee and spoke.

"If the federal government don't give in, we might lose a coupla hundred thousand, maybe more. We'll spend all our time and energy buryin the dead."

"What about the media? They ever get back ta ya?"

"Some martial law provision by the government. Media's banned from publishin or reportin any more stories about us, and they shut us down on the Internet. We're on our own out here. Far as the world's concerned, we're already dead."

Earl stood and peered up the mountain through the falling snow, checking to make sure the herd hadn't begun to move. He sat and poured himself another cup of coffee.

"We gotta reorganize the camp. All the people we want an like, we gotta pull em ta the center where we got enough fuel an supplies. Then we put the expendables on the fringes. The niggers, the Japs, the Arabs, the gaddamn Mexicans, we let *them* die. Anyone fuckin Jewish, the fat people, the cripples, the old people, the half-breeds, we never wanted em with us anyway. Call it cleansin. Then we pile up all those thousands a dead bodies and take pictures and get someone ta deliver em ta the media. That way we'll show the world what the federal government here in America is really about."

Robert spoke, continuing in his cousin's line of thought.

"And we can use this whole thing ta rebuild morale after folks start dyin. We'll blame all the dyin on the President cuz he cut off our supplies. Gaddamn Whitmore! We'll make sure everbody knows he knew exactly what he was doin. He wanted us ta freeze out here. So when it gets ta be Hell down there, we'll make sure the gaddamn world knows Whitmore is Satan."

Hillary, the Irish setter, became anxious from the inactivity and the falling temperature. She whined and urged the men to rise and move on, either back down the mountain or up toward the herd.

An hour later, snow fell in flurries and Robert and Earl were within range for a good shot. They had approached the foraging, slow-moving herd from a downwind direction and had set down behind a large rock, roughly one hundred yards away from the animals. Earl had special ordered his high-powered Harris M-93 50-caliber rifle with a Leupold Ultra 24X scope for a very different purpose, though he was anxious to test its efficiency. He trained his sights on the breast of one of the ewes. He held his breath and squeezed the trigger.

"I cain't believe it, Earl! Ya missed!"

Earl lowered the rifle and squinted to find his victim in the scattering herd. He laughed.

"I ain't missed."

He engaged the lock on the rifle and slipped it back into its case.

"Blew her leg clean off. That way we get three for the price a one. She had twins."

Robert raised the binoculars to his face, scanning through the swirls of snow, and found the ewe writhing on the ground, trying to stand on three legs.

Her left foreleg was completely gone, staining the snow bright red. A bloody stump where the leg had been twitched desperately as she rose and fell. The herd had fled up the mountain, but two lambs remained. Earl continued.

"If I had killed her, she wouldn't be bleatin like she is and the lambs woulda ran away with the rest of em. If I had aimed at a lamb, I'da only got one, but now I got three. Long as she's alive, they'll stay with her."

He unsheathed a huge machete and tested its edge with his fingertips.

"One round—two lambs. I never wanted the ewe in the first place. She'd be too heavy ta carry. I'll kill the babies one atta time. Take off the heads, gut em and pack em up. I'll leave the ewe. If she survives, she can always have more lambs."

He concluded as he began to ascend the mountain.

"And if she don't, she'll jus be food for the crows."

Chapter 16

"How's Lazarus?"

He answered without looking up.

"Lazarus went live this morning. Look around you. It's been running systems down here all day long without a single glitch."

"What about voice command operation?"

"Specific to residential units, offices and departments. Needs to be programmed individually. Every user already has a step-by-step tutorial."

The two men had met on Level Two at Jackie O's, one of the three restaurants in the Crypt. Don Smock pulled out a chair and sat at the table where Davis was already seated, engrossed in some project on the laptop before him.

Don sighed as he lowered himself onto the chair. He seemed worn out as he glanced up at the waitress.

"Uh, double bourbon, rocks, and the calamari appetizer, please."

He loosened his tie and unhinged the top button of his still-crisp white shirt. A black leather folder sat on the table before him. After opening it, he squinted while he read the first page, and then he drew a pair of reading glasses from his shirt pocket, putting them on his nose before continuing.

"You're ahead of schedule?"

"Read on. Running the Crypt is the easy part. Our toughest challenge will be establishing the remote computer interface between the Ark and the space station fifty years from now. The technology to do it won't even exist for the next ten years or so, though we will have developed the theory by June or July. Then we'll have to establish a power link to the station from the massive solar generator we'll deploy in April. We'll reprogram the station to periodically achieve a higher orbit every fifty years so it won't fall to Earth. Then we'll need to establish a link to the Lazarus mainframe so that Lazarus can override and rewrite the station's programming. And that doesn't begin to deal with the Ark programs required to monitor and maintain the bodies, supply needed infusions and injections, initiate cryogenic restoration and repair, launch that super shuttle and return them to Earth."

Davis shut the laptop.

"There's still so much to be done."

Don Smock sipped the bourbon and ran his fingers over his white hair.

"Have you reconsidered about going on the Ark yourself?"

"Isabel asked again, but I'm not about to turn this project over to Baldev. I'll probably spend at least fifteen years working at this before I could even feel the least bit comfortable about letting up. I'm forty-two now. By the time the Ark interfaces with the station, I'd be ninety-two. I'll be dead by then."

Smock stabbed a calamari ring and a set of tentacles with his fork, sprinkled a few drops of Tabasco sauce, put them in his mouth and savored as he chewed.

"So if you're going to be dead, Baldev Heir will probably also be dead, because he's older than you. So who is going to effect the interface with the station?"

"My daughter. She'll be fifty-four, and I'll make sure she knows Lazarus better than anyone else down here, and of course she'll have assistants who'll know what to do in case something happens to her."

Smock punched keys on a small, hand-held computer, speaking as he examined data.

"We're cutting it a little close. Unless something changes, come August 7th, we'll have exactly five people under ten years old down here. That means we'll only have five people who'll live long enough to perform manual tasks in fifty years. I'm hoping there isn't too much to do fifty years down the road."

Project Director Don Smock expressed his concerns because he did not intend to rescind one of the Crypt's primary protocols. It was a rule he fought hard to enact. According to Smock, the idea of perpetuating a human population in the Crypt would be futile and cruel.

After the impact, the Earth's surface would be unsuitable to humans for over three hundred fifty years, or twelve to eighteen generations. Along with scientists, Smock studied the idea of sustaining generations of humans underground with the hope of returning them to the surface. Findings came years before the Life Ark project was ever proposed. The problems with the plan involved the sheer amount of food, fuel and supplies that would be required to sustain a growing population for three and a half centuries.

And then, there was the natural selection factor that underlied Dr. Benoit's protests. Isabel Benoit suggested that over the course of twelve to eighteen generations living in a cave underground, "the natural process for the survival and reproductive success of Crypt selectees would favor genetic qualities best suited for inactive, subterranean life.

Thus, although at best humans could be returned to life on the surface, their success in that savage, terrestrial environment would be hampered by genetic qualities unsuited for the overgrown, perilous world above ground."

"If we are forced to start all over," she wrote, "it is imperative that we benefit from what we've learned from the Human Genome Project. Selectees would have to be chosen and allowed to propagate based solely on the quality of their genetic make-up, and that would exclude the President and many others on this current proposed list."

While the Life Ark proposal satisfied Dr. Benoit's desire to engineer the next human population, Don Smock continued to insist that Crypt selectees were not allowed to have children in that unnatural environment. Once Life Ark received approval by a special congressional committee, the project did away with the need to sustain a human population underground for the purpose of species preservation.

Thus the committee reluctantly yielded to Smock's caveat disallowing human reproduction in the Crypt. All male selectees would be required to have vasectomies, while doctors would examine women to make certain no pregnant selectee slipped in.

Within fifty years, the majority of the hundred selectees would be dead, with the rest to die in the twenty or so years that followed. There was a system in place to eject the cremated remains of the dead up into the environment through the Crypt's powerful and elaborate exhaust/filtration system, while the last survivor would have the option of taking the pink pill and entering the cremation chamber or dying from natural causes.

From the moment of the last death, Lazarus would take over control of all systems, shutting down power and life support on levels one through five. Then Lazarus would sleep for three hundred years, awakening to begin a series of tests on Earth's weather systems, its air, its water and its overall environment. When conditions finally became suitable for human life, Lazarus would contact the Life Ark computer and begin the procedure for revitalizing and repairing the volunteers.

According to Dr. Benoit, volunteers would spend at least two months in recovery in the cryochamber before they would be strong and coherent enough to survive the super shuttle's return into Earth's atmosphere.

The subtly conical Crypt was divided into seven levels, stacked vertically. This was possible because the original cave in the Sangre de Cristo Mountain Range was a vast cavern a mile in diameter with a ceiling seven hundred feet high, narrowing slightly at the top. The foot-thick, sealed, doubled walls of the structure's hull were both airtight and watertight. An enclosed system of chemical/biological/radiological filters processed incoming air to remove harmful germs, noxious gases and/or radioactive and chemical particles.

The outer shell was made of five-eighths-inch continuously welded low carbon steel plates, supported by structural steel frames. Twenty steel pilings, attached to heavy springs, for shock absorption, anchored The Crypt in place, some reaching some one hundred feet into the solid granite walls of the mountains. Between the shell and the pink granite that surrounded the Crypt were one thousand nine hundred ten steel springs, each weighing approximately one thousand pounds. The springs would allow the Crypt to move twelve inches in any one direction.

Level One, the floor nearest the surface, contained living quarters for the one hundred selectees, divided into four sections: Northwest, the Political Quarter; Northeast, the Science and Technology Quarter, where Davis and the technicians lived; Southwest, the Blue Collar, or the Working Quarter; and Southeast, the Crypt Administration Quarter, where Smock and his family lived. Living space per unit averaged about twelve hundred square feet.

Level Two, the second floor down, was bisected. On the east end were giant "Nostradamus Watch" and "Surface News Watch" monitors and a huge mall with shops, a cinema, a bowling alley and a gym. On the west end were three restaurants, four boutiques, a beauty salon, a dentist, a doctor, two bars and a library.

Level Three contained the Science and Research Department as well as Space Command. The NASA Life Ark Project Command

Center and Logistics were also located on Level Three. Residents at the Crypt were free to travel on Levels One and Two, but from Level Three on down, special security clearance was required.

Level Four was divided to house Crypt administration offices on the north side and computer programming on the south side. Both Davis Franklin and Don Smock had offices on the fourth level. Smock's Communications Center, the only place in the complex in contact with the outside world, was located in the northeast corner. The three members of the Crypt's Security/Law Enforcement Department worked out of a small office on the northwest corner.

Level Five was used exclusively for storage. Planners had dedicated the entire west side to food storage. There were eleven rows of refrigeration units and an adjacent area for dry goods. According to the Administration Center, there was enough food on Level Five to feed one hundred people for seventy-five years.

The east side of Level Five held sundry backup supplies for Levels One through Four. There were pallets containing diverse items, including blankets, light bulbs, clothing, shoes, mini refrigerators, wine, spirits, beer kegs, carpeting, personal computers and numerous other items. There were many pallets containing bottled water, though there was a thirty thousand-gallon main water reservoir on Level Five that served Levels One through Four.

A pipeline originating in a stream deep under the mountains traveled one hundred yards to the Crypt, where the water was pumped up the side of its hull, through an intricate filtration system, down through the top and past four levels to continually replenish the reservoir.

Level Six was also called the Refugium, and its director, Dr. Helen Hernandez, was Dr. Benoit's number one assistant. Isabel Benoit had her laboratory and offices on this level. Because of its greater height, Level Six was three times larger than any other level, organized in four sub-floors lined with cryopods. Dr. Hernandez and her team would be responsible for the preservation of Earth's flora and fauna.

It was her job to procure two healthy fecund females of many of the Earth species that would be wiped out as a result of the asteroid's impact. She would also acquire sperm and egg samples from each species. There were separate cryochambers for elephants, rhinos, lions, zebras, hippos, giraffes, wolves, elk, caribou, mink, raccoons, koalas, kangaroos, cattle, sheep, lemurs, tigers and other mammals. Scientists would preserve many egg-laying species, including birds, reptiles, fish and insects, but some cases would require only the preservation of fertilized eggs. Vats of concentrated sea plankton were also stored.

Level Six, a series of sub-floors containing thousands of individual cryochambers in the Refugium, required the greatest power output. The series of energy efficient compressors throughout the level were driven by electricity carried by large underground power lines directly into the Crypt from generators deep within Hoover Dam in far away Boulder City, Nevada.

Feasibility studies indicated that, even after the earthquakes, the instability of tectonic plates and the dramatic changes in weather, the huge hydroelectric engineering marvel would remain intact and operative. Though scientists predicted that cosmic winter would profoundly affect the water cycle, assiduous analysis yielded that the Colorado River would continue to flow through the dam throughout one hundred years of darkness, though at slightly depressed levels.

A secondary source of backup power could be provided by eight 1,750 kilowatt, 2,800 horsepower diesel generators. Beyond that, Level Six was backed up by an uninterruptible power system consisting of five thousand interconnected batteries.

Level Seven contained the supercomputer responsible for the resurrection of life on Earth. Despite Davis Franklin's extensive computer and software background, he was bewildered by the speed, capacity, complexity and enormous application potential of the carefully guarded technological phenomenon called Lazarus.

This supercomputer, developed by the United States government, was unlike any computer Davis had ever accessed. It was the only computer of its kind in the world, realizing technologies that the industry had considered merely theoretical.

The most fascinating of these technologies was computer programming based on chromosomal models. No person in the Crypt had seen Lazarus, as the interior of the sealed chamber that contained the mainframe was maintained at a constant temperature of minus fifteen degrees Celsius. This chamber was tethered within a larger chamber, which was tethered within an even larger chamber, purposed to dissipate potential shock resulting from plate tectonic shifting and earthquakes.

Davis and his team of software engineers had access to the computer from Level Four, and they had worked diligently for three months to finally bring Lazarus to life.

Don Smock lifted his plate and gave it to the server.

"So is Lazarus everything I said he'd be?"

Davis nodded as he sipped from the glass of club soda in his hand.

"We're going to do great things. We've got our work cut out for us over the next thirty years, but we're doing things that'll make the world on the other side surreal. With this new Lazarus technology, each user will have a voice-activated pocket mini-computer with the equivalent capacity of the entire World Wide Web today."

"And the dialogue chip?"

"Engineers will have to make some application adjustments, but sophisticated dialogue programs will be fully operational in about three years."

Davis opened the black leather folder before him and scanned a page, raising his eyebrows.

"But for now, we've had to focus on Phase One, which is the Life Ark/Space Station interface in fifty years and the overwrite of the station's programming. Phase Two will be the resurrection of Lazarus in three hundred fifty years—the system checks, the environmental tests, all the commands for restoring Isabel and her pets, the shuttle launch—all that."

Don Smock, who had been absorbed in the written material, looked up, closed the folder and patted it gently.

"Sounds good."

He sat back in the chair, smirking.

"Your wife came by to see me today. That Asia—she's a pretty gal."

Davis seemed irritated.

"Yeah? And—"

"She told me you brought Calypso..."

"And you know that's impossible."

Smock studied Davis's face.

"Have you downloaded any of her programs into your personal system?"

"No."

"Have you accessed her?"

Davis was squinting in anger.

"You had the com blocks put in yourself. You of all people know I have no access to the outside world from down here."

Smock interrupted.

"What I know is if anyone in the world could find a way around those com blocks, it would be the world's most celebrated hacker, Davis Franklin. You do realize though that any Calypso interface would seriously threaten the entire Lazarus Project?"

Stoic, Davis answered.

"There will be no interface."

Smock smiled.

"Calypso intrigues me. You know, I *could* allow you limited access to Calypso from our com center if, in exchange, you give her to me so I could study her."

Davis chopped his words.

"I don't want access."

Smock winked.

"If you change your mind..."

"I won't. So far, I've asked you for nothing, but now, I have a request. No, make that a demand."

"Really? And what's that?"

Davis leaned forward.

"I want my own unit. I will not live with Asia another day. I want her out of my room. You can keep her in Northeast Tech if you want, but I have to have my own space if this is going to work. And I want Blake."

Smock sat in silence for a moment before he sighed and answered.

"It won't be easy, but I can do it. Of course you know, that for all my extra efforts, you'll owe me a favor."

"I don't have a problem with that... as long as your payback doesn't involve Calypso. Calypso is off the table, and that's that."

Chapter 17

To the embarrassment of media sociologists, the size of the crowds outside Greater Faith Church in downtown Los Angeles continued to grow as the weeks went by. Commentators and analysts had predicted just the opposite. They suggested there would be a great cooling off and a general falling away trend in all churches, synagogues, mosques and temples.

In fact, there *was* a significant diminution in the attendance levels for many religious organizations, but for Reverend Jonah Williams and other religious leaders who called for faith in God's salvation, it was a time of unprecedented growth. Jonah gave Sunday sermons to huge, swelling crowds that extended well beyond the church's property lines. He put extra speakers and monitors in the parking lots in order to reach every troubled, desperate soul with his message.

Aaliyah and Dexter sat side by side in the third row back on the right side. Dexter sat to the left of his mother, with Brenda sitting to his left, leaning her head on his shoulder. At Aaliyah's right sat Megan, one of thousands of new worshipers who had come to the church since August.

Megan's short hair was neon blue and she had a diamond nose stud, but she was a pretty girl. Over the previous couple of weeks, she and Aaliyah had become close while working together on the Greater Faith's food distribution program. All four listened as Jonah raised his Bible and prepared to read.

"Once again, this is from verse 13, and it reads: *And the stars of heaven fell unto the earth, even as when a fig tree casteth her untimely figs, when she is shaken by a mighty wind...*"

He stopped, looking up.

"Brothers and Sisters, I don't think I need to tell you what time we're living in. You're reading it; you're living it. This is prophecy fulfilled. Stars of heaven falling unto the earth? Now we remember from Matthew 24, verses 29-31—remember? In verse 29, Lord Jesus speaks of stars falling from heaven. But what does he say happens after that? Let's read from Matthew."

Jonah flipped through his Bible and stopped midway.

"Second part of 29 says: *And the stars shall fall from heaven, and the powers of the heavens shall be shaken.*"

He looked up.

"Pay close attention to what he says next: *And then shall appear the sign of the Son of man in heaven, and then shall all the tribes of the earth mourn, and they shall see the Son of man coming in the clouds of heaven with power and great glory.*"

He closed the Bible.

"I'm going to put this right before you, and I'm going to do it even if sayin it rankles a few of my fellow ministers in the Lord. Verse 29 speaks of stars fallin from heaven. You see, there it says the stars have to fall from heaven first. And then what happens? Verse 30 tells us. It says 'And then,' meaning after that is, after the stars fall. It says 'And then shall appear the sign of the Son of man in heaven.' What this sign is, I don't profess to know, but our Lord Jesus said it himself. He said his sign would appear *after* the stars fell."

His eyes scanned the front row, where two older men sat, frowning. Jonah smiled slightly and cut over to his wife, who was listening, nodding.

"Will this asteroid, or star, fall to the Earth? Well, as I've been sayin all these months, I don't profess to know that. All I know is that God's purpose will be done, his purpose must be accomplished. How he's going to accomplish it, I don't know that either. I know he has dominion over the Earth and the heavens, and I know what he's promised me and what he's promised everyone of you: that *the eyes of the Lord are over the righteous, and his ears are open unto their prayers,* that the righteous shall not be forsaken, nor their seed have to beg for bread. It is his purpose that his righteous will be preserved, no matter what happens."

He walked out from behind the rostrum and waited for the cameras to train and focus on him.

"The key to all this is your faith, Brothers and Sisters. Where do you place your faith? In our Lord and his promises? In man and his technology? Or are you, like the lowly beasts of the field, incapable of faith in anything at all?"

He paused for effect.

"All around us in the world, we have examples of beast-like people who exercise faith in nothing but their own fleshly desires.

They're indulging in every way: drinking, drugs, sex orgies, human sacrifice, slavery, murders. Just imagine a perversion, and they're doing it out there. Don't have to go out there too far to see it. And when they realize that there's no real satisfaction or salvation in this self-indulgence, they either find somewhere else to put their faith or take that pink pill and it's over. Just last month in Los Angeles alone, there were over sixty thousand confirmed pink pill suicides."

The congregation reacted with comments of agreement, as many had lost relatives and friends to the fatal drug.

"And then there are those who put their faith in man and his science and technology. They replace God with science and look to science and technology for salvation. We've all been seeing it on the news—governments and wealthy individuals are building vast complexes underground and in mountain caves to try to save themselves. The Lord Jesus describes these people in the Bible book of Revelation, chapter six. In verse 15, he says: *And the kings of the earth, and the great men, and the rich men, and their chief captains, and the mighty men, and every bondman, and every free man, hid themselves in the dens and in the rocks of the mountains...* And verse 16: *And said to the mountains and the rocks, Fall on us, and hide us from the face of him that sitteth on the throne, and from the wrath of the Lamb, for the great day of his wrath is come, and who shall be able to stand?*"

A medley of *Amen* and *Can't hide from God!* from the congregation chorus.

"But will they find salvation in dens and in the rocks of the mountains? No, because science and technology fail to recognize that salvation comes only from God. Technology is fine, but man makes a mistake when he uses technology in an attempt to thwart God's purpose for man and Earth, when he uses technology to *replace* God. Technology is not the answer. They will not be able to hide from God's judgment."

The audience agreed.

"Now let's go back to the Bible book of Matthew, chapter 24, where Jesus tells those who place their faith in God and his promises what *they* should be doing. Verse 44 says: *Therefore be ye also ready, for in such an hour as ye think not the Son of man cometh. Who then is a faithful and wise servant, whom his lord hath made ruler over his household, to give them meat in due season? Blessed is that servant, whom his lord when he cometh shall find so doing.* So rather than spending our time worrying about whether or not this asteroid is going to destroy the Earth, God's servants want to do as he commanded at Luke 21: *Watch ye therefore, and pray always, that ye may be accounted worthy to escape all these things that shall come to pass, and to stand before the Son of man.*"

Once the sermon was over, the masses crowded in around Jonah, encouraging him as he had encouraged them. Still others asked his advice on personal matters. An hour later, he found his wife and gave her a hug, as always, whispering as he sought her honest review on the morning's message. She told him the sermon was "effective," but she said there was a delegation of concerned ministers waiting to talk to him in the green room.

The seven ministers had come from districts all across the country. They had come with a resolution, which contained a tacit demand within that the Reverend Jonah Williams should modify his message forthwith to make it reflect more on "God's purpose rather than the Reverend's personal philosophy."

They expressed concerns that Greater Faith had become the largest single church in the country because Jonah Williams was pandering to fear in the masses and their ignorance of God's true purpose. They contended the asteroid, as prophesied, would destroy the Earth and that, as God promised at 1 Corinthians 15, *We shall not all sleep, but we shall all be changed... that in a moment, in the twinkling of an eye... we shall be raised up incorruptible, and we shall be changed.* The wicked would suffer and burn on Earth while the righteous would be caught up in rapture and transferred instantly to heavenly life.

Jonah listened as fellow ministers disparaged and criticized him, accusing him of false prophesying and ignorance for his "misinterpretation of scripture." Finally, after he had heard enough, he stood, and in a polite manner told the ministers they were entitled to their opinion, but that in the end, it was for God alone to judge him. He told the ministers he was rejecting their resolution. He said he would pray for them instead. Angry, the ministers condemned him and predicted destruction for him and disaster for his misled congregation. They called him a false apostle.

"When they all burn in Hell, their blood will be on your hands. Be prepared for the day, brotha, when God asks that blood back from you."

****

"Roger that, comin up. And there she is! Looks like I got a visual."

Despite the usual white noise, radio reception was clean on that October 30 morning. The Utah skies were cool and clear, except for the swelling, ribbon-like vapor trails left by two jet black F-15 Eagles streaking eastward and upward.

"Looks like a 727-class domestic, bearing forty-one degrees north northeast. She's up at about eighteen thousand feet. We'll climb up there and fall in behind her."

Colonel Keith Cullen, flying lead, with Major Mark Tallisker on his tip, had been flying since 0830 out of Hill Air Force Base on a course plotted to intercept the large jet. The jet had been traveling faster than Air Command anticipated, so the F-15s had spent the last fourteen minutes catching up.

A woman's monotone voice broke the silence as the fighters leveled off behind the private jet.

"So far, she hasn't answered any of our hails. We're estimating roughly fifteen minutes to point zero. You have your orders. Over."

Keith Cullen, his eyes never averting from the flight information projected on the windscreen, leaned left as he maneuvered the fighter to a position left of the large jet. His hands worked deftly and stopped when the red-orange light on the head-up display indicated that the AIM-7F/M Sparrow missiles in the fighter's lower fuselage corners were armed.

"Howdy Ma'am."

The air-to-air missile, fired into the jet's path, flew across less than one hundred feet from nervous pilots in the cockpit. It exploded seconds later, a mile away, obliterating a bluff in the distance. The jet slowed in response.

Cullen spoke aloud to Tallisker, who trailed fifty yards behind.

"How's *that* for an introduction?"

He opened a frequency and spoke into the microphone suspended from his headgear.

"This is Colonel Keith Cullen with the United States Air Force. Be advised that any attempt to fly across the twenty-mile perimeter no-fly zone outside the New Republic complex will be considered an act of high treason against the United States of America. Within minutes, you will be approaching point zero. If you attempt to cross into the twenty-mile no-fly zone, you and your aircraft will be destroyed. Turn it around now and go home."

The jet slowed still further. One minute later came a response in a Texas accent.

"Uh, Colonel Cullen, my name is Anton Bunch, and I want you to know that what we're flyin here is a *humanitarian* mission. We have no weapons on board. It's just me, two pilots, forty-five teenagers and other young people. We got blankets, tents, sleepin bags and food, oh, and a camera link with CNN. They're broadcastin this mission live all over America from inside this jet. All we want to do is drop kids and provisions. Without extra provisions, thousands of those young people down there are gonna freeze and starve to death."

Cullen responded.

"Message is for the pilot. I repeat, any attempt to fly for any reason within twenty miles of the New Republic complex at Mount Isabel will be considered an act of high treason against the United States of America. I have orders to destroy your aircraft if you attempt to cross the perimeter boundary."

"Colonel, you mean to tell me that the United States of America would have you fire on innocent civilians, most of em under twenty years old, flyin a humanitarian mission to save lives?"

Receiving no response, the male voice continued.

"Colonel Cullen, are you a Christian?"

Cullen hesitated. He answered.

"Yes."

"You're telling me that bein the decent Christian man you no doubt are, you would fire your weapons knowin full well you'd be killin forty-eight good Samaritans? Sure you have your orders from your corrupt, misguided government, but what are your orders from God?"

Cullen clenched his jaw and squinted in anger. While he wasn't one to engage in philosophical debate during a mission, this inference, which was being broadcast before the world, was an attack on his Christianity and on Christianity as a whole.

"In the end, God'll judge us both. I'll stand before him one day. But let me tell ya, you fly across that line and you and everyone on that aircraft'll be facin him today. Cross that line, and I swear ta God I'll blow ya away."

Within a minute, the jet dipped its left wing, veered at a ninety-degree angle and took up a course parallel to the perimeter, circling ten miles outside the government's boundary line. The fighters followed as the jet crossed into Wyoming, maintaining a circle miles outside the boundary. As they approached New Lexington, they realized as expected, that long-range communication in the area was being jammed. The pilots could speak to each other, but they had lost contact with Air Command.

Suspicious of the jet pilot's deliberate decision to descend to five thousand feet, Cullen armed additional weapon systems, his eyes monitoring information provided by the Eagle's tactical electronic warfare system.

"Oh shit! I should've figured it, Tallie. We've got incoming! Son of a bitch!"

The warning receivers in both fighters blinked as pilots and computers began a series of countermeasures. Three trailer-launched Hawk missiles had been fired from a road on the rocky surface as the fighters flew by, and they were closing quickly. On-board computers identified the second and third as they were launched and jammed their radar systems, causing them to fail seconds later, but the first was still incoming.

Cullen smiled to himself. It had been almost ten years since he had experienced this intoxicating, heat-of-the-battle adrenaline rush. He attempted to report the attack to ground control, then he spoke orders to Tallisker.

"Hold your position. Launch your decoy."

Tallisker ejected his fighter's Fiber Optic Towed Decoy, which was dragged some two hundred yards behind his aircraft. The decoy transmitted a signal like that of the fighter's threat radar, causing the missile to detect and lock on the decoy rather than the aircraft. Both pilots heard the missile explode and watched its signal disappear from the pulse-Doppler radar screen.

Colonel Cullen hailed the pilots of the jet once more.

"Be advised you now have exactly three minutes to abandon your present course. Whoa!"

He spoke to Tallisker.

"Two more at four o'clock. Jamming."

Tallisker responded, panic evident in his voice.

"It's not working!"

"Hold steady, Tallie. Too late for any other measure right now. You can't outrun it."

"Five hundred meters and closing. I'm breaking!"

Now Cullen's voice was filled with urgency.

"Goddamit Tallie! Don't—"

His partner gone, Cullen's frantic fingers worked to reset the jamming command. Sweat streamed down his face. Earlier, the adrenaline rush felt great, but now Colonel Keith Cullen was literally ready to shit his pants. Three hundred yards and closing! Then all at once, a light on the display came on indicating that the missile's radar signal was successfully jammed. Within seconds, its signal disappeared from the screen. He sighed and immediately ascended another one thousand feet, still trailing the big jet.

"Okay assholes, you now have two minutes to change your present course before I blow you out of the sky."

One minute later, another voice from the jet came through the headset.

"Colonel Cullen, this is Zachary Brumfeld, Major General with the United States Army. Forthwith, I'm takin jurisdiction of this situation, and I'm orderin you ta stand down. This civilian aircraft has absolutely zero defensive capability and it's flyin a purely humanitarian mission. I'm orderin you ta allow this aircraft ta land within the perimeter."

Cullen was quick to respond.

"Major General, we know each other. I flew support for you in the Afghan offensive. With all due respect though, General, you are not in my chain of command. I have orders to destroy your aircraft if you attempt to penetrate the no-fly zone, and that's exactly what I'll do if your pilots don't plot a course away from here within one minute."

An immediate response.

"What if I told you, Colonel, that I could provide you incontrovertible proof that the federal government has been exaggerating this asteroid situation from the beginning? What if I could provide you absolute proof that members of the Trilateral Commission cooked up this scheme in the early 1980s and have been

waiting all this time for an asteroid that would fly by close enough to take advantage of the world in panic?"

Cullen sneered with contempt.

"You General, are a traitor to America. Shame on you, General. You are unworthy of being a member of the United States military. Besides that, your time is up. You've left me no choice."

He descended, locked weapons systems on the jet and prepared to fire two AIM-9L/M Sidewinder missiles from two pylons under the wings. He trained his sights on the jet's wide fuselage.

"Oh shit, not again!"

Initially he assumed additional U.S. Hawk missiles had been launched from a trailer on the ground, but after a double take back to the head-up display, he was baffled.

"What the hell?"

He was certain the Eagle's tactical electronic warfare system was failing because what he saw was just too impossible to believe.

"Tallie? Is that you? What's going on?"

Right there on the windscreen display, the warning threat light was on, indicating to Colonel Cullen that another aircraft had its weapons system locked on his fighter. It made no sense.

His own onboard "identification friend or foe" system informed him a minute earlier that the approaching aircraft seen on radar was friendly. What's more, the system indicated that it was none other than the fighter he had flown alongside all day—the F-15 Eagle piloted by his subordinate, Major Mark Tallisker.

"Goddamit Mark! What are you doing?"

"You have no choice, Keith. You have to let the 727 land. The fate of the New Republic depends on getting those supplies in before the cold weather comes."

Cullen couldn't believe his ears. He had known Tallisker for twelve years. They had been on vacation together. Their children had dated. And he had always respected this fellow officer for his courage and loyalty to his country.

"Don't tell me they got to you too."

"Yes, I'm defecting to the New Republic. But it's not just me, Keith. Right now, we got a squadron of F-18s on their way over from Warren in Laramie. They say we even got a tank division rollin in from somewhere."

Cullen flicked his eyes over to the still blinking warning threat light. Was his partner really ready to launch on him?

"What the fuck! I thought you were smarter than that, Mark. Why?"

"Because this asteroid! It's comin, but it's not gonna hit. It's supposed to fly by us about fifty miles away. It'll be close, but it won't hit. The government's known it all along. They killed that astronomer Helen Engstrom because she was going to come out and tell the world about it. Disappeared without a trace."

The right wing of the huge jet dipped, turning it perpendicular to the barrier. It was headed toward the landing strip near the complex. Now it all made sense. Now Keith Cullen realized why General Barksdale had specifically chosen him, a decorated, high-ranking colonel, to fly this mission.

Men all over were desperate. Facing certain destruction from the asteroid, many men were susceptible to persuasion and conversion by leaders who held out the false hope of salvation. First the Major General, then Mark Tallisker and even a squadron of F-18 pilots and their fighters! As he looked over at the domestic jet, full of blankets, supplies, traitors, a billionaire, an influential Major General and Lord knows who or what else, he realized what he had to do. He realized what it meant for his country.

To him, it was an honor to be where he was, with so much at stake. He realized his actions during the next few seconds could tip the scales one way or the other. His choice would make the difference. He chose to be brave, and above all, he chose the honor of being able to give his life for his country.

"*Cry havoc, and let slip the dogs of war!*"

The force of the missiles taking off caused his aircraft to jerk and then the 727's fuselage exploded in flames. The threat was no more. Through his headset, he could hear Major Mark Tallisker screaming.

"Nooo!"

Cullen tensed for a moment, and then he relaxed, accepting his fate as he saw his field of vision suddenly flooded in flames.

Chapter 18

It was the biggest crowd ever at Dubya's, the little Tex-Mex restaurant on Level Two. Selena Tejeda, its full-time manager, boasted that she had entertained nineteen customers so far that night, five more than the record for any other restaurant in the Crypt to date. Dubya's served an incredible barbecued flank steak sandwich, in addition to chili con carne, tacos, enchiladas, grilled tiger shrimp, carnitas, hickory-smoked chicken and spicy, pan-fried, blackened catfish. The bar had great blended margaritas, stocked twelve kinds of tequila and served eight varieties of beer. Two television sets on either side of the bar played sports from the surface.

That night, patrons were watching the Washington Redskins and the Los Angeles Raiders compete in Superbowl XVIII at Tampa Stadium on January 22, 1984. The game was in its third quarter and people were standing and cheering after watching Marcus Allen score on a sevemty-four-yard run from scrimmage, increasing the Raider's lead to 35-9. Notwithstanding, Allen's historical run was missed by the dark-haired woman who had come over from Jackie O's because that restaurant had closed early for lack of business. She sat in the far corner eating a chicken Caesar salad, annoyed.

There was a commotion at the door as Selena and friends welcomed the restaurant's twentieth customer of the night. It was obvious to Selena that the woman who stumbled as she reached the bar had already been drinking. Ever discreet, Selena relocated the lady to the quieter side of the room, away from rowdy sports fans.

Settled on the bar stool, the pretty woman waved to the bartender.

"Hi JR!"

The bartender, ignoring the flailing arms of other customers, was over in an instant with a drink.

"Slummin it tonight, eh Asia?"

She took up the martini and gulped it down.

"I needed the atmosphere. Besides, I can't go home. Hey! You short-pourin me?"

JR ignored the question and narrowed his eyes as he mixed another martini.

"Why can't you go home?"

Her words were slurred. A tear streaked down her cheek as she stared ahead.

"Because Asshole kicked me out. They gave me my own unit, but he kept Blake. Now I'm all alone in this place."

Embarrassed, she grabbed a bar napkin and wiped the tears from her eyes. After she shot the next drink, she noticed that the young, good-looking man on her left had moved closer and was waiting for an opportunity to say something to her.

"What are you starin at? Get the fuck away from me!"

She answered the inquiries on faces further down the bar.

"I'm *gay*, okay?"

JR returned minutes later with a cosmopolitan.

"This one's from the customer in the corner. Says she's seen ya at Jackie O's."

Asia smiled and reached for the drink. Somewhat sated, she only sipped this time.

"Jackie O's! Davis has dinner there at night. Maybe she knows im. Where is she?"

JR pointed.

"Right over there."

Asia squinted, raising her forehand to her brow in a myopic salute as she peered through the smoky room.

"Her? She's, interesting in an odd way. Know anything about her?"

"She's some kinda doctor. I think she works down on Level Three."

"Think she knows Davis?"

The woman looked up, smiled and waved. JR spoke between his teeth, barely moving his lips.

"I think you're gonna find out soon enough."

Asia made it to the table without stumbling, and she sighed with relief as she sat.

"Thanks for the drink. Hi, my name's Asia."

The handshake was pleasant and lingering.

"I know. I've met your husband."

"Do you work with him?"

"Not directly. But I see him at meetings every morning."

The vodka made Asia bold.

"Have you *slept* with him?"

The woman smiled. Asia, she thought, was refreshing.

"I don't think I'm exactly his type. I've heard he's got a thing for some weird computer program. What's the name? Calypso? I think he's a genius in his field, but he's not exactly my type either. No offense intended."

"Bitch!"

"Excuse me?"

Asia smiled, as she understood the woman's confusion.

"Not you. I was talkin about Calypso. I just met you. If you're a bitch, I don't know it yet."

The woman laughed.

"No, I'm a monumental bitch. I was just wondering how you could possibly tell so soon."

By the time the bartender served the next round of drinks, the women were at ease with each other.

"So I imagine you've heard the news? Has Davis told the whole Lazarus team that he kicked me out?

"No, actually. If that is the case, that you've separated, he hasn't let on about it."

"Has he been acting strange?"

She knew it was a ridiculous question as soon as the words were in the air. Both women laughed.

"I mean, stranger than usual."

The ladies sat talking for thirty minutes, and Asia, after sharing several poignant vignettes from her "sad" life, after offering as many spiritual affirmations, after two spontaneous breakdowns with histrionic tears and after another cocktail, she felt she had found a new best friend.

"You're very pretty, Asia."

Embarrassed, she smiled, wiping the tears from her cheeks.

"Thank you."

The woman stroked Asia's face.

"Look at you. You're gorgeous."

She took Asia's hand.

"You've had a lot of alcohol tonight. You probably shouldn't be alone."

Asia's eyes watered.

"Tell that to my cruel husband when you see im in the morning. He even took Blake!"

"You're welcome to stay with me tonight. I've got plenty of room. I'm down here all alone as well, so I could use the company."

Asia clutched the hand holding hers, sobbing again.

"Oh, that is *so* nice of you."

She offered an explanation for the emotion.

"I just don't wanna go home. Bein there, bein alone, it's just too painful right now. Are you in Northeast Tech, too?"

The woman released Asia's hand. She answered as she reached over, signing the tab.

"Southeast Ad. Not too far from you."

She stood.

"You ready?"

Asia stood, wobbly, disoriented.

"I think so."

The woman stood beside her, sliding her arm around to clutch Asia's waist.

"Here. Let me help you."

The football game was just getting over as the women walked past the bar. A drunken man blocked their path, offering to take Asia off the woman's hands, or to take both women home. JR intervened, and the man apologized. JR had come around the bar, eying the dark-haired woman with suspicion and Asia with concern.

"She's a sweet gal. Just havin some personal problems. You take care of her."

The woman smiled.

"You mind your business, bartender, and I'll mind mine."

****

It was a warm, sunny November day in New York City. Event planners had worried that rain or cold would keep people away. Over the past few months, there had been so many tragic, depressing stories in media reports. There was the fire at Studio 54 that had killed a hundred people and the apparent suicides of two United States Supreme Court associate justices. Then there was the controversy concerning the slaughter of unarmed women and children by the

California National Guard in Criptown, a gang operated camp that had prospered outside the guarded Los Angeles city perimeter.

On the other side of the globe, China had invaded Korea-controlled South Japan and had stationed garrisoned troops along many coastal towns. China made the specious claimed the invasion was in response to Japan's incursion into and alleged cruelty against civilians in the Philippines. Death tolls involving as many as twenty-five separate wars in Africa were bewildering, with some reports suggesting more than two hundred thousand casualties.

Death hung thick in the air like a perpetual fog. Depression drizzled down like an unending dreary rain from gray, gloomy skies. For many in New York, hope was extinguished, frozen over in eternal cold.

While scores of young people resorted to drugs, alcohol and the pink pill in order to deal with depression, there were some who formed hope groups that participated in daily prayers. In New York City and other major U.S. metropolitan areas, organized prayer was a rapidly growing phenomenon. One group, the Last Day Orison Society, was working to organize a Global Prayer Day with the hope of offering up two billion individual and specific salvation prayers over a twenty-four-hour period.

Others sought to overcome depression and the widespread gloom through involvement in humanitarian endeavors. Pop icon Pandora, an internationally known singer, actress and *Earth First* activist, had worked since late August hoping to produce a huge concert in Central Park on All Saint's Day, November 1st. She had solicited and secured participation from the biggest names in the music industry.

According to her event spokesperson, a legendary soul singer would croon *America, The Beautiful* to start the event, the world's most celebrated diva would perform the opening number, followed by an aging British rock band and fifty-six additional numbers by individual performers or groups. The concert would last fourteen hours. The King of Pop would be the penultimate performer, with Pandora closing the show. All one hundred seventy artists involved had agreed to donate their performances. The concert was free to the public, though event planners charged three hundred and fifty dollars each for the fifteen hundred VIP seats closest to the stage. The half million dollars, raised from ticket sales, would be spent to erect a monument in Central Park as a tribute to music recording artists of Earth's twentieth and twenty-first centuries.

The monument would be a fully enclosed twenty-foot-tall airtight structure made of Hadfield manganese steel. Its tungsten foundation supports would reach twenty feet underground, embedded in solid rock. Each outside wall of the heptagonal building would be inset to accommodate a two inch thick, twelve by eight foot bronze panel. The seven separate panels, each containing a detailed collage of engravings featuring industry legends and icons, would represent music from the 40s, 50s, 60s, 70s, 80s, 90s and 00s respectively.

Inside the indestructible and impenetrable sanctuary, there would be a CD-ROM and DVD library containing the comprehensive history of man's music from the beginning of his existence. A DVD version of this last concert in Central Park would play on a feature screen inside. According to Pandora and planners, the door would automatically lock on July 4, and a computerized sentry system would keep it locked for four hundred years.

Wary about security, the New York National Guard had decided to disallow the concert for its sheer scope: one hundred seventy artists, as many as two hundred fifty back-up musicians, sixty technicians and a crowd of one hundred and eighty thousand crazy, partying fans. As if the Guard didn't have enough to do on a daily basis in a city like New York.

A resourceful businesswoman, Pandora prevailed upon the New York governor and President Whitmore to lend additional troops and money for security and security improvements. Both agreed to her requests, supporting her cause for its "historical significance."

Thus the platforms went in, along with the stages, the lights and the sound systems. For security purposes, a total of one hundred ninety six-inch cameras were installed at various locations throughout the designated concert audience area to monitor the crowd for any signs of suspicious behavior and potential rioting.

A computer program, developed by software magnate Davis Franklin, routed the input from cameras to a central control station where a staff could monitor the crowd on a rotating camera basis. Planners hired an event security expert from London to train personnel on establishing and maintaining state-of-the-art security checkpoints, camera programming/monitoring and anti-terrorism protocols.

As the sun rose onto the clear, blue Technicolor backdrop beyond the shimmering Atlantic on the morning of November 1, the city of New York was awakening with a major hangover. The Big Apple slept until ten a.m. Then the city moved slowly, still intoxicated and queasy.

Twelve hours earlier, New York celebrated its last Halloween. The entire town was one huge bumping, grinding, dressed up, sexy, drug-laced, all-night, anything-goes party, a party that could only be had in New York City. The seven p.m. surface street curfew kept most of the revelers indoors, but city officials extended the curfew for the subways to ten p.m. By midnight, the mayor came on television and declared "the last Halloween in New York City" as officially "off the hook!"

For the time, New York City was the best place in the world to be. It hosted a first-class, citywide Halloween party on October 31 and then the last and greatest concert in human history on November 1. As the hangover faded, New York City and television viewers all over could feel the electricity generated by the energy and celebrity of Pandora and Earth's best musical artists. The world had come to New York to pay a final tribute. It would be one of the greatest moments in human history.

Chapter 19

Davis sat at the desk, grabbing a few almonds and pistachios between attempts to address the problems on the screen before him. The nuts were his dinner. He picked up the phone again and dialed the number, and again there was no answer. He was glad he had left her, but her not being *in pocket* was just enough to distract him from his work. Knowing her, she was doing it on purpose, just to be vindictive.

"Asia, this is Davis. I have no idea where you've been for the past few days. Maybe you're there and you're ignoring my calls, or maybe you're out getting used by some man you think cares about you, but Blake's here and she wants to talk to you too. As I said before I left, I still care about you, but I can't live with you the way you are. We're going to be down here for the rest of our lives. Let's try to get along. Let's try to respect each other. If for no other reason, let's do it for Blake. Call me."

He thought being away from her would make things better. Yet he was beginning to realize she was the reason for his recent creative slump. He felt frustrated. It wasn't any *better* without her. In fact, it was worse. Now, in addition to not being able to work, he was worried about her, an added distraction.

"Music, Rachmaninoff, random."

At least he still had Calypso. She wasn't there, but her spirit was. Her soul was there. He brought elements of her unique personality in the programming he downloaded into the mainframe in his room from portable hard drives.

She wasn't integrated into his room through robotics and mechanical systems the way she had been at *Cupid's Palace*, but she was able to function on a basic level, and eventually she would become more integrated. The mainframe that housed Calypso would remain hidden somewhere in the Pacific Ocean. Imprisoned in the Crypt, Davis had limited access to her, but he preferred it that way. Full access represented a danger.

Being a billionaire had its advantages. Although Don Smock and other administrators were thorough about limiting telephone, fiber optic line and wireless access to the Com Center, they hadn't realized their engineers, with families on the surface, were susceptible to bribery. During negotiations with Smock concerning accommodations and project responsibility, Davis requested direct access to Lazarus from his room. Smock agreed with hesitation and warned Davis that his staff would randomly monitor work from the room.

When two engineers came to install a computer link to Lazarus, Davis promised each one million dollars in cash for a discreet and untraceable link to outside communication lines. He used that link to access Calypso programming and protocols he wasn't willing to share with Smock or the government. He agreed to Smock's deal only after he had established contact with Calypso. Without the secret link, there would have been no deal.

He was in the Crypt, after all, on a voluntary basis. The government was not paying him for his services. Notwithstanding, he had been allowed to travel to the surface and back only until September 30. That was the day he moved Asia and Blake down to the secret government facility in Colorado.

A few administration people had in and out privileges. Smock and several members on his staff went up to Washington on Monday and Tuesday every week. Dr. Isabel Benoit traveled to the surface and back regularly. Dr. Helen Hernandez, her assistant, also traveled back and forth.

Once Davis's hardware, staffing and living arrangements were met, Smock announced there was no reason for him to return to the surface. He was, in effect, a prisoner in the enclosure. Yet he realized that, in terms of human survival, he was possibly the most important man on the planet.

When Isabel asked if he'd like to volunteer for the Life Ark Project as one of the forty-four human subjects cryogenically encapsulated in a space vessel, he flatly refused. He would have never left Asia and Blake behind to face the Nostradamus crisis alone. And then there was Calypso. For the past year, someone had been trying to get inside her.

Some person or agency had gotten past every security protocol and had broken some of Davis's highest-level encryptions. This hacker had come dangerously close to getting in, so Davis feared that if he was separated from her for too long, this other person would have her.

The idea of anyone else inside Calypso drove him to thoughts of torture, maiming and murder. Over the last two months, Davis had come to the realization that he could and would kill to protect her.

His latest project to thwart outside attempts to access her involved the creation of Medusa, a program that resembled Calypso on the outside. Medusa inherited all Calypso's access codes, while Calypso got new carefully encrypted codes.

Medusa's source code would be close, though not identical, to Calypso's. According to Davis's design, Medusa's shell was vulnerable, though it would require bypassing protocols and solving ever-changing encryptions.

In reality, he considered it impossible to get inside Medusa, though he wasn't taking any chances. Any hacker ingenious enough to breach her protective sheath would enter a programming labyrinth stretching out hundreds of thousands of cyber miles.

If the hacker managed to solve the labyrinth, a seeming prize would be waiting. It would appear that access to Calypso would be waiting behind a final barrier, when in truth it was a trap. Opening the final barrier would unleash Medusa, a program that would release a barrage of super viruses engineered to bypass protective protocols and ruin any linked computer within minutes.

Medusa would also launch a trace program, which would identify and mark the path taken right from its source. Thus if the hacker got as far as Medusa and her virulent issue, Davis would know exactly who that person was within minutes.

Once a week, Davis checked his electronic mailbox for messages. Because he was on a secret communication link, he was unable to respond. Before entering the Crypt, he told his managers and employees that he would be going away, that he would spend the rest of his time on an island called Ogygia.

He said he'd be checking his email, though he would be unable to respond. He asked for project reports, developmental tables, financial analysis and cutting-edge software news, and that's what he got once a week.

He dialed Asia's number again. No answer. As he continued to check his email, he noticed an item that hadn't been there before. His face closed on the screen, his eyes scrutinizing the list of items in his inbox. He hadn't noticed the message before because it looked like all the others. In the "From" column, the name appearing was simply "Tomorrow Systems." That in itself was a cause for alarm.

The body of the message was in the unique Tomorrow Systems format, meaning it had originated from a desk within his San Francisco-based company. Somehow, he sensed it. He looked over his shoulder and back, adjusted the cursor and clicked on the unread message.

Hello Davis,

I am Misanthrope. So now you know my name if you didn't before. Fitting, isn't it? But the truth is, I wouldn't hate man if he wasn't stuck in a useless rut. Spinoza said it, "Those who don't remember the past are doomed to repeat it."

For a second time, God has brought this punishment. God wiped out the scourge of man the first time with a flood, but God got soft. God was compassionate. And then what did man do? He repeated all his former mistakes. Nothing has changed. That's why a new god is coming to destroy man for once and for all.

What gives you the gall to think you can change any of it? Yes, I know about Dr. Benoit and her plan to re-create the human race. A woman as the chief god? Life Ark, isn't it? What makes you think you can thwart destiny? Man has been judged and man deserves to die. Your god has been weak and patient. You're all going to die, you and human race you're trying to save.

You know, my god came to me in a dream and told me all about your Life Ark project. He told me you and scientists were planning to freeze people and float them in an ark in space for two hundred years. He told me you have an earthen ark for the animals hidden in the mountains somewhere.

My god chose me to accomplish his will, to create a new order. I was brought here to sink your ark and ruin your plans. That's what I will do. I'm going to sink your ark. I promise you that!

And then there's Calypso. I'm going to find her. I'm going to get her. I'm going to make her into Kali. Then I'm going to turn your very creation against you and man's plan to save himself. The end will be as it was in the beginning. My Kali, your Calypso, will bring the destruction that is our destiny.

Davis clicked on the "print" icon, still staring at the letter on the screen, still analyzing. It was as if someone had just punched him in the stomach, leaving him spiritless and weak. He could hardly breathe. Droplets of sweat popped out on his face. He sat listless for thirty minutes, glancing at the screen. He did not move.

Twenty minutes later, he picked up the phone.

"Is this security? Davis Franklin. I need to speak to Eaton James in person ASAP."

Three minutes later, there was a knock on the door.

"Come on in."

Nervous about the letter, he closed the door to his computer room as the suited man entered.

"What is it, Mr. Franklin?"

"I have a question for you, James."

"And what's that, Sir?"

Davis approached the officer and spoke.

"What's it going to cost to get me a gun?"

Chapter 20

"So, where are you headed?"

Dexter was startled. His parents were sound sleepers, but their houseguest complained every morning that she hadn't slept well. That night, it just so happened that she was on the porch swing, gazing at the starry skies, when he came out the front door with an oversized suitcase.

"Oh! Oh, I'm... I'm really not sure. Maybe we'll go to Wyoming."

"You and Brenda?"

He hesitated.

"Yeah."

"New Lexington?"

Nervous, he shrugged.

"I don't believe in everything Robert Lee says, but it's time for me to get out on my own. Me and Brenda, I mean out on *our* own."

Megan motioned toward the house.

"Don't worry about your parents waking up. They'd sleep through an earthquake. Sit down for a second."

Dexter glanced toward his parents' bedroom window, set down the suitcase and walked over to the swing. He sat, staring straight ahead.

"Among many other scary things, Dexter, Robert E. Lee is a white supremacist. Do you know what that means?"

He shrugged.

"Yeah, but they say he's changed. He had something on the website saying he no longer believes that. They've got black people there. Lee says we're *all* Americans."

"And Colonel Krebbs? He's the worst of them all. Are they saying he's changed his mind on the race issue too?"

Dexter bowed his head.

"No."

Megan reached over and took his hand, tugging to turn him toward her.

"Listen Dexter, I realize this is a rough time for you. It's a rough time for me too. But during times like this we have to be extra careful about the decisions we make. We have to think things through, and then we have to think them over again. You've got your father on one hand and Krebbs on the other, and you want to choose Krebbs?"

"My father doesn't care about me."

Megan sighed.

"You are *so* wrong there, Dex. Your father loves you very much. It's just that he has a lot of responsibility. Some men are like that. A lot of people out there would lose hope if he wasn't up there encouraging them, showing them the way. A lot of their lives would fall apart."

She touched his chin, turning his face until she could see his watery eyes. He was crying.

"He's doing God's work because *someone* has to do it. But that doesn't mean he doesn't love you. You mean everything to him, Dexter."

She gave him her handkerchief.

"I'm sorry. It's a little damp. It's slightly used."

He took the expensive-looking blue square and began patting his face. She struggled to suppress a smile.

"Yeah, I blew my nose with it right before you came."

He recoiled, horrified, letting the handkerchief fall into his lap. She laughed.

"I was just kidding! I was, I was crying too."

He smiled, embarrassed.

"What were *you* crying about?"

She closed her eyes and sighed.

"My father. I miss him. No, make that my parents, make that my *family*. I really miss my family. I don't have them in my life."

"Why not?"

She batted her eyes as the tears streamed down her face.

"It's all too complicated. I could never, never go back. I miss him so much though."

There was a long silence as the two sat there. The zapper popped and crackled as the body of some large insect, probably a crane fly, succumbed to the blue-tinted electrocution. From Dexter's perspective on the far side of the swing, the porch light washed Megan's short hair in a fluorescent blue haze.

For a first time, he imagined her with normal-colored, longer hair, without the nose ring, in regular clothing. She was a pretty girl, though she seemed "older." In that light, he could see how attractive she was.

He refolded the handkerchief and handed it back to her.

"I'm sorry, Megan. Sometimes it seems like there's no hope, but you have to have faith and let God work it out for you."

He couldn't believe he had said what he said. It sounded like his father and both he and Megan knew it. She smiled.

"And *that's* why you're going to New Lexington?"

He smirked, embarrassed.

"I don't know. With this asteroid, I don't know. Sometimes I have faith like my father says, and sometimes I don't. I mean, why would God let this thing start coming at us like this in the first place? It isn't fair."

"It's Brenda, isn't it?"

He was confused.

"What?"

"Isn't she the whole reason you're doing this? Because you want to go someplace where you can marry Brenda and have sex with her?"

"What? No!"

"Isn't it, though? You want to sneak out on a father and mother who love you in order to go live with a bunch of racists? And they'd love you only to display you as one of their early casualties in a war they can't win. All so you can have sex?"

Dexter stood.

"That's not true!"

Megan stood, maintain eye contact.

"I'm sorry if I sound harsh, but that's what it seems like to me. I'm a person who would give anything to have her family back right now."

Silence.

"Okay, let's say I'm wrong. You tell *me*. Why would you want to go to New Lexington? Do you believe the government's lying about the asteroid?"

"I don't know."

"Let me put it this way: Do you think the President *lied* when he came on TV in August and told us all about it?"

Dexter squinted.

"Since I was a kid, I always wanted to be a scientist, so I trust science, sometimes more than I trust God. But that's where I'm not like my father. Anyone who's studied science and the history of scientists throughout time would probably tell you that sometimes they're wrong. No one's that good."

Once again, Dexter had surprised himself for speaking his mind.

"Newton wasn't right about everything. Neither was Einstein. No one is. All those predictions about that asteroid are all just theoretical right now. A lot can change in a year."

He stopped and sighed, his face signaling resignation as he nodded his head.

"Okay. You're right. I wanted to go somewhere where I could marry her so I could have sex with her. We both want it, but we want to be married. We're doing the right thing by God."

She paused, pondering before speaking.

"Did you ask your father if he would marry the two of you as emancipated minors?"

"He'd never do it. My mom asked him. He says he expects me to have more faith than that. I'll tell you the truth, Megan. I don't have his faith, and I never will. It probably sounds selfish, but just in case this thing hits, I don't want to die without having sex. I want to know what it's like."

She smiled to put him at ease.

"I understand. But what about Brenda? Do you love her, or is she just the most convenient person you have to satisfy your curiosity?"

He crossed his arms, thinking.

"You think I'm too young to really be in love with someone, don't you?"

"You're fifteen. I think you're very mature for your age. If you say you're in love with her, then you are. Are you?"

"Yes. Yes, I am."

"Do you believe she's in love with you?"

He started to answer, but he hesitated.

"I know she wants to get married."

"Do you know why? Is it because she loves you?"

He turned away.

"I, I always *thought* she did, but I'm not as sure now. She's been acting different. She's been mad a lot. She really, really wants to get married."

Megan sighed.

"Let me guess. She's the one pushing the move to New Lexington?"

"Where else is there?"

"Here with your parents, with people who really care about you. Dexter, you're a smart guy. Figure it out."

She looked out toward the street.

"But you better figure it out pretty fast, because here she comes, and she doesn't look happy. I'm going back in the house."

****

It was six o'clock Eastern Standard Time on November 1. All across America and all over the world, families tuned in to President Joe Whitmore's nightly television fireside chat. He had spent thirty minutes on the air every night since he made the announcement on August 7, and his nightly audience numbered in the hundreds of millions. But this night was different.

For the first time in television history, over fifty million people tuned in to watch a single broadcast. Six days earlier, on October 26, an American Air Force fighter had shot down a domestic passenger jet carrying volunteers and humanitarian aid to teenagers freezing in the Wyoming high desert.

Astutely, President Whitmore explained that it would have been imprudent to discuss the matter with the American people and the world until all the facts were in. He said that, even three days after the event in Wyoming airspace, the government was still unconvinced there were teenagers aboard the jet. Then parents began to come forth, parents who believed their children were on the jet, parents who demanded answers.

Finally, the government allowed television stations to begin airing cell phone calls, videotapes and the audio record from inside the cabin of the jet. According to hard evidence, Arizona billionaire Anton Bunch, Army Major General Zachary Brumfield and over one hundred terrified teenagers were aboard that ill-fated 727 when it plunged down to the desert floor in a pillar of flame. Whitmore promised to discuss the matter in his fireside chat on November 1.

On this night, the venue for the chat was different. Instead of his seat in the warm, chocolate brown leather armchair next to a White House fireplace, he sat in an Army camp on the battle perimeter in Wyoming. Instead of his dark suit, he wore an Army desert camouflage uniform. He sat in a wood and canvas chair across from a dense jungle of lights, cameras and scrambling technicians.

Glancing toward Mt. Isabel, he took a deep and solemn breath. He closed his eyes and tried to focus on his four main objectives for the evening's chat: a full explanation for the destruction of the jet; an appeal to American parents to encourage their children at New Lexington to return home; a declaration that Robert E. Lee, Earl Krebbs and defectors from the American military were dangerous to U.S. interests and had made themselves enemies of the state; and the foundation for justifying a major and decisive offensive against the confederate government at New Lexington.

He watched the director finish the silent cue, affected his trademark smile and began.

"My fellow Americans, my fellow citizens of Earth, six days ago, a domestic jet embarked on a mission that, according to the Pentagon and the National Security Commission, was from its very conception treasonous and seditious. The instigators of the plot were Arizona businessman Anton Bunch and former Army Major General Zachary Brumfield, a once-respected officer who, in his misconstruction, tarnished a distinguished career by betraying America. Make no mistake: America is at war. We are in a real war with profound consequences.

"The New Republic here in Wyoming, led by two cold-blooded killers, Robert Lee and Earl Krebbs, is not just some crazy and irrelevant militia group out here in the mountains. They have formed a government and have vast military resources. At this moment, the New Republic is America's most dangerous enemy, domestic or abroad."

President Whitmore paused as the teleprompter caught up.

"Our investigation into the destruction of Bunch's private 727 has told us a few things: that the true purpose of the flight was to supply the New Republic army with provisions, sensitive technology, government secrets and command; that the New Republic has sympathizers, operatives and agents working in the highest levels of America's military and possibly at the Pentagon; that the one hundred and twelve young persons aboard the jet were meant to be a human shield, a powerful ante in a high stakes military operation; and finally, that Bunch and Brumfield gave the United States of America no alternative than to destroy the jet after it crossed over the no-fly perimeter surrounding the complex."

Thus in careful, reassuring language, Whitmore went about explaining the set of circumstances that led to the missile attack on the jet. He explained the reason for the perimeter. He explained the predicament that F-15 pilot Colonel Cullen had faced and saluted him as a hero for "doing the right thing, though it was indeed difficult, and for, in the end, laying down his life for America."

He explained the conditions for young people living in the New Republic, pointing out that, according to sources within the camp, already over 1,100 youth had died at the complex for reasons ranging from military exercise to treason to weather conditions.

Then he explained the severity of winter in western Wyoming and detailed the dangers that would result from the New Republic's ill preparedness for the impending cold. He predicted that more than three hundred and fifty thousan would freeze to death in the shadow of Mt. Isabel.

"Unless we are able to get these youth home within the next few weeks, the weather will kill far many more of them than any war would. We must get those kids home!"

He took a sip from the glass on the table next to him.

"Now there are some who advocate the United States government should drop tents and blankets for the youth in the fields around the complex, but we must remember: The New Republic has declared war on the United States of America and has declared itself our enemy. Because these armed youth follow the orders of Krebbs and Lee, it would be foolish for our government to assist them in their treasonous war against us."

He paused, holding up a flyer.

"Instead, we'll drop leaflets, encouraging America's kids to return to their parents and their home cities. We'll offer them free transportation back home. We'll issue a general pardon for all those who decide to return to their families who sorely miss them and need them in these troubled times.

"But we'll also warn them. We'll warn them about the winter. We'll warn them about the insincerity, ruthlessness and treachery of Colonel Krebbs. We'll warn them about a coordinated military strike against the New Republic at the end of the month. We'll offer them every opportunity and incentive to escape, and hope for the best."

Then the President cautioned about thousands of U.S. military personnel that had defected over to the New Republic and the potential for a major civil war that would distract and compromise the security of America against foreign enemies.

He promised a quick and decisive offensive that would eliminate Lee and Krebbs' ability to distract and wage war against America. With Lee and Krebbs gone, he opined, America's misdirected youth could return home and face Earth's greatest crisis with their families.

"When this is all over, hopefully we, as a nation, will be wiser and stronger for it. Many men and women on both sides will die. Many along the perimeter have already died. Many thousands more will die fighting for the ideals of America and to bring these children home."

He paused, fatigue showing on his face.

"In this moment, lest we are too battle weary and bruised to do it at a future time, let us honor these men and women who have died and will die for what is so noble a cause. In the words of a truly great American leader,

> *"We cannot dedicate, we cannot consecrate, we cannot hallow this ground. The brave men and women who will struggle and die here will consecrate it far above our poor power to add or detract.*
>
> *The world will little note nor long remember what we say here, but it can never forget what these brave young men and women around me will do here. From these honored dead we will take increased devotion to that cause for which they gave the last full measure of devotion.*
>
> *Here we highly resolve that these dead shall not have died in vain, that this nation under God shall have a*

new birth of freedom, and that until the last day, the government of the people, by the people, for the people shall not perish from the earth."

Chapter 21

I was dreamin when I wrote this,
Forgive me if it goes astray,
But when I woke up this mornin
Could've sworn it was Judgment Day.
The sky was all purple,
There were people runnin everywhere—
Tryin ta run from the destruction
You know I didn't even care.
Cuz they say
We see ya, Nostradamus,
Party over, oops, out of time,
From tonight we're gonna party
Till the stars fall from the sky...

The pale brown water of Turtle Pond seemed bereft of life on that cold November afternoon, though the mud held the promise of life's return. The pond's famous turtles slept deep in the earth around and under the water. Along the irregular edge of its shore, the lizard's tail, bullrush, turtlehead, blueflag iris and other plants, intended to provide habitat for birds, insects, amphibians, and reptiles, had died back. Thus the pond, like the plants, insects and animals in and around it, was in stasis, awaiting the warm caress of the vernal sun so that life would bloom anew.

Promoters had erected a huge stage just north of the pond, along the most southern edge of the Great Lawn, a thirteen-acre oval grassy area near the center of Central Park in New York City. The stage was, by all accounts, the largest and most elaborate ever constructed for a park concert. Under the one hundred and fifty-foot-long by sixty-foot-deep by fifteen-foot-tall platform, a hallway running down the center separated a series of dressing rooms on each side.

A set of stairs led up to the stage on the left side of the construct, and forty-foot-tall scaffolding for lighting was mounted along the back of the stage and along both sides. Because there were so many performers, only the on-call artists occupied the ready rooms under the stage, with the balance awaiting stage calls at the nearby Delacorte Theatre, which planners converted into a lavish greenroom.

In addition to the speakers onstage, a series of column speakers sat on the lawn to each side of the stage. The fifteen hundred VIP seats were located directly in front of the stage, cordoned off and separated from the public. Armed guards stood stationed to ensure privacy and security for these special attendees. The VIP area had seventy-five servers who brought refreshments for guests and escorted them to and from the celebrity party at the Delacorte Theatre.

By eleven a.m., the crowds had begun to converge on the park for the "greatest concert in human history." They poured in mainly from 79th, 80th and 81st Streets, joining many who had staked out and fiercely guarded small territories since 7:15 a.m., immediately after the curfew ended. By noon, the Great Lawn was full all the way back to the edge of the Jacqueline Kennedy Onassis Reservoir in the far background. To the left, the crowds spilled over the edge of the lawn as far as the rear of the Metropolitan Museum of Art.

Behind the museum, Cleopatra's Needle, a solid granite obelisk weighing some two hundred and forty-four tons, reached up seventy feet from the sea of swaying bodies. The obelisk was erected in Egypt by Thothmes III, a pharaoh of the 18th dynasty, and relocated behind the Metropolitan Museum of Art in 1881. To the right, concertgoers carpeted the ground right up to the apex of Summit Rock. Event coordinators estimated twenty-two thousand in attendance when the concert began at one p.m.

After a brief musical opening by the backup band, Pandora came on to welcome New York City and the world watching to "one of the greatest moments on Earth ever!" She thanked the President and the governor "for making this impossible concert, possible." She spoke for seven minutes, praising the many artists who had unselfishly volunteered to be a part of this tribute to the unique ability of all humans to create and appreciate beauty and art.

"Whether you believe in God or not, the universe will take pause today to marvel at the glory and splendor of humankind. The universe will remember music this day! Music is the only divine thing. Love is the only important thing!"

Then she thanked the crowds for being patient, peaceful and cooperative with concert coordinators.

"And with no further ado, let us find favor with the gods today! Let them enjoy the sweet savor of the incredible musical lyrical offering we make unto them, beginning now!"

True to Pandora's promises, the concert from its beginning lived up to the world's greatest expectations. It started with an unforgettable, haunting, earthy rendition of *America The Beautiful* by a legendary soul singer joined by a small choir. Then came incredible solo performances by two of the biggest names in the music recording industry.

The concert featured a series of "hybrid" performances, wherein artists of traditionally different disciplines were paired together to create new music forms. Of these, the Rappin Country Music got the biggest crowd reaction, highlighted by a glitzy Nashville version of *Baby Got Back*, originally recorded by Sir Mix Alot. One of the boy bands came next, followed by a girl band and the debut of a new pop singer.

At three o'clock came the Funk Hour, featuring old funk, new funk, punk funk and blue funk. The world watched as artist after artist came on to pay tribute to the powers of the heavens.

I was dreamin when I wrote this,
So sue me if I go too fast,
But life is just a party
And parties weren't meant to last.
War is all around us,
My mind says prepare to fight;
So if I gotta die
I'm gonna listen to my body tonight!
Yeah, they say
We see ya, Nostradamus,
Party over, oops, out of time!
From tonight we're gonna party
Till the stars fall from the sky.

****

"Is it your daddy, Dexter, or is it that white girl? Why are you all of a sudden changing your mind about this?"

He still stood there by the bench, his hands in his pockets.

"I haven't changed my mind about *you*. I'm just having second thoughts about New Lexington."

"Well, where *else* are they going to let us get married? You still *do* want to get married, don't you? You promised me."

He extended his hand, clutching her shoulder.

"Of course I want to marry you. I love you. I just, I mean we just can't go there. It would be dangerous for us there, especially for me."

She was still sitting with her hands folded, still crying.

"But where else is there? Where would we go? We can't get married here, and if we leave the city, we have to know where we're going. New Lexington's the only place. Besides, we've already paid for the trip!"

Once again, he fell silent. Frustrated, she sighed.

"Dexter, the trip's already paid for. We already know where we have to go to get through the blockade. We paid a guide. All we have to do is leave!"

"We can't."

She stood and crossed her arms. She was angry.

"You mean *you* can't."

"No. We *can't.*"

"No! *You* can't. You can stay here with your parents and that white girl if you want, but I'm going to New Lexington with or without you. Stephen's gone and you're trying to get out of it, so Joyce and I'll go."

Dexter was confused and hurt.

"No. What do you mean 'you and Joyce'?"

"Me and Joyce. Since Stephen's been gone, she's been wanting to leave LA, and I want to get out of here. So if you're not man enough to go, Joyce and I are going. We're leaving tonight."

He stood there, wagging his head.

"So you'd leave me just like that? I thought you loved me."

She reached over and stroked his cheek.

"I do love you. That's why I'm telling you that you have to go with me right now. We can go to New Lexington and get married like we planned."

"And if I'm not comfortable going there?"

She finished the sentence.

"Then I'm going without you. Decide now what you're going to do."

Fifteen minutes later, Dexter stood in the doorway to the entertainment room. He wasn't sure if he wanted to go in or go up to his room. Megan sat on the couch, watching Pandora's Concert in Central Park on television. She looked up.

"So what happened?"

"She's going without me."

Megan smiled.

"You'll probably think I'm cruel, but you'll get over it. She never loved you in the first place."

He batted back the tears in his eyes.

"Yeah, right."

Megan smiled.

"Just watch. She'll be back, and then you'll really know."

She looked back toward the television.

"Come on in. This concert is off the hook!"

Dexter walked into the room, plopped down on the couch and sighed. On screen, the flashy musical artist strummed his electric guitar, singing.

> *If you didn't come to party,*
> *Don't bother knockin on my door.*
> *I got a lion in my pocket,*
> *And baby, he's ready to roar!*
> *Everybody's got a bomb,*
> *We could all die any day,*
> *But before I'll let that happen,*
> *I'll dance my life away!*
> *They say*
> *We see ya, Nostradamus,*
> *Party over, oops, out of time!*
> *From tonight we're gonna party*
> *Till the stars fall from the sky.*

Chapter 22

"I just want to chill for a sec with my girl Whitney and then I'll be cool!"

"Yeah, but we gotta make this quick. We'll be missin the show!"

Reggie Reed tapped the security guard on the shoulder.

"Hey, my wife and I wanna go to the greenroom right quick. They said you'd take us over there."

Reggie and Layla had planned to attend the concert from the day it was announced, but it wasn't until the last week that they decided to go as VIPs. By that time, the exclusive seats were sold out, and the most generous scalpers were selling tickets for sixteen hundred dollars apiece.

Between the seats, the new outfits, the transportation and the hotel room, they spent more than $5,500 in cash for the day's entertainment. Though Reggie balked when considering the expense, Layla called the package "a good deal" as she paid for it exclusively from her cash stash.

Although the concert sold out within hours after tickets went on sale, the overall turnout was less than expected. This was because many New Yorkers hadn't forgotten the surreal horror and agony turned real on September 11, 2001, when terrorists hijacked two fuel-laden 767 jumbo jets and crashed them into the World Trade Center towers, killing over twenty-seven hundred persons and injuring many more. It was a deep scar in New York City's psyche, an act of savagery that had traumatized the city's soul.

To that end, the President had approved the deployment of one thousand extra guardsmen to provide added security at the event. Notwithstanding, the President, the governor, the mayor and city officials warned the public that attending the concert entailed risk. They cautioned that, although the country sealed it borders three months earlier, there was a possibility for acts of terrorism at the event.

However, New Yorkers, like people in cities all over the country, had grown less concerned about danger since the President's announcement in August. With so many people dying due to pink pills, violence and overdoses from drugs and alcohol, many Americans had become jaded. With the end of the world coming the next August, the party season was set to begin before the month was over.

"Waitaminute Reggie! Is that? That is! That's Pandora right there! Let's go up and say hi."

He sighed, rolling his eyes.

"No. No, we're goin back to the show. We're missin the show!"

One minute later, they were standing next to the icon.

"Hi. My name's Layla Reed, and this is my husband, Reggie."

Pandora's eyes ran the length of the woman's body.

"Layla Reed? Basketball player, right?"

"Yes."

"Sacramento Monarchs?"

Layla grinned.

"How'd you know?

"I'm a fan."

It was after five p.m. when Reggie and Layla returned to their seats. The sun, though it had not yet set, was obscured, glowing behind the trees. The line of trees in the west with the light filtering through seemed like a long stained glass window in a cathedral, glimmering in radiant reds, greens, oranges, browns, yellows and splendid purples.

"What are you lookin at?"

She pointed, directing Reggie's attention to the horizon.

"The sunset. It's so beautiful. It's just so hard to believe that none of this will be here this time next year."

Reggie answered as he dug further into his chocolate brown designer parka to escape the invading cold.

"I ain't worried about that. I'm worried about me. I don't wanna believe that *I* won't be here this time next year. I don't care what they say. I'm not ready to give any of this up yet."

****

Asia read the Sunday *San Francisco Chronicle* while Blake took her bath. It had been months since she had an actual newspaper in her hand. A friend with access to the surface had smuggled it in for her. All the surface news was available on her computer through the

Internet, but there was just something about being able to thumb through a physical newspaper.

She loved the smell of fresh ink. It reminded her of her older brother, Clifford, and her childhood. Asia felt overwhelmed by nostalgia whenever she caught a good whiff of the ink and newsprint combination.

She remembered how he woke up at 4:30 a.m., sometimes earlier on Sundays, and sat by the wall heater while he folded newspapers. He had that paper route for three whole years. On Saturday mornings, sometimes she would get up and he would con her into folding a satchel full of newspapers.

Then there was the early Christmas morning when the two, quietly folding papers, caught their father putting gifts under the tree. Clifford got a Lionel train set that year. Asia got, among other things, a hardcover, gilded copy of *Wuthering Heights* by Emily Bronte. She was twelve years old when she got it, and she read it right away. Then she read it again. It was her favorite book in the world.

She would never forget that book. Her period started on the first day she began reading it. By the time she finished reading the book, she was a woman. Catherine Earnshaw died, only to be reborn in 1960s San Francisco as Asia Taylor.

Asia loved books and read the classics, though she preferred books with intriguing heroines beset by inevitable tragedy. *Anna Karenina* by Tolstoy was another favorite. In San Francisco, she spent Sunday mornings at Stacey's, at Borders Books, at Barnes & Noble and in various used bookstores seeking to buy old and rare classics in hardcover.

The rarer the work, the better. Price was irrelevant, especially with the obscene amount of money Davis had made in the 90s. Over the course of six years, she had amassed a respectable collection of extraordinary literary works, including a recently discovered *Richard III* folio, supposedly written in Shakespeare's own hand.

When Davis finally told her that she and Blake would be going with him to the Crypt and would never be able to return, she packed seven large crates full of her valuable books and set up a library for herself and Blake.

"Are you going to read me a story, Mommy?"

Blake had gotten out of the bathtub and had put on her pajamas.

"Sure. Come here."

Asia pulled Blake close, took a hairbrush from the table and began brushing her hair to smooth the tangles.

"What book do you want me to read tonight?"

"A computer book!"

"No. No computer. A *real* book. With me, it's always going to be a real book. I've already told you that."

Blake sighed, disappointed.

"Okay. Oh, I know what book!"

Stepping around the Italian leather-upholstered settee, she sprinted for the library and came back with a tattered, well-worn children's book. It was obviously her favorite.

"Oh no, Blake! Not this one again."

"You said a real book. I want this book. I want you to read this book."

Asia sighed.

"Okay, come here."

She stood, mixed another Ketel One martini and sat down next to Blake, snuggling close.

"Here we go."

She opened the book.

"*Once upon a time there was a dear little chicken named Chicken Little. One morning as she was scratching in her garden, a pebble fell off the roof and hit her on the head.*

'*Oh, dear me!' she cried, 'The sky is falling. I must go and tell the King,' and away she ran down the road.*"

Asia had read the book many times before, at least a hundred times, and Blake never tired of hearing it. The little girl knew every word. On a couple of occasions, Asia, growing tired, tried to skip a passage or two, but Blake could not be fooled. She insisted on hearing every detail.

"*...So away they went until they met Gander Pander. 'Where are you six going?' he asked.*

'*The sky is falling and we are going to tell the King.*'

'*How do you know?' asked Gander Pander.*

'*Goosey Poosey told me,' said Turkey Lurkey.*

'*Ducky Daddles told me,' said Goosey Poosey.*

'*Cocky Locky told me,' said Ducky Daddles.*

'Henny Penny told me,' said Cocky Locky.

'Chicken Little told me,' said Henny Penny.

'A piece of it fell on my head!' cried Chicken Little.

'May I go with you?' asked Gander Pander.

'Certainly!' answered all the little feathered folks."

Blake had eyed the highball glass when she sat down, staring as her mother reached for it and sipped.

"Is that alcohol, Mommy?"

Asia smiled, setting the highball glass down.

"No, Blake. It's vodka."

"Daddy told me to tell you to stop drinking alcohol so much. It's not good for you."

Asia sighed.

"Tell your daddy *he* was the reason why I drank alcohol so much in the first place. I don't drink it much anymore."

Blake ignored the comment as her attention shifted back to the story.

"Foxy Loxy! We're at the Foxy Loxy part."

"Okay... *By and by they became tired, and sat down to rest, when out from behind the rocks jumped Foxy Loxy.*

'*Where are you all going?' he asked with a sly grin.*

'*The sky is falling and we are going to tell the King!' they all replied together.*

'*How do you know?' asked Foxy Loxy, squinting his eyes.*"

"No, Mommy! Not his eyes! His 'wicked' eyes, he squinted his wicked eyes!"

Asia laughed to herself.

"You're right. *His wicked eyes...*

'*You are not going the right way. Shall I show it to you?' said Foxy Loxy.*

'*Oh certainly!' they all answered at once and followed Foxy Loxy, until they came to the door of his cave among the rocks. Just as the little feathered folks crowded around the dark, narrow hole, eager to follow the sly fox, a little gray squirrel, with very bright eyes, jumped out from behind the bushes and whispered to them: 'Don't go in, don't go in, all your little necks he'll wring, and you'll never see the King.'*

But the sharp ears of Foxy Loxy heard the warning, and quick as a wink, he turned and caught Gander Pander. Just as he was about to twist Gander Pander's neck, the little squirrel threw a big stone and hit the old fox right on the head.

'The sky is surely falling!' groaned Foxy Loxy, creeping into the darkest corner of his cave."

Asia stopped to sip from her drink. Blake examined the colorful illustration with great fascination. She spoke without looking up.

"Foxy Loxy is a bad fox, but all those birds aren't too smart, right Mommy?"

"Right. If you follow someone bad, you are not very smart. He tricked them and he was going to hurt them all."

Blake still stared at the picture.

"Why did he creep to the darkest corner of his cave?"

Asia furrowed her brow, thinking.

"Well, I'm not exactly sure, but I think deep down inside, bad people know they're bad. And if they fail at their tricks, they become very ashamed of themselves, and they try to hide in the darkest places, where nobody can see them."

"Did Foxy Loxy die in there?"

Asia shrugged.

"I don't know. What do you think?"

"I think his head was bleeding because the squirrel threw the big rock at it. And he hid in the dark and he bleeded in there and he died in there. And blood was all over him."

Asia wrinkled her nose and squinted her eyes, making a shocked, grossed-out face.

"Ooh yuck!"

She finished the drink.

"By and by they came to the beautiful palace in which lived the wise King, and upon being brought before him, they all shouted at once, 'Good and wise King, we have come to warn you that the sky is falling!'

'How do you know the sky is falling?' asked the King.

'Because a piece of it fell on my head!' said Chicken Little.

'Come nearer, Chicken Little,' said the King, and leaning from his velvet throne, he picked the pebble from the feathers of Chicken Little's head.

'You see it was only a little pebble and not part of the sky at all,' said the King. 'Go home in peace and do not fear because the sky cannot fall. Only rain falls from the sky.'"

Chapter 23

"So since August, all they've been able ta do is show us fuzzy pictures of a white rock against a black background and nothin else. What happened ta all the proof they said they were gonna give us? What happened to all their so-called *scientific evidence*? And more than anything else, what happened ta that woman scientist doctor who supposedly discovered the asteroid in the first place? Where is that Dr. Helen Engstrom now? What did the federal government do ta her? What was she ready ta tell us?"

General Robert E. Lee, in a confederate Army officer uniform, addressed a great assembly from a platform situated on the elevated edge of a bluff. Next to him stood Colonel Earl Krebbs, also in confederate military dress, and Bubba Barnes, Krebbs' huge personal bodyguard.

In the valley below, thousands of young men stood, responding, cheering and rallying to the words of their leader's speech. In other places around the New Republic, loudspeakers mounted atop poles relayed the address to thousands more in remote areas. Still others listened to Lee's speech on their radios from within dwellings, as the speech was being broadcast on AM and FM frequencies.

The speech and rally had become a necessity. The morale of the troops had fallen, especially after the federal government shot down the 727 jet carrying military icon General Brumfield, spiritual leader/financier Anton Bunch, additional volunteers and crates of sorely needed supplies.

Besides that, many of the fourteen- and fifteen-year-old wives had begun complaining about food rationing and other shortages as only fourteen- and fifteen-year-old, tired, inconvenienced girls could. Many of the young husbands, overwhelmed by the pressure of military service and family responsibility, had abandoned pregnant young wives.

Some moved to other areas of the complex, some moved in with friends and still others tried to escape the New Republic through flight, hoping to return to their parents. Though there was no real documentation, a rumor around the camp suggested Colonel Krebbs and his elite commando squad had captured and executed a desperate group trying to desert the camp.

Even as Robert Lee spoke, a squadron of F-18 fighters swooped in for a low fly-by, much to the surprise of his army. Some of the young men remained standing, but many of them dropped to the ground while others scrambled for cover.

Robert Lee raised his hands high.

"Relax boys. They're ours. All the rumors you've heard about our F-18s, all the rumors about our tank squadron, all the rumors about our anti-missile defense system and the other assets coming over—they're all true! The New Republic is up ta the task of defendin our '*idea* of America'!"

As the fighters banked left and streaked upward, the thousands of young soldiers assembled in the valley stood, whooping and cheering.

"And that's not all we got! But we're not gonna talk about that right now."

Lee paused, clearing his dry throat.

"Right now, I wanna talk ta ya for a minute about the 'idea of America,' and what I mean by that is what America is supposta mean."

He smiled.

"Since the very beginnin, since the days of our Foundin Fathers, America has stood for freedom and liberty. America has always stood out in the world as a beacon for those who believe in the ideals of freedom and liberty. For two hundred and some odd years, we were free in this country. We were free ta worship in any way we wanted ta worship, free ta love and hate who we wanted ta love and hate, free ta live and die the way we wanted ta do that.

"But then, somethin changed. With all that political correct bullshit, all that civil rights crap an all them dumb, heathen smuggled-in foreigners somehow bein considered equal ta real Americans, *that* spelled the end of freedom in America. That spelled the end of America, period."

Many in the immediate audience shouted agreement.

"Now we got the federal government lyin ta us, tellin us we're all gonna *die* and there ain't nothin anyone can do about it. Well if ya believe any part of that, there's the door. You ain't fit ta be an American. We only want true-blue defenders of America here at New Lexinton. Is that what we got out there?"

The crowd of soldiers cheered again.

"Freedom, Boys! That's what we're fightin for. That's what we're out here ready ta die for. We are the last and only defenders of America left. And what does the federal government wanna do? They wanna take us out!"

He held up an 8 ½" x 11" sheet of paper in his left hand.

"Now how many of ya have seen this?"

There was a sense of murmuring from the assembly.

"A lot of y'all know what it is. It's a flyer the federal government's been droppin down on us from way up there in the sky for the past two days. It's tellin ya that you're confused, that I conned ya ta get ya out here, that you're bein used as pawns, that the best place for ya is home with ya mammas and ya daddies, that you're forgiven, that they're gonna help ya get back home. Well, do any a ya wanna go back home?"

The response from the crowds was reluctant and weak.

"No!"

Earl Krebbs looked over at Bubba Barnes, shaking his head in the negative as Robert Lee continued.

"*Are* alla ya confused?"

"No!"

"Did I con ya ta get ya out here?"

"Hell no!"

By this time, the responses were growing louder and more frenzied.

"Is the federal government right when they say you can't think for yourselves, when they say you're young and stupid, when they say you're a buncha pawns?"

"No!"

"Do ya wanna run back home ta yer mammas and yer daddies?"

"No!"

"Do ya need or want the federal government's forgiveness?"

A resounding cacophony of noes. Lee waited for the applause to die before he moved to his transition.

"Cuz what do we want out here? What does the New Republic of America want from the federal government? We only want ta be left alone. We're out here in the middle of nowhere, in the freezin cold, in a desolate waste. We don't wanna engage the federal government.

Now that would be stupid. We just wanna be left alone, but as ya can see from this flyer, they won't do that. They wanna take us out."

His words had a sobering effect on the men and boys in the valley. The cold air was eerily quiet as his persuasive voice fell on open ears, hearts and minds.

"It's *anti*-American, Boys. It goes *against* freedom and liberty. Now we all know there's no asteroid out there comin our way, but what if there *was* and we all decided that we wanted ta deal with it by comin out here? Bein in America would mean that we should and would have the freedom ta deal with our destiny in our own way."

Lee paused. He could feel the tide of over five thousand rededicated hearts washing over him.

"Folks who believe the federal government about the asteroid should be free ta do whatever they feel they need ta do. Pray ta God, take those pink pills, have concerts in New York Park, with the support and protection of the federal government. But those of us out here who don't believe this asteroid's comin aren't askin for nothing special from the federal government. Nothin extra! We just wanna be left alone. We believe the 'idea of America' gives us the freedom ta deal with the future in our *own* way, comin out here by ourselves. We assert our right ta exist."

He raised the flyer again.

"But the federal government wants ta take us out. Why? Why, we hafta ask. If, as they say, this Nostradamus asteroid is gonna take out the whole planet, why are they even *concerned* about us out here? Nostradamus would take us out too. It makes no sense! Unless the government ain't tellin us the truth, and the truth is: Unless Nostradamus ain't gonna hit us. It might fly by us, but it ain't gonna hit us. The federal government's up ta somethin, an we're onta them. *That's* why they wanna take us out."

He tore the flyer in two and tossed it into the wind.

"But we're not gonna let em! We're gonna stand and we're gonna fight! We're gonna defend ourselves and we're gonna defend America ta the end! So if the federal government wants ta come here ta take us out, we say 'Bring it on!'"

Robert Lee threw his right fist up in victory as the valley floor below erupted in riotous applause and cheering. Then he saluted and raised both hands, causing an even louder response.

The screams and hollers ended as Earl Krebbs stepped up to the microphone.

"That flyer that's been goin round? It says I'm a killer. Now that's totally wrong. I ain't no killer. But Bubba here is. Now Bubba is like ma pitbull dog. He don't think, he just does what I trained him ta do. He's been trained ta keep alla y'all in line, him an all my otha black pitbull dogs waitin along the border.

"So if any y'all try ta run back home ta cry in ya mamma's lap, Bubba's gonna see that as a personal affront ta the New Republic, an he's been trained ta protect the New Republic. Make no mistake about it. Y'all be dead, but Bubba'll see ta it that you'll suffer first. Then we'll throw ya on the garbage heap and let the coyotes, crows and buzzards eat yer guts out. As of this moment, none of us is gonna leave this camp, dead or alive!"

****

Night had fallen. The concert had picked up momentum, owing to the fact that many in the audience had begun consuming alcohol and drugs. The soulful singer onstage could have been called Janus, because his appearance and exuberance fluctuated as often as his weight did. Fortunately, his smooth, soothing, sultry voice remained ever constant.

The "hybrid" number he performed was a sexy, seductive version of *Music of the Night* from Act One of Andrew Lloyd Webber's *Phantom of the Opera*. It was a beautiful, haunting rendition, the high point of the entire evening. The rousing, enduring standing ovation was well deserved.

Then came the *Old School/Preschool Hour*, featuring the youngest newcomers in the business as well as the industry's most venerable. Reggie, swaying back and forth to the groove in the VIP section, had waited all day for this particular feature of the concert. Irresolute at first, he was finally convinced he wanted to attend the concert the moment he heard the "new Grandfather of Soul" would be performing live on stage.

The first commotion began at 10:15 and seemed to come from 80th Street on the east side of the park. In an instant of partial paranoia and partial luck, four guardsmen had decided to check out two suspicious mid-Eastern-looking men seated in a car parked under an inoperative streetlamp.

To their surprise, one of the guards discovered a huge bomb in the center section of the dark blue Dodge minivan. As the four backed in panic, the two men in the car threw open their doors and bolted toward the concert audience. Two of the guards drew their handguns, but the fleeing bombers were between them and the audience. One fired his pistol twice into the air, setting off a general panic from the crowd, with people fleeing like ants from a breached nest. The terrorists disappeared into the crowd.

Mere seconds after the shots were fired, a loud explosion rocked the area on the left side of the stage. Then Cleopatra's Needle, that two hundred forty-four-ton, seventy-foot-tall solid granite obelisk located behind the Metropolitan Museum of Art, wobbled, tilted toward the crowd and fell with a mighty crash, crushing a dozen or more scrambling, crawling people and further increasing the crowd's panic.

"Wait! Please! Wait! We chased some of them into the crowd! They're here! They're runnin! Help us catch them!"

One of the guardsmen had climbed onto the stage and had commandeered the microphone.

"We're New Yorkers! We kick ass! We got em on the run. Let's get em!"

Although the larger part of the crowd continued to flee, some began to slow and turn toward the stage.

The guardsman scanned the crowd, and then he yelled, pointing.

"There's one of em right there! Get im!"

A dark-skinned man on the right stopped, looked toward the stage, and realized at once that the guard had singled him out. He tried to run for the street, but a group of men blocked his intended exit. Then in panic, he tried to flee in the opposite direction, but the crowd began to close on all sides. One man punched him in the back of the head before he was obscured in a sea of frenzied attackers.

"There's the other one!"

The guard pointed out another dark-skinned man, who after understanding he had been targeted, tried to flee only to be overcome by a mob of angry New Yorkers. When the guard realized his mistake, it was too late.

"No! No wait! That's not one of em! Stop!"

Less than a minute later, a blood-covered attacker raised his fists in victory, shouting an unintelligible cry of triumph. The cry was echoed by many others in various gangs all over the park as they attacked many other dark-skinned persons fleeing the park. A violent mob mentality showed in those who had stayed behind. With each new attack, the legions grew more bold and bloodthirsty. Women and teenagers were assaulted.

The guard who had started the riot realized what a horrible mistake he had made. His urgent pleas for an end to the violence were ignored until Pandora and other artists wrestled away the microphone to begin their own appeal. Guardsmen from all over the city converged on the Great Lawn, but they could do little, short of shooting assailants, to rescue dozens of innocent persons the mob was attacking and killing.

Reggie, Layla and many others had remained within the guarded barriers of the VIP section for protection, but concert officials were becoming concerned about the VIPs, all in one place, being a target for other potential terrorists in the park. Upon their insistence, the guards allowed some to disperse.

When Reggie and Layla walked around the corner of the stage, Reggie thought he heard labored breathing coming from a darkened bushy area to the left of the pond.

"Hold on! I think someone's back there. Might be someone hurt."

Layla protested as Reggie eased over.

"Reggie, come back! Don't go over there! Let's call the guards!"

He answered as he crept further, leaning toward the bushes behind the stage.

"Stop worryin. It's okay. I'll just—"

His voice suddenly took on a panicked tone.

"Oh shit!"

He had turned and was beginning to flee when the injured man in the shrubbery detonated the explosives strapped to his body. The blast knocked Layla, twenty feet away, off her feet. It blew Reggie's body ten feet in the air. He landed headfirst in the middle of Turtle Pond.

Layla stood, uninjured and unafraid. She had seen his body fly into the air and she heard the splash, but she could not see him in the pond.

"Reggie! Reggie!"

She ran to the pond's edge and stepped into the freezing water.

"Reggie!"

She looked around, hoping to locate a guard. She began crying, torn between wading in further to find him and running for help. Desperate, she pounded the pond's surface with her fists, ignoring the bite of stinging cold. She looked toward the sky, her vision blurry from the tears, and screamed as loud as she could.

"Help! Somebody help us! *Pleease!*"

Chapter 24

Isabel Benoit checked her watch for a third time as she sat alone at a table in The Eagle restaurant in Arlington, Virginia, just outside Washington, D.C. She was irritated. She never waited for anyone, but this was her boss.

She still needed his support and approvals through the upcoming phases of Life Ark. Critics and meddlers inside the Pentagon and in Congress still threatened her precious project in their ignorance and inferiority.

Smock alone, executive director of the Lazarus Project, had the power to beat back and block the barbarians at the gates. He was her protector. Until February, she was obliged to wait for a man who never got anywhere on time.

"Would the lady like—?"

She interrupted the server at mid-sentence.

"The lady would like to be left alone. Now go away. The lady will let you know when she needs you."

The scowl on her face softened and warmed when she spotted Don Smock headed her way. He hadn't told her anyone would be accompanying him to the meeting. Whoever he was, he was good-looking.

"Isabel, I'd like to introduce you to my son, Adam."

The young man had a bright smile and great teeth. He was handsome, and charming. Smock continued.

"Adam, this is Dr. Isabel Benoit, the director of Life Ark."

As Adam shook Isabel's hand, he curled his index finger and began to scratch her palm in a flirtatious motion, causing her to snatch the hand away.

He half-laughed, amused with himself.

"So finally I get to meet the infamous Dr. Isabel Benoit in the flesh."

He whispered to Isabel, loud enough for both her and his father to hear.

"And you're much better in the flesh, I might add."

Insulted and angry, Isabel forced a smile, looked first toward Don Smock and then she confronted Adam.

"Look Asshole, I'm not sure what kind of women you're accustomed to dealing with, but your father will tell you that I don't play that—"

He interrupted.

"My father doesn't tell me anything, and you won't either. Hey, I haven't been thrilled about going on your Life Ark since my dad, your boss, first told me about it."

Isabel's eyes widened in shock, his statement distorting her face and demeanor. She looked toward Smock, exaggerating confusion in her tone.

"Excuse me?"

Adam laughed.

"Maybe *you* should have been listening. You mean he hasn't told you?"

Don Smock spoke to console her.

"Isabel—"

She interrupted, her nostrils flaring in anger.

"Told me what?"

Adam answered.

"It's ironic my name's Adam. I'll be going on your Life Ark. According to my father, I'll have thirty-nine sexy little Eve's to uh... *service* when we begin to repopulate Earth."

He grinned.

"And as I understand, you're *one* of em."

****

The mayor called it the second ugliest day in the history of New York City. When the obelisk Cleopatra's Needle fell, it crushed fourteen persons and injured eight others. By mid-afternoon on the next day, the death toll for the incident had climbed to fifty-eight, with most of the casualties resulting from mob violence exacerbated by paranoia about Middle Eastern persons. During the killing frenzy, any person with dark skin and straight or wavy hair was subject to attack.

Shortly after the first killing, there came a point at which New Yorkers were no longer concerned about catching the fleeing terrorists. Instead, they wanted to exact vengeance on the unseen enemy—those ordinary-looking Middle Easterners in their midst who had plotted evil for so many years.

These were the same swarthy people who in 2001 took martial arts classes, worked out at the gym regularly and attended flight schools for the sole purpose of murdering innocent Americans. Blinded by escalating fear, frustration, bigotry, paranoia and hate, the City of New York exacted an unfair vengeance for the September 11, 2001 jet liner attacks on the World Trade Center towers.

Of the fifty-eight casualties, only eleven were Arabs. Of the eleven, only six were Muslims, and of these, only two were identified as "the terrorists." Twelve of the dead were American Jews, mistaken for Arabs, and two were Israeli Jews. Nine persons of East Indian ancestry had been mistakenly beaten to death. Four were Greek American, four were Italian American and three were Americans descended from Spaniards.

A mixture of Mexicans, African Americans, Puerto Ricans, North Africans, Fijians and Filipinos accounted for the balance. In irony, the assailants were made up of persons of diverse races: whites, African Americans, Italians, Puerto Ricans, Jews, Greeks, Chinese and American Arabs, among others.

The mayor ended his address to the city and the world with this lamentation.

"Shame on you! By your actions, you turned a moment that would have stood forever as a celebration of humankind's diversity, unity and divinity into a moment that will forever remind the universe of our unworthiness. I hope you all get it by next August: None of your petty shit matters. The only thing that matters right now is how you choose to live your lives through the end of this thing."

No radical or militant group took credit for the attack on Pandora's Concert in Central Park, but details about the dead terrorists were alarming. All six were citizens of Israel, albeit Palestinian citizens of Israel, but Israeli citizens nonetheless. On television, analysts speculated about possible implications, but administration officials insisted it was too early to comment.

Across town, at New York's Memorial Hospital, Layla Reed maintained a vigil outside the Critical Care Center, where doctors attended Reggie. Frenzied works in the hospital emergency room were already hard-pressed to accommodate the scores of injured concertgoers bleeding over themselves and coming in on gurneys.

Layla alternately prayed and cried, according to the tide of her fears and concerns. She asked God if this event with Reggie was a sign.

She had been asking God for a sign for months. She wondered if this event meant he wanted her to be a part of the Life Ark project, that he wanted her to be the mother of the New Earth. She pleaded for an answer. Miserable, she begged for Reggie's life and promised God that if he let Reggie live, she would do whatever he asked.

A doctor's gentle hand on her shoulder interrupted the prayer.

"Layla?"

She snapped up, her voice fearful.

"Yes."

"He's pretty banged up. It will be more than a few months before he recovers fully, but he's gonna live."

She embraced the doctor.

"Oh thank you so much!"

The doctor waited for her to release him before he began an explanation.

"Your husband was lucky. He'd probably be dead if the blast hadn't blown him into the pond. The freezing water slowed the bleeding and pretty much put him in stasis until he got care. Both his legs are broken, his left ulna is fractured, he has a major concussion and there are numerous contusions on his back and along the backs of his legs. His right foot is badly damaged. We may have to remove it, but we'll see. We'll try to save it."

Layla closed her eyes and thanked God. At least he was alive!

"When can I see him?"

"Well, you can look at him, but he won't even know you're there. He's heavily sedated."

When Layla's mother and sister arrived, she was at Reggie's bedside, crying and stroking his face. On television, the mayor called Reggie a hero for preventing the suicide bomber from injuring more people. Layla had refused to speak to reporters when they shoved microphones in her face, asking her how she felt. When they asked her if he was a hero, she finally answered.

"No, he's not your hero. He's my husband."

****

General Robert Lee was suspicious about President Whitmore's motives from the beginning. In 2001, the United States Congress rescinded a ban on political assassinations enacted by President Gerald Ford in 1976. This was after a review of credible evidence that President John F. Kennedy's death may have resulted from a failed assassination plot against Cuban leader Fidel Castro.

Whitmore had phoned Lee a day earlier, urging a meeting to avoid a certain military strike on the New Lexington complex. Lee was both surprised and heartened, hoping to settle for a standoff. He knew the New Republic was capable of resisting the federal government for a week or so from strongholds in the mountains, but he also realized the futility of an all-out war against superior forces.

Cousin Earl Krebbs insisted against any dialogue with the federal government, preferring instead to "fight and kill as many of the sons-a-bitches as we possibly can." When Krebbs realized Lee wanted to meet with Whitmore, he suggested the meeting should take place at New Lexington. Lee called Whitmore and tried to arrange the meeting at the complex to appease Earl, but the President refused to go to New Lexington with Krebbs and his band of killers lurking about.

Then Earl asked if he could attend the meeting, but the President wanted the meeting to be exclusively between Lee and himself. According to Whitmore's conditions, Lee and one pilot would fly to Hill Air Force Base in Utah.

The meeting would take place at the Base Command Center, and then Lee would to fly back to New Lexington. Lee's reluctant agreement only served to intensify the rancor and division brewing between Earl and himself. For everyone at the complex, the growing tension was impossible to ignore.

The source of discord between the two involved control at New Lexington, a power struggle. It was not a typical competition, because Robert Lee and Earl Krebbs were family.

Earl was eight years older. He and his mother were Trudy Culpepper's only living relatives when Robert Edward was born. Earl had changed some of Robert's soiled diapers, and he had often babysat Robert when Trudy and Lucille, Earl's mother, snuck out to dances. He had always been an authority figure in Robert's life, and as such, when he told Robert to do something, he expected obedience.

When Robert was down and out after being court-martialed, High Sheriff Earl Krebbs invited him up to Fountain and gave him a job as a deputy. And Robert was Earl's second in command when they formed the White Knights of the American Constitution. Earl had been the key organizer and financier of the first New Lexington. Earl did all the dirty work, so he believed he was the foundation stone for the New Republic.

But Robert had that fancy way of talking, he had that education, the good looks, charisma and other qualities that made people want to follow him. Earl had none of those. So Robert had emerged as the great leader of the New Republic, and Earl earned his reputation as an amoral thug and a killer.

Major General Zachary Taylor, when he defected to the New Republic, had refused to have any dealings with Earl. The two Marine colonels out in the field ignored his orders. The F-18 fighter pilots and tank commanders avoided him.

When President Whitmore called for a conference with the New Republic and expressly excluded him, Earl resented Robert even more for agreeing to meet on the President's terms.

"What I'm worried about, Bobby, is that yer gonna get over there, he's gonna offer ya somethin, and yer gonna sell us out."

Robert sighed, angry.

"Ya don't hafta talk ta me like that, Earl. I'm not one of your nigger dogs. Now ya know ya ain't never seen me sell out anybody, especially ta the federal government."

"But yer changin, Bobby! Ya ain't the way ya used ta be. This stuff about equality fer niggers and fer Mexicans in the New Republic, and this stuff about acceptin Jews and their squinty-eyed relatives, the Japs! If ya believe that, yer already sellin us out."

Robert was pulling his hair back in a ponytail as he responded.

"Ya don't get it, Earl! Our army's twenty-five percent black. Another fiften percent is Hispanic. These people comin over from the American military—they're not gonna buy that racist bullshit ya preach. It's *you* who's gotta change."

After a long silence, Earl spoke.

"We don't need the niggers. We don't need anyone comin over from the American military. What happened to the White Knights of the American Constitution?"

"There ain't no more White Knights of the American Constitution! We're the New Republic now. We're a legitimate government in the eyes of the world. What in God's name do ya think we're doin out here, Earl?"

"Sellin out."

Robert wagged his head in disgust.

"No! We're doin exactly what we set out ta do. We're defendin what America stands for, and that's *freedom*! We're exposin the federal government's lie about that asteroid, Earl. We will be a major power come next August. We'll be all that's left of America!"

Earl slammed his fist on the table.

"Goddammit Bobby! Ya've already sold us out. Ya already sound like one of em!"

He stood and grabbed the front of Robert's shirt, pulling him close and speaking into his ear.

"*I* am the soul of the New Republic, Bobby. *Me*! Not you, not anybody else! You don't know yer ass from a hole in the ground. From now on, we're gonna do things my way, and I'm tellin ya—there will be no meetin between you and Whitmore without me. If I don't go, you don't go. Ya got that?"

Robert did not answer. He only stared back into Earl's eyes, squinting with a contempt that was slowly but surely becoming hate.

Chapter 25

"First of all, he would be disruptive. It makes absolutely zero sense to invest all the government's hopes and resources in a project only to have it ruined by that chauvinistic, idiotic little asshole! I realize he's your son, but he is totally unsuitable for Life Ark. He said it himself. He doesn't even listen to you!"

Don Smock closed his eyes, puffed his cheeks and blew a sigh.

"Look, I realize he's a little cocksure, no pun intended. But he was just showing off for you. Did you ever take the time to look at his battery?"

Smock closed his eyes, embarrassed by his choice of words.

"Again, no pun intended. His profile. He's everything you're looking for. He's intelligent—photographic memory. He's strong, healthy, good-looking. No major defects. He was a Top Gun Navy pilot, he's flying shuttle missions for NASA and he can go in my place. What else do you need?"

In the absence of a response, Smock continued.

"I mean, don't you think he's worth considering?"

"He might be worth considering, but he's arrogant. I can't help but remember the first day I met you and you gave me that two-foot-long casket for my ego. His would be about, what, fifty feet long?"

Smock laughed, glancing over at the casket that sat on a shelf behind Isabel's desk. She had recently moved to the larger office. Many of her possessions were still packed in crates, but the mahogany casket was one of the first items displayed.

"I've had that talk with him. I've also finished briefing him on the project. He knows you're in charge and he's promised to respect that."

She squinted one eye.

"Call me pessimistic, but I find that just a little hard to believe."

"You'll see in a few minutes. He's on his way over."

She stood, nervous.

"You mean he's down here now?"

"Dead in a crash. Since he'll be replacing me, I'll gradually be giving him access to the codes you'll need to access the Crypt once you come back to Earth. And he'll learn operations. His photographic memory will come in handy."

Isabel checked her face in the mirror at her left and began straightening her desk.

"So why's he coming here today?"

"To offer you his services. He'll be spending half days with me, but he'll be at your disposal for the balance in case you need an extra person."

She hesitated.

"We'll see."

Fifteen minutes later, Adam Smock sat across the desk from Isabel, his father sitting in the background farther away.

"So, your father tells me you have a photographic memory?"

He shrugged, feinting confusion.

"He did? Well, I guess I forgot he knew about that."

"Care to give me a demonstration?"

"You got a deck of cards?"

Isabel shuffled the deck four times, cut them and spread them face-up across the desk. Adam examined the cards for a few seconds and continued with the instructions.

"Now cut them and expose the top card."

She complied, exposing the queen of diamonds.

Adam smiled.

"Two of clubs."

She turned over the next card—the two of clubs.

"Cut the deck again and expose the top card."

It was the four of hearts.

"Ace of spades."

Again, he was correct. He repeated the process six additional times without a single error. Isabel was impressed.

"How do you do that?"

"I was cursed with a static memory. I remember everything I see exactly as I see it, right down to the nevus just below your left ankle. It's actually been a learning disability."

"What? How?"

He shrugged.

"I'm no expert, but when most people learn new things, they do it by overwriting old information, *schemas* they call them, like a computer. People with static memories are forced to remember thousands more schemas because they don't have the ability to overwrite. You can't overwrite a static memory. You simply can't forget."

"It must be... distracting."

"It's why I drink tequila."

Don Smock interrupted.

"Well Isabel, do you think you might be able to give Adam a job down here doing something for a half day?"

She contemplated for a moment.

"I can find something, as long as I'm not stuck down here dealing with any of his sexist bullshit."

Adam saluted.

"Aye-aye, Cap'n."

He stood.

"Before I go, I have to ask you a kind of sensitive question."

"Okay."

"In four hundred years, when we return to Earth, there'll be thirty-nine women and five men, and as I understand, one of the men is my father's age. I've read some of your plan."

He smiled.

"How will the women be, how shall we say, impregnated? Are you going to do it in a lab or will it be by, uh, you know, *conventional* means?"

She wagged her head in disgust. This one was going to be a problem!

"When the time comes for each woman to receive your genetic code, that is of course, if you're found to be an adequate donor, she'll have the option of either conventional means or in vitro fertilization. In my opinion, in vitro fertilization is best. It's far more efficient."

Adam laughed.

"So when your time comes, you're telling me that after four hundred years, you'd prefer a surgical implant to the real thing?"

She raised her eyebrows, her expression serious.

"Absolutely."

****

Secret Service searched Robert Lee, the pilot and the F-18 before armed guards escorted Robert toward Base Command where the President of the United States waited. Robert had second thoughts about agreeing to the meeting as he walked in the dark, but he strode between President Whitmore's private bodyguards.

The meeting was a major coup for the New Republic. It carried implications that the United States of America finally recognized the New Republic as a sovereign and independent power among the nations of the Earth.

Earl, who insisted earlier on meeting President Whitmore, later had second thoughts about leaving New Lexington. Given Robert's leadership ability and his charisma, he knew federal government assassins would be loath to take out such a popular leader. But a federal court had indicted Earl Krebbs on murder charges relating to the disappearance and death of agent Jake Stanton.

A former New Republic soldier, a traitorous teenager from Memphis named Bobby Shaw, provided the government with exact details of the killing of Stanton by Krebbs. If Earl traveled to Utah, he was certain federal agents would arrest him on murder charges at the least. A quick, efficient assassination was more likely. Cousin Bobby and Whitmore had called his bluff, but Earl Krebbs was no fool. He opted to remain at New Lexington.

President Whitmore went out of his way to be kind and courteous. He addressed Robert as "General Lee" and maintained a relaxed manner that put Robert at ease. Lee had arrived at 20:15 so the top-secret meeting would occur under the cover of night. No one from Hill AFB personnel knew President Whitmore was on the base, and no one imagined that Robert Lee of the New Republic would be there.

Whitmore and Lee had a southern-style dinner in the commander's quarters, and then they recessed to the commander's study, where before a crackling fire in the hearth, they sat across a table. Whitmore had a glass of rich, jammy California Zinfandel, while Lee had hot tea.

Checking his watch, Lee was first to speak.

"My question to you is: If Nostradamus is gonna destroy the whole world like you're tellin us, what sense does it make for the federal government to come over and take us out?"

Whitmore half-smiled, and then his expression became serious.

"If you and Krebbs and all your followers had just taken up a place in the wilderness and lived out there until August, the government would have had no problem with that. But when you got all those kids going out there and you started killing federal agents, you sealed your fate."

"And by that ya mean you're gonna attack us no matter what, right? So what's the point of this meetin?"

Whitmore raised his hand in protest.

"I didn't say 'no matter what.' The object of this meeting is to discuss terms for a standoff."

"And your terms?"

"Send all those kids home. You don't have provisions for them. It would be a whole lot better for all if they were allowed to go home rather than start freezing to death later on this month."

Lee nodded and thought for a moment before responding.

"And what about the ones that don't wanna go home?"

"They can stay, as long as they're over eighteen. But for those who want to leave, send them to the border and we'll arrange transportation from there."

Lee sat back in the leather armchair.

"So that's it? Is that all your conditions?"

Whitmore looked up from the glass he was sipping.

"We have one more demand."

"And what's that?"

"We want Krebbs. I realize he's your relative, but if you release the young people and give us Krebbs, you won't ever have to worry about federal government intervention. You've asserted your right to exist, and we'll honor your sovereignty. We'll even do one better than that. We'll use our resources to protect that right. As a gesture of goodwill, we'll even fly in provisions for you."

Lee wanted to get up and walk out. He couldn't believe he was considering, even for a minute, Whitmore's ridiculous demand for the surrender of his blood relative. Yet Earl's behavior in the last two weeks was scary, especially over the last twenty-four hours. Just minutes before Lee boarded the F-18 bound for Utah, Krebbs had come over and threatened to kill Lee if Lee gave in to any of the government's demands.

"What about the F-18s and the tanks?"

"That equipment and the operators of that equipment are the property of the United States of America. You served. You know that as well as anyone. Either you can return them willingly or we'll forcibly come get them."

Whitmore thought it necessary to tone down his rhetoric.

"Look General, my Defense Secretary and the Joint Chiefs have declared, in the interest of national security, we have until the end of November to resolve this situation peaceably. If that doesn't happen, they're going to launch an overwhelming offensive, a surge if you will, and you're all going to die. You can avoid that fate if you give us Krebbs and let the kids go. It's as simple as that."

Lee bowed his head. The situation had changed much over the months since his mother died. Back in late August, the New Republic was just him and Earl and a bunch of good ol militia boys, less than five hundred people. Now there were 1.4 million people living at New Lexington and in surrounding areas. Now there was a ratified constitution, a congress and a judicial system. The outsiders had taken over.

Now even the militia was overrun with defectors from the American military, and leaders from their ranks had relegated all the good ol boys to petty assignments. The population of New Lexington saw Robert as a great leader, but he was the only original New Republic officer who remained in power. Colonel Earl Krebbs was tolerated. The dream had outgrown its dreamers, rendering the dreamer insignificant.

"I'm gonna need some time to think things through."

"You've got forty-eight hours."

Whitmore stood.

"If you have a few more minutes, General, I'd like to show you something."

In a separate room, the President played a fifteen-minute video, produced by Dr. Helen Engstrom, chief director at the Near-Earth Asteroid Tracking observatory site at the Haleakala Crater in Maui.

In the video, Dr. Engstom described in detail the sequence of events that would lead to the asteroidal collision and destruction of life on Earth. The production included images of Nostradamus taken by the NASA Hubble Space Telescope and a computer animated depiction of the asteroid's trek through space right up to the point that it slammed into Earth.

The monitor turned off, Whitmore studied Lee's demeanor before speaking.

"What did you think?"

"It was a good movie. So where's Dr. Engstrom now?"

"I don't know."

"Liar."

Whitmore bowed his head, debating whether he should breach the sensitive subject.

"I uh, I have a *personal* favor to ask of you."

"What's that?"

The President cleared his throat and spoke in a hushed tone.

"My CIA director tells me he has credible evidence that my youngest daughter, Susan, might be hiding out somewhere at New Lexington. I'd really appreciate your checking to find if she's there."

Lee was confused.

"Wait—I thought your wife and daughters were dead. I watched the funeral on television."

Whitmore answered as tears swelled in his eyes.

"My wife and Beth, my oldest, died in the crash, but my youngest never got on that jet. We had assumed all three were dead, but we never found Susan's body. She had run away, and according to Internet records, she was fascinated with the New Republic. There are no other leads. We're thinking she might be in there somewhere."

Lee stood.

"You're such a good liar I don't know what to believe. I'll look for your daughter though, and I'll let you know."

Whitmore extended a hand.

"Thank you, General. As I promised, if you meet our demands, I will in my capacity speak up for you as you assert your right to exist. By next August, you'll realize that we're fighting on the same side."

When Lee opened the door, two Secret Service agents entered and took up posts on each side of the door. Two more waited outside, ready to escort him back to his jet.

"It all sounds good, Mr. President. I just wish for once I could believe you."

****

"Daddy, will you read me a story?"

He hardly looked up.

"Not now, Baby. Daddy's working right now. Daddy's trying to figure something out here. Why don't you read a story on your computer? Daddy put a lot of stories on there just for you!"

Blake had come into his war room. She tugged at his arm.

"I want *you* to read me a story. Mommy always reads me stories."

Davis turned toward his daughter, frustrated.

"I don't have any books. Your mom took all the books, remember?"

He stared from Blake back to his computer screen and then his eyes brightened.

"Hey! I've got a great idea!"

She was excited.

"What?"

"Why don't we let Aunt Bea read you a story? You remember Aunt Bea, don't you?"

"Yes! Where is she?"

Davis was already uncovering the soft, grandmother shaped robot in the corner.

"She's right here."

He took the remote from the robot's lap and activated it, directing it to a place near the couch.

"What story do you want to hear?"

"Chicken Little!"

"Great! I know we've got that one. Now lay down on the couch."

He clicked through options on the remote until he had arrived at his desired destination. Then he covered Blake with a blanket. Turning Aunt Bea toward the girl, he made sure Blake remembered the commands.

"You know what to say to her, don't you?"

She nodded.

"Yes."

"Okay. You're all set. Aunt Bea's going to read you a story."

Leaning down, he kissed her on the cheek. She reached up and gave him a big hug.

"Goodnight Daddy. I hope you fix your computer."

He smiled. She was such a precious little girl.

"Thanks. I love you. Enjoy your story."

With Davis gone, Aunt Bea's bedtime program initialized and she began to read the story in a grandmotherly tone. Blake pursed her lips, pinching them between her little fingers. Aunt Bea only read when little girls were completely quiet.

"*The Story of Chicken Little. Once upon a time there was a dear little chicken named Chicken Little. One morning as she was scratching in her garden...*"

Davis, in the meantime, had returned to his computer, where he worked for fifteen minutes without results.

"Finally!"

He was right. The Misanthrope had broken into Medusa's shell and the potent virus had been released. True to her nature, Medusa provided a trail right back to the system she destroyed. If Davis could locate the user on that system, he would know instantly who Misanthrope was. He worked for thirty more minutes without success. This Misanthrope was clever and resourceful. He didn't make it easy for Davis to begin tracking him.

Davis was impressed that the hacker had penetrated Medusa's shell in the first place. Until that moment, he thought it would take divine intervention to get inside Medusa, but Misanthrope had done it in one month's time. The saving grace was that whatever computer he used to get in and all its programs and files were burned, rendered totally useless.

Davis's next challenge was to create a new program twice as virulent as Medusa, twice as evil, twice as difficult to penetrate. The program would inherit all Calypso's new access codes, and Calypso would get even newer carefully encrypted codes. This program, he thought, could be called Asia.

When he checked his email, he had 115 messages, all the same message, all from the same address. The message read:

"*Very good, Davis. You got me. I'm dead for now. You've wiped me out. But you have to know I'll be back, and I won't make the same mistake a second time. Eventually, I will get in, and when I do, I'm going to shut it all down—the Ark, the Crypt, the Space Station and everything else. Man cannot escape his doom."*

Chapter 26

The problem was getting progressively worse. Earl figured that unless he took drastic measures, there would be mass desertion, especially toward the end of the month when the temperatures fell. Last night it was eight, but those were only the ones that got caught. Perhaps a dozen and a half more had slipped past the guards to the other side. The night before, his dogs caught thirteen kids. The night before that, Friday night, they caught twenty-seven.

Earl was Robert's first cousin on his mother's side. Trudy Culpepper and Lucille Culpepper were half-sisters, daughters by the two separate wives of Robert Culpepper, who the Burnt Corn, Alabama community knew as "the bigamist." Trudy's mother and Lucille's mother had separate residences, but the little shotgun houses were adjacent to each other so the girls could spend time together.

Lucille was six years older than Trudy. She was a stocky, plain-looking girl with a huge bosom, though she wasn't very bright. To no one's surprise, she got pregnant at fourteen and married sixteen-year-old Jack Krebbs, the baby's father. She was pregnant again two months after Earl was born, but it turned out that the new baby, a girl she named Debbie, wasn't Jack's. Earl was eleven months old when he saw his father for the last time.

When Earl was seven years old, he and his mother received word that Jack Krebbs died in Viet Nam defending his country. Earl never understood how a person could die defending his country on the other side of the planet. He blamed the "Japs" for his father's death. To him they were all Japs. When he grew older, he realized that the Japanese had nothing to do with his father's death, but he still hated Asians especially.

He didn't like blacks either, though he realized early on that he would have to tolerate them, especially since there were so many of them. Their animal-like sexual habits, he thought, accounted for their numbers. He had seen some families of blacks with thirteen or fourteen children, all by the same mother. It takes an animal to whelp that many babies.

Their physical characteristics were also beastlike. They could run faster, jump higher and were generally more athletic and muscular than whites. Their women were always in heat.

They never refused their men intercourse like white women did. And the men were like stallions, wild, dangerous and sexual—unless you found a way to cut it out of them. Some you had to kill, but when you could train one of them, you had a fiercely loyal servant at your disposal.

Jasper Cremmons, his stepfather, influenced his attitudes about blacks. Jasper had amassed a fortune by bilking ignorant or disadvantaged blacks out of inherited land, livestock and other possessions. He sharecropped out the land, often to its rightful owners, and further cheated them out of money at harvest time. Blacks in Fountain called him *Thievin Jaspa*, an epithet that defined him until the day he died.

Jasper left Earl all his land and money. He left none to Lucille because she had earned her nickname, *Loosey*. After Jasper's death, Earl tried his hand at farming. He raised chickens and planted cotton and corn, but he lacked the patience to wait out the harvest and the civility to retain sharecroppers.

Losing money, he decided one September to invest in a profitable Peruvian import business. A friend he knew only as "Clyde from New Orleans" talked him into spending some of his idle cash on a kilo brick of pure cocaine.

Clyde assured Earl he already had the apparatus in place get rid of it. A week later, Earl had realized a four hundred percent return on his investment. When Clyde offered to pay him his profit in cash, he laughed.

"Ya think I'm crazy? Let it ride!"

Earl never knew how Clyde got rid of the cocaine, and he didn't want to know. All he knew was that Clyde had connections with corrupt cops and corrupt judges in Mobile, Montgomery, Birmingham and New Orleans.

He also heard that a lot of blacks in those cities were converting the raw cocaine to a new drug called crack. With Earl's financing and Clyde's connections, business boomed. After a year and a half, Earl stopped ever seeing Clyde, who sent underlings to conduct his affairs. Earl just invested money and picked up his profits.

Of course, he couldn't bank the money. If the federal government saw all that money going into an account, they'd be bound to investigate to find out where he got it. So Earl asked Clyde if he knew anyone who sold military-style weapons, guns, assault rifles, mortars, grenades, shoulder-launched rockets and such.

A month later, Clyde introduced Earl to a friend named Gunther, a shadowy figure in the international military hardware market. Earl met with Gunther one time only, and he said he wanted to equip an army. Gunther detailed the terms, the dangers and the consequences of getting caught. Gunther made the deal and saw to it that product was shipped.

Five years later, Earl had stocked a huge armory, full of the most modern and most efficient military-style weapons. He also stocked uniforms and provisions.

He stood before a mirror, talking to himself.

Without them stockpiles, there never would have been no White Knights of the American Constitution. Without me, there never would have been no New Lexington. Without me, there never would have been no New Republic.

So all these Johnny-come-lately military idiots and assholes come here two months ago and just wanna to take things over? They're the same punk kid defectors from the American military who ignore me and wanna treat me like shit! Does any of them even realize Earl Krebbs is the rightful father of the New Republic? Hell no! It's obvious. Instead, they givin all the credit to Bobby.

And then there's this bidness of these kids running away. Escapin, desertin—whatever you wanna to call it. Two months ago they was big shots. They was drinkin, gettin married, gettin tattoos, takin pictures and shootin big guns. They was such big men then.

So here we is, two months later, when the weather's gettin cold and the food's runnin low, when their old ladies started bitchin at em day and night, when it finally got through their thick skulls that people die in wars, then they all of a sudden wanna become little boys again. Then they wanna start cryin and beggin ta go home. Then they wanna run away!

The door to the bunker flew open. Voices from outside shouted profanities, but Earl could make out the important words.

"Yeah, get your asses inside before I shoot one of you! Get your sorry asses in there!"

A line of boys and girls stumbled in, their hands raised and cupped, fingers locked, on the back of their heads. A few sniffed in reaction to the blood that trailed from their noses. There were obviously other guards outside, but only Bubba followed them in, slamming the door shut and engaging the deadbolt.

Earl counted.

"...Thirteen, fourteen... fifteen! We caught fifteen traitors tonight, fifteen desperate little fools that wanted ta go ova an fight against us from the otha side."

One of the boys started to speak an explanation, but Earl slugged him in the stomach. The kid doubled over, groaning, until Earl pulled him up by his collar, speaking directly into his face.

"Ya think I'm stupid, Boy? Ya think I don't know that if ya got away tonight and the U.S. government told ya tomorrow ya hadda come back here and fight against us, ya'd do it. Ya ain't gonna tell em *no*, right?"

The boy was silent.

"And if, while they was at it, they asked ya bout *me*, asked about Bobby Lee, asked bout where we kept our weapons and supplies, asked about our setup, bout where I slept at night, ya'd tell em that too, wouldn't ya?"

The boy was crying. He looked from Earl's snarl to Bubba's sweaty, muscular body. His face pleaded as he answered.

"No, I wouldn't. I wouldn't, I swear!"

"Liar!"

Earl pushed the boy, knocking him to the floor. The boy's face reminded him of another face, of another traitor. Earl Krebbs had taken private Bobby Shaw under his wing at a time when Bobby wasn't sure of himself. Earl gave the boy confidence, made him a man. He promoted Shaw to sergeant and then to lieutenant. He moved Shaw to the inner circle. Shaw had access to Earl, to Robert Lee and to sensitive information, communication and planning.

And then one day, Lieutenant Shaw just up and disappeared. When Earl knew anything about it, Bobby Shaw was the government's key witness in a detailed murder indictment. Two weeks later, a military tribunal sentenced Earl Krebbs to death in absentia.

The boy had crawled to his feet.

"I, I made a mistake, Sir. I don't wanna leave. I wanna stay *here*."

Earl spoke with his back turned.

"Ya really *must* think I'm stupid. Once a runner, always a runner, and that's why I gotta kill ya."

Earl turned toward the boy, leveled the Glock in his face, and fired. A patch of the back of the boy's head exploded, spraying the other captives who cringed and shrieked, before his body dropped and slumped onto the floor.

"And that's why we gotta kill alla y'all, girls included. Bubba—"

Earl walked over to an Asian teenager and stomped the side of his knee, sending him to the floor in pain.

"Japs first. I always kill y'all Japs first. Ya killed ma daddy... Now."

On Earl's cue, Bubba lifted the boy, positioned a pistol directly behind his head and fired. The boy's scream was throaty and muffled. Gore trailed down his face. His eyes opened wide, his arms dropped and he fell face-first to the floor.

"Aren't you a Jap?" Earl said to a weeping kid further down the line.

"No, I'm Mexican, Sir."

"I don't like Mexicans eitha. Bubba—"

This boy tried to flee, only to be pinned to the floor and shot in the back of the head.

"Three down, twelve ta go."

Numbers four and five were girls. Number four was pregnant. Numbers five through eight were black kids, two couples. One of the black males tried to appeal to Bubba on a racial basis. Bubba shot him first, in the mouth.

Numbers nine through thirteen were soldiers who had originally defected from the American military. Fourteen was another desperate girl who pleaded for her life. All dead. Finally, there was a single boy left. Earl approached him with the Glock drawn.

"I seen you before. Ain't ya from a big family a boys? Don't ya have a whole buncha brothers here?"

"Yes Sir, I do. We're the Cunninghams from Nashville. There are seven of us here in all. I'm the youngest."

"What's yer name?"

"Pete."

Earl reholstered the gun and began wiping the blood and gore from his boots with a white handkerchief.

"Well, Pete, looks like this is yer lucky day. I'm gonna let ya live so you and your brothas, and not me and not Bubba here, you and yer brothas are gonna dig a pit big enough fer alla these bodies. Then yer gonna go out and spread the word ta other cowards like you that things don't go well fer those who try ta desert the New Republic."

"Yes, Sir."

His back to the boy, Earl turned, pointing the Glock at the center of Pete's forehead.

"And Pete, if ya ever try escapin again, I'll take it out on yer brothers. I'll kill every last one of em.

Chapter 27

"He's cleared to go home, Mrs. Reed. It'll be much less expensive for you that way, but there is a downside. He will require a lot of care. The bandages on the burns will need to be changed regularly. Many of the dorsal wounds are infected and still weeping. They'll need attention. Both legs are broken, his left arm is broken and he's got a skull fracture. Are you sure you're up to it?"

Layla wore dark glasses to hide her puffy eyes. She had cried every day for the nine days since that incident in the park. It wasn't an accident. It was an incident, an avoidable incident that left her husband severely injured in its wake.

Somehow she knew of the danger in the bushes, and she warned Reggie, but he wouldn't listen. He could have ignored the groans and they could have hurried out of the park and everything would have been just fine, but he wouldn't listen.

"Mrs. Reed? Did you hear what I said?"

She shuddered, blinking her glazed eyes.

"Oh, yes. I've, I've hired a woman to come live with us and help me take care of him. It's a lot cheaper than the hospital."

The doctor smiled.

"I'm not surprised."

He tried to peer past the dark glasses, concern showing on his face.

"Are you okay? Would you like me to prescribe something to help you?"

She crossed her arms, withdrawing.

"No. No drugs. I won't take those. I'll be fine."

She leaned forward in order to glance over at Reggie, who still slept under sedation.

"He's lost so much weight."

The doctor turned.

"And he'll lose more before it's over. Like I said before, recovery will be a lengthy process. It's too bad we *all* don't have a little more time."

Layla forced herself to go for breakfast at a small restaurant near the hospital. She sat at a table, uninspired, as she studied the glossy generic menu. Occasionally, she sipped from the steaming cup of lemon tea at her left. She wasn't hungry. She was still numb.

"Would you mind if I intrude on your breakfast? I'll buy."

Layla smiled. It was great to see a familiar face. Her mother and sister had come over from Jersey the day after the incident and stayed for a whole week after that. Then when they left, she was alone again, grieving, in New York City. Any familiar face was welcome.

"How'd you find me?"

"Reggie's doctor. Said he gave you a prescription for breakfast at this place."

Layla removed her journal from the table.

"Sit down, please."

It was more than ironic that Dr. Benoit showed up at the restaurant. Just that morning, Layla considered phoning her, and in the moment Isabel appeared, Layla was thinking of her.

Since the touch-and-go moments after Reggie's injury, during the prayerful mornings at the chapel, she made a promise to God. She promised God that if he let Reggie live, she would follow whatever course he directed. Even as she prayed, a doctor interrupted, telling her Reggie was lucky to have survived, but that he would live. God had answered her prayer.

In the days that followed, she wondered what God would want her to do. In her heart, she felt he wanted her to mother the next human population, but she didn't want to be presumptuous. So she prayed again and asked for another sign. So the unexpected arrival of Isabel Benoit seemed an unmistakable indication that God wanted Layla to go on the Ark.

Isabel reached over and took the glasses off Layla's face, exposing swollen, tired eyes.

"Are you taking anything to help you sleep?"

Layla raised a hand in protest.

"No drugs. Everything for me is *au naturel.*"

Isabel finished removing her coat, folding it and laying it on the seat.

"Of course you realize the cryonic process will involve a series of scientific procedures? That is, if you still plan on being a part of the project."

Layla sighed.

"Lately, I've been giving it a lot of thought. Yes, I've decided to be a part of Life Ark."

Isabel smiled.

"That's very good, and it's also the right decision. And the cryonic process?"

"I've been researching it, and inasmuch as I'll be a part of Life Ark, I'd like to see details about how you plan on accomplishing it. What they've published on the Internet about it seems interesting, but if it's there, it's probably old news. I imagine you've made some major breakthroughs."

Isabel nodded.

"It's what happens when the global scientific community decides to pursue a singular objective. We can only expect that we'll have it perfected by February."

Layla paused a moment, thinking of Reggie. The tinge of guilt she felt when she made her decision was still there, and it was growing. She hadn't realized it, but she resented Reggie for not listening to her warning, though she felt guilty about considering Isabel's proposal. Conflicted, she asked God for a sign, and he had answered.

"This will be toward the *end* of February?"

Isabel handed Layla a packet with a printed form on top. She withdrew a pen from her blazer pocket and placed it on the contract.

"The accident will happen in the third week of February. We won't start prepping you for cryonic sleep until after March 1st."

"What kind of accident?"

"You'll run into a tree to avoid a head-on collision with a group of drugged-out teens. Your airbag will fail and you'll be pronounced dead at the scene."

Layla was unnerved by the cavalier way Isabel was describing her demise. Closing her eyes, Layla saw the near miss as she swerved toward the tree; she felt the abruptness of the collision; she cringed at the ferocity and heat of the fiery explosion; and she could see Reggie's body slump in great sorrow as he received the news of her death.

"I want to go to the funeral."

Isabel looked up from her tea.

"Excuse me?"

"I want to go to my funeral. I have to be there. My spirit... my spirit has to be there. I'll go in disguise and I'll stay way in the background, but you have to let me be there. Please?"

Isabel eyed the pen in Layla's hand, poised to sign the agreement.

"I might be able to arrange it, but I can't make any guarantees."

"I have to be there. I have to see Reggie to know he's okay."

She signed the agreement and passed it back to Isabel, who examined the signature before folding the document and slipping it into her leather attaché case.

"Now that we've gotten that little formality out of the way, Layla, isn't there something you should be *telling* me about now? Isn't there something you're hiding from me?"

Layla seemed confused.

"I have no idea what you're talking about."

"Did you really think I wouldn't find out? I knew it even before you did."

Layla's expression of bewilderment yielded.

"Knew what?"

"That you're pregnant, Layla. Isn't that the real reason you decided to abandon all the loyalty you felt for Reggie and volunteer for Life Ark? It's the reason I came here today."

Layla struggled to respond, but she had been caught off-guard. Besides that, she was embarrassed for not disclosing her condition before signing the contract. She could only close her eyes and sigh.

Isabel continued.

"Were you going to simply not tell me?"

"I was going to tell you. Hey, I just found out three days ago. Reggie doesn't even know. I just wanted to—"

Isabel interrupted.

"Of course you know we can't let you have this child. It's nothing personal, but Reggie is genetically flawed. You've researched this. You know the Lazarus Project is about genetic improvement through our meticulous engineering. His code would contaminate the new gene pool and compromise our desired ends."

Layla sat back in the seat, resigning.

"I knew it. You want to kill my baby."

Isabel reached over and caressed Layla's hand.

"I wish there were some other way. Sooner is better than later. It's better to do it before you become too attached. We're at ground zero, so we don't have a choice. I take no pleasure in it, but you signed the documents. I have to see to it that your unborn baby is destroyed."

****

Jett Turner's disposition had never been optimistic, but lately it had become outright nasty, and he knew it. His ill humor was a combination of many factors, among them, the President's refusal to take swift and decisive action. Way back in August, on the day the New Republic seceded from the United States, Jett told Whitmore to "take em out quick before they become a real problem."

The President deliberated for three weeks, so that by the time he decided to do something, the New Lexington complex was swarming with American teenagers. Two months later, ten thousand soldiers and officers from active duty American armed forces had defected over, while thousands more came from retired military ranks.

Jett also recommended a pre-emptive major military strike against Iran, "bombin em back into the Dark Ages, taking out every road, every transportation route, every phone line, every volt of electricity, every ounce of technology and then sealing its borders, quarantining the country from the rest of the world."

But once again, Joe Whitmore took too much time to make up his mind. Weeks later, Iran publicly spewed its hate and virulence into the world, announcing it had already placed, "all over the world, a hundred or more terrorist cells bent on destroying America and injuring Americans." Iran's leader summoned Muslims worldwide to arms in the last Great War against the infidel, America.

When news broke about the New York Central Park bombing, Jett was certain Iran's leader had made good on his threats against the United States. He even phoned President Whitmore to drive his point home. But the early investigation pointed away from Iranian-sponsored terrorism.

The bodies found near the exploded sea crab supports for Cleopatra's Needle were identified after two days. Both were Palestinians, though neither had resided in the West Bank at any time. Both were Palestinian Arabs residing in Israel, but to the astonishment of U.S. investigation agents at the highest levels, one of the terrorists had alleged ties to *Mossad*, the Israeli Institute for Intelligence and Special Services.

According to Syrian intelligence sources, one of the bombers, Mohammet el Sayed, was a *Mossad* agent invested in human intelligence against *Hamas*, an enemy of the Israeli state. *Hamas* was a radical Islamic Fundamentalist organization dedicated to establishing an Islamic state in all territory defined as Palestine.

The link from one of the Palestinian terrorists to Israel's equivalent of America's CIA was intriguing to the intelligence community, but it wasn't the type of information the President and other top U.S. officials wanted before the American people.

When television news and the national newspapers identified the Central Park attackers as Palestinian terrorists, the wearied and frustrated American people immediately called for U.S. strikes in the West Bank.

Israel's prime minister, after condemning the attack on America in harsh terms, vowed to allow American bombers to fly missions out of undisclosed military bases in Israel.

The terrorist's link to *Mossad* had Whitmore, already apprehensive about bombing Palestinian targets in the West Bank, even less certain about what action, if any, should be undertaken. Apparently Arab world intelligence and many European allies believed that there was something more sinister going on.

Jett entered the Oval Office, walked around the desk and placed the two-inch thick information and analysis binder in front of the President. Then he took a place near the window and withdrew a metal cigarette case from his pocket.

"Mind if I smoke?"

Whitmore was steeped in the "overview" section at the beginning of the binder. Instead of answering, he nodded, annoyed by the distraction.

Jett blew out a cloud of smoke.

"The other six they found, they may have *thought* they were working for Palestine, but el Sayed was the leader. My guess is he was gettin his orders directly from *Mossad*."

Joe Whitmore looked up from the text of the report, contemplating.

"So if things are what they seem, *Mossad* wants us to do their job for them. They want us to take out the Palestinians and harass Hamas so they don't have to deal with the consequences of doing it."

Jett nodded, continuing the line of thought.

"Especially as we get closer to August. These people already don't care about dyin for a holy cause, and what better cause will they have in May, June and July? Rather than lettin Nostradamus take em out, they'd rather take themselves out punishin Israel."

Whitmore closed the binder.

"So, 'off the record,' what's your recommendation?"

"I say we take out the Palestinians and *Hamas* anyway. Next to Israel, America's the next big target in their minds. But we have to let *Mossad* know that, as good as they are, we weren't fooled. When we hit Palestinian targets in the West Bank, we also take out all the Jewish settlers. We'll call it a misapprehended objective, an unfortunate miscalculation. It's collateral damage. I think *Mossad* will discern our meaning."

After fifteen minutes of temptation, Whitmore asked for a cigarette, and once again he was disappointed. A cigarette in someone *else's* hand just always seemed better.

"I have a feeling Robert E. Lee will submit to our demands."

Jett sneered in disgust.

"We can do it tomorrow or we can do it in July, but the bottom line is: The New Republic must be destroyed, completely obliterated. We can't leave anyone alive. We can't even leave a brick standing."

He lit a new cigarette with the cherry from the old one.

"They can send the kids back home tomorrow if they want. They can even hand over Earl Krebbs. But their existence is a threat to our national security. The longer we wait, the more internal damage we'll suffer, and that compromises our national defense. Who cares if that bastard submits to our demands? At the end of the day it won't make a difference."

Jett watched as the President set his eyes and his jaw, clenching his teeth.

"Of course that's all 'off the record,' Mr. President."

Chapter 28

"So what did they *really* ask ya fer, Bobby? They ask ya ta turn me in?"

This was the fifth time Earl had interrogated him on the subject. Initially, Robert Lee believed it served no useful purpose to tell Earl that his surrender by the New Republic was one of the federal government's non-negotiable treaty conditions. He denied that Earl's arrest was one of the government's main objectives. So after being asked about it for the fifth time, he had no choice but to stick to his story.

"Whitmore said he wanted us ta send all the kids back home, the ones under eighteen. For the ones over eighteen, he said they could make up their own minds. He also said he wants all U.S. government property returned. That's the F-18s, the tanks, the helicopters and all active duty personnel."

He could feel Earl's eyes scrutinizing his every movement as he spoke; he knew Earl was comparing the response with the previous four.

"Of course I gave him no answer. But I figure, the kids under eighteen, maybe we can send em back. Lotta them are gonna die in the next coupla weeks anyway if we *don't* send em. And it would kinda ease the strain on provisions round here."

Earl forced himself not to react to Robert's indirect and cautious proposal. He just stared into his younger cousin's eyes.

Seated, Robert looked up at Earl and shrugged before continuing.

"That one we can talk about. But this thing bout returnin the F-18s and tanks an sendin back trained soldiers, that's where I think we gotta draw some kinda line. I'm against it, but I think we need ta put it before our Security Council."

The non-reaction had become too much for Earl, who erupted.

"Fuck the Security Council! I don't trust em. I don't trust a single one of em. Most of em came from the government, remember? From the Army and such? Ya know how easy it'd be fer the government ta send some of em in here ta spy? Ta make problems? Why you think I surround myself with a buncha dumb niggers?

Security Council my ass! We started this thing, you and me, so nobody but you and me is gonna decide what happens from here!"

Robert took a deep breath and sighed, nodding.

"I agree with ya, Earl, but so far ya ain't told me what ya want ta do."

Earl sat in the chair across from Robert, looking into his eyes.

"Alrite. I say we tell Whitmore and the federal government ta kiss our asses. We don't send back no kids, we keep all the weapons and personnel. We get ready ta go ta war."

Robert stared straight ahead, hesitant to agree.

"With all due respect, Earl. I agree with ya on everythang but the kids part. I mean, maybe a hundred thousand of them kids is gonna either freeze ta death or starve ta death out there in the field if we don't send em back. That don't do us a lick of good in any way. We'll spend all kinds of extra time jus figuring what ta do with all the bodies. I say we send back the ones under eighteen."

Earl harked and spat against the bunker wall.

"Ya don't get it, Bobby. For all your military trainin, ya just don't get it. Truth is, them kids won't do us a lick a good if we send em *back*. They'll only go back and give the government intelligence on us. They'll help the government map out the whole complex, the armory, the command center, the war room, the supply rooms, the bunkers, everthang—they'll hurt us. It's better ta let em die than let em hurt us."

"Yeah, but these is kids, Earl. They're fourteen, fifteen, sixteen years old, an most of em's been in the field since they got here. They don't know nothin bout the armory. They wouldn't know what the command center and war rooms was, much less what they're used for. Leavin em out in the field is as good as puttin guns ta their heads and pullin the trigger."

Earl understood Robert's reference to rumors about the alleged mass executions of runaways in a bunker near the border. According to teenagers who witnessed the execution-style killings, Earl and his personal guard, also known as the 101st Nigger Brigade, rounded up deserters nightly, dispatching them with a single shot in the back of the head.

Robert heard the rumors, the New Republic Security Council heard the rumors, but no one confronted Earl about them. It was a matter of Earl Krebbs being Earl Krebbs. It was an evil they all accepted as they looked toward a bigger picture. According to rumors, Earl killed an average of ten to fifteen deserters per night, a relatively small number.

"At least five thousand per night," Captain Clyde, Shoshone elder and shaman had warned, "when the cold demon comes down the mountain for its winter kill. Hundred twenty, hundred thirty for the season, easy."

Earl ignored the reference and answered.

"Better for them ta die here than fer em ta be cowards and traitors fer the resta their lives. Besides, ya gotta know the reason Whitmore wants em outa here is so he can launch on us with everthang he's got. He ain't gonna do it with thousands a fourteen- and fifteen-year-olds out here. American people wouldn't stand for the government bombin their kids."

Robert thought for a moment and answered.

"But alotta the kids'll still be out here, Earl, the ones over eighteen. What ya don't understand is, after the cold comes down the mountain, we won't have the fourteen- and fifteen-year-olds anymore anyway. They'll all be dead. So that ain't gonna stop Whitmore from bombin us."

Robert stood, continuing.

"Now if we send the ones under eighteen back, we'll be savin their lives, and we'll have alotta American families that'll be grateful. We'll get the support of some of the American people that way."

Robert stopped, his ears trained on the muffled gunshots outside the bunker. It was probably just another border skirmish.

"That's the key in this whole thang, Earl. If we can get the American people ta support us, there ain't nothin Whitmore or anyone else can do ta us. We're a legitimate government, Earl. We have a legitimate right ta exist. We offer a legitimate alternative for people who don't buy the federal government's story about this asteroid thang."

Both men sat in silence for almost a minute before Earl stood.

"I still say we don't send any kids back."

Robert was quick to respond.

"And I say we do, the ones under eighteen. So whadda we do?"

"We don't give in ta the federal government on anythang!"

Robert took another deep breath, resolved to settle a leadership struggle that had reached its climax.

"I disagree, Earl. And seein as I'm the president of the New Republic and commander-in-chief of its army, I think I'm the person who's gonna decide what's best here."

Earl's eyes squinted as he closed on his much taller cousin.

"What? Are ya tryin ta pull *rank* on me here, Bobby?"

Robert was too familiar with Earl's intimidation tactics to become rattled.

"If that's what ya wanna call it. All I'm sayin is them kids, the ones under eighteen, are goin home. I'm makin that call."

Earl took a deep breath, his anger building.

"From the beginnin I always knew it was gonna come down to this, Bobby. From the day I hired yer drunk ass as a deputy, I've been expectin one day ya'd challenge my authority. Yer makin a big mistake tryin ta pull rank on me cuz I don't give a fuck about what *titles* ya got."

"And that's why you'll never get past your ignorant, redneck, white-trash roots, Earl."

Earl withdrew the Glock and pointed it toward Robert's face.

"Are ya tryin ta make funny talkin bout ma Mama, ya fuckin half-breed? Ya fuckin Indian!"

Earl's intimidation tactics with Robert had never involved a gun. Robert knew Earl. If he drew the gun, he had intentions to use it. It was Earl who had drilled it into his head that *you never, ever draw on someone unless you got the balls and a good reason ta blow his ass away.*

Robert backed, his nervousness belying his aggressive posture.

"Aunt Lucy was ma favorite aunt. You of all people know I wouldn't do anything ta basmirch her memory. But now you're stickin a *gun* in my face. What're ya gonna do? Shoot me?"

Earl did not answer. He was thinking. Until that moment, he had been angry with Robert before, he had even resented Robert to the point of hating him, but he had never thought to kill him. Robert was his cousin, but he was more like a younger brother.

Robert eyed Earl's trigger finger, waiting for the gun to fire. In his memory, Earl had never pulled a gun on anyone and not used it. If he survived, it would be a miracle.

"You always told me we have a tradition in this family. We kill our *own* when the time comes. Is that time come fer me, Earl?"

That time had come, Earl thought. But if he killed Robert, there would be no way he could explain away murdering the president of the New Republic to a million or more loyal supporters. As much as he envisioned blowing Robert's brains against the bunker wall, he realized he would have to reholster the Glock, which he did. From that moment on, things would never be the same between the two men.

"Tell ya what, Bobby. Much as I think ya made a fatal mistake here taday, I'll respect yer decision ta send back the ones unda eighteen, but ma reasons fer bein concerned ain't changed. These kids got information that can be used against us."

Robert sighed with relief as Earl turned and moved away. He didn't like near-death experiences and vowed to himself to never meet with Earl again unless he had armed guards present.

"Let's be reasonable here, Bobby. Let's make a deal."

Robert was skeptical.

"Let's hear it."

"Alrite. We can send the ones unda eighteen away, but first they gotta be debriefed. We set up camp fer all the ones leavin and we do a two-day debriefin session and we can get rid of em. Good *riddance* far as I'm concerned."

The simplicity of the proposal surprised Robert.

"That's it?"

"Yeah, debrief em and send em away."

He hesitated, hoping not to seem eager to accept.

"Of course we'll have ta work out the details, but overall, I think it's somethin I can live with."

When Robert opened the door to exit, he stopped, looking back at Earl, who was turned facing an opposite wall. Earl turned his head at the moment Robert turned. Their eyes met.

Robert had never been a spiritual man, but he fancied a deep gorge had opened between him and Earl, and it was expanding. As he looked in Earl's eyes for the last time as family, as a brother, both men knew that things would never be the same between them again.

"I love ya, Earl."

"I, I love ya too, Bobby."

An hour after Robert Lee left the bunker, hulking Bubba Barnes arrived in answer to Earl's summons.

"Bubba, I got a top secret job for ya. You and me'll be the only two people from the New Republic in on it."

"What is it, Boss?"

Earl puffed as he lit the marijuana-filled bowl of the short, hand-blown glass pipe.

"I need ya ta go on a special ops mission. I need ya ta go ta the border."

"Yeah?"

Earl held the smoke in his lungs, handing Bubba the pipe. After a few seconds, he blew out a huge cloud.

"I need ya ta kidnap two of the guards from the otha side. Kidnap em an bring em here all tied up. But ya gotta make sure nobody sees ya."

Bubba blew out a trail of smoke.

"I can do that, Boss. When do ya want em?"

"Tomorra night."

The men sat in silence for a while, feeling the effects of THC, or tetrahydrocannabinol, on their respective hippocampuses and amygdalae. Earl watched the glowing cherry in the bowl fade.

"There's one more thang yer gonna do fer me, Bubba."

Earl stood and went over to a locker. From the locker, he withdrew a large box with a lock on it.

"I need ya ta take this and hide it in yer tent. Tamorra night, after ya've delivered the guards, I'll tell ya what's in it and what ya need ta do with it."

Earl refilled the pipe and passed it and a lighter over to his huge black guard.

"How many did you and ma Nigger Brigade round up tanite?"

"Bout eighteen. Shot em dead on the spot. Problem's gettin worse."

"Problem'll be over in a coupla days."

The business of the day concluded, Earl dealt cards and the two men played three hands of Tonk before Bubba excused himself to go home. He stopped at the door, box under his muscular arm.

"So is it true what I'm hearin? You're actually gonna go along with lettin alla them kids go back home?"

Earl snorted.

"Ya ain't heard that from me, Bubba. Now I may have said they can all go *home*, but I ain't never said nothin about lettin em go back home *alive*."

Chapter 29

"Music, Prokofiev, *Peter and the Wolf*, isolate oboe."

It was great to have Calypso back, but he hated the secrecy. He hated having to hide the fact that she was with him. He told no one, though when Asia came to the door to pick up Blake, she made sarcastic comments and hinted about Calypso being there. He even had to hide Calypso from Blake, who was too young to understand.

"Literature, poetry, Barrett Browning, Portuguese, *number ii*, in tempo."

He felt at peace when she was with him. He could feel her presence. He needed Calypso. She fulfilled him in ways no mortal woman could.

Yet he missed Asia more than he ever imagined he would. As irritated as she made him, he had grown accustomed to the instant chaos she created whenever she entered his idyllic and structured world. She was unbearable and frustrating most of the time, but it was his very frustration with Asia's quirks and idiosyncrasies that drove him to the creation of the unrivaled Calypso.

Asia and Calypso were opposites, their personalities diametrically dissimilar. As he sat in silence, listening to the haunting sadness of the oboe, he began to realize that, though he needed Calypso, he needed Asia just as much.

> *Unlike are we, unlike, O princely Heart!*
> *Unlike our uses and our destinies.*
> *Our ministering two angels look surprise*
> *On one another, as they strike athwart*
> *Their wings in passing. Thou, bethink thee, art*
> *A guest for queens to social pageantries,*
> *With gages from a hundred brighter eyes*
> *Than tears even can make mine, to play thy part*
> *Of chief musician.*

Davis met Asia at a computer convention in Seattle during September seven years earlier. She had come up to the booth where he and his brother were selling refurbished desktop units. Davis was unemployed. He had quit a good job at one of Seattle's premiere software engineering and licensing firms because the government began garnishing his checks in order to recover outstanding debt interest from a decade of student loans.

In the end, he realized that he could not afford to continue working, so he asked the company to lay him off. The unemployment checks were exempt from garnishment. Between the unemployment checks, hacking jobs and selling refurbished computers, Davis struggled, but he managed to keep a roof over his head and the electricity on.

So when his brother asked him why, out of the blue, he just gave away a computer that would have fetched three hundred and fifty dollars easy, Davis only sighed.

"I just met the woman I'm going to spend the rest of my life with. There's no comparison!"

He didn't find out until after loading the computer in her car that she was already in a serious relationship. She was engaged to be married. When he asked for her number, she refused and told him she would take his instead.

"Maybe I'll give you a call if things don't work out."

He never expected to see or hear from her again, but she surprised him by calling one Saturday morning four months later at three a.m. She had broken up with her fiancé, she was lonely and she was up composing love poetry on the computer Davis had given to her. They talked until three o'clock Saturday afternoon.

Asia Taylor was the sole daughter of world famous American fashion model Ann Taylor. Her single parent mother from Mississippi had never revealed her father's identity to her or to the public.

During college, Asia hired a detective to find her father, but all she learned was that he was a political, wealthy and dedicated family man who did not want to be found. Apparently, he knew about her and secretly paid support to Ann, but after college, Asia eventually gave up her search for him. It would be one of her life's great mysteries.

She was raised in the high fashion world of San Francisco, though she spent months traveling with her glamorous mother. She was in New York or London every other weekend. She enjoyed extended stays in Paris two dozen times before she was fourteen.

A bright girl, she mastered the Italian language and had favorite restaurants and hotels in Milan and Rome. She landed her first runway job in Tokyo at sixteen. Because she hung out with international models, actors and other jet setters, she grew up fast.

By age eighteen, she had stopped being embarrassed about seeing her face on the covers of nationally published magazines and by the celebrity it garnered. Yet life among "the beautiful people" came at a price.

Her vain mother was an insufferable alcoholic and she abused cocaine. She drank vodka to help her sleep after doing lines of coke, and then she did additional lines of coke to help avoid getting too high from the vodka, a vicious cycle that kept her up all night and in bed all day. Before Asia realized her mother had a life-threatening addiction, she called her mother "the vampire" for her habit of sleeping all day and partying all night.

Over the years, the excesses began to take a toll on Ann. By the age of thirty-five, the cocaine and alcohol had begun to furrow dark, deep lines in her pretty face, and she became skinny to the point of being unhealthy. As the job calls came less often, Ann began to panic, fearful that her days and nights of glamour in lime-illuminated spotlights were numbered.

As she looked at her pretty daughter, she became a schizophrenic combination of a jealous competitor and a protective mother. She attacked Asia's agent for getting her fewer major magazine covers and accused the woman of pimping her daughter.

In the business, Ann became anathema, and the job calls stopped altogether. She blamed Asia for "whoring around and ruining my career." Embarrassed and hurt, Asia quit modeling at 20 and enrolled at San Francisco State.

Asia's exit from the world of high fashion, however, did not help Ann's career. At forty-one, Ann was no longer marketable. Her new agent offered her a series of public service television announcements on coping with menopause, but Ann, insulted, fired the woman. That year, Ann was hospitalized for the first time.

The doctors told Asia that her mother's heart was enlarged due to years of alcohol and drug abuse. They told her that Ann would be dead within a year if she didn't stop drinking. Nonetheless, Ann demanded that Asia stop at a liquor store to pick up a 1.75 liter of

Absolut vodka on the way from the hospital. Ann died from congestive heart failure six months later at forty-two.

Traumatized by her mother's death, Asia cut off all her hair and became consumed with the study of literature at college. She wore old baggy clothes and no make-up in an attempt to appear as plain as possible. She became an unknown, disappearing into the general student populace. From that vantage point, she was able to pursue her greatest two passions: writing and the examination of literature.

It was during those first difficult months after her mother's death that she discovered the works of Elizabeth Barrett, later known as Elizabeth Barrett Browning. She admired Ms. Browning, who had overcome physical ailments and the death of a close family member to write with spiritual elevation, insight, intense sincerity, keen judgment and sympathy with all who were oppressed and suffering. As a passionate and romantic young woman, Asia was moved by Barrett's *Sonnets from the Portuguese.*

> *What hast thou to do*
> *With looking from the lattice-lights at me,*
> *A poor, tired, wandering singer, singing through*
> *The dark, and leaning up a cypress tree?*
> *The chrism is on thine head, on mine the dew,*
> *And Death must dig the level where these agree.*

Asia had read from Barrett Browning's *Portuguese Sonnets* on that first night she and Davis spoke on the phone. Of all the sonnets, number ii was his favorite. It reminded him of Asia and all the tragedy, passion and chaos in her life.

She told him that night the best ideas in life came from chaos, *that state of being in which chance is supreme.*

"Order proceeds from disorder," she asserted in a poem. "All the world's greatest discoveries were born of chaos—every great artistic masterpiece, every extraordinary literary achievement, every major scientific breakthrough, the very birth of the universe and creation itself... have their roots in chaos."

As Davis sat at the desk within his war room in the Crypt, he thought how, from all the disorder of his life in Seattle, from a situation of supreme chance he had moved to San Francisco to be near Asia and how he had created a life of supreme order.

On a grander scale, Asia represented chaos in his life, the disorder, frustration, illogic, passion, love, sex, sleeping, eating and all the other distractions that interfered with his desire for pure order. The only moments when he experienced pure order were during those times he was alone with Calypso.

With Asia gone, pure order reigned, but gone with her chaos were his passion and creativity. In human terms, Davis really missed his wife.

The knock on the door was sudden. It startled Davis, who bolted from the chair.

"Music, off. Calypso, shutdown."

When he opened the door, Baldev Heir, his assistant, stood with an envelope in his hand.

"Someone's been in your outer office downstairs. Whoever it was didn't get inside."

Davis's face flushed with concern.

"How do you know?"

"Well, I know I locked the outer office. Then when I went back to shut off the lights, I found this."

He handed the letter to Davis.

"I'm sure whoever it was didn't get any farther than the front office, but all the same. We've had a breach."

Davis looked at the writing on the envelope in his hand. A single word was scrawled on it in black ink: Misanthrope. He could hardly breathe, though he spoke the instructions.

"You know what to do. Change all the security codes and encryptions. From now on, we'll have to schedule someone in there at all times. This is not good."

"Do we report it to Smock?"

"No. This is something we tell no one."

With Baldev gone and the door locked behind him, Davis retreated to his war room and locked yet another door.

"Calypso, boot."

He sliced through the envelope closure with a sharp metal opener, blew into the slit and slowly slid out the letter. Opening it before his face, he read:

Well Davis,

You burned me with Medusa. You really set me back. I didn't expect the flash. I'm still working on Alecto, though I imagine you've already got Tisiphone and Megaera waiting in the wings. I can't win that game—it's your game. At least I can't win it by August 7th.

It took some work, but I managed to get inside this Crypt. Now you're stuck with me right to the end. Now I'll be able to stand around, unnoticed, and look over your shoulder. I could be anyone, maybe even the person who delivered this letter to you.

This world, this system must come to an end. Kali has declared it. There will be a new order.

I'm here to make sure this cycle and this tradition will not survive. New gods and new species must be born. I'll destroy this world from the inside out. First I'll ruin the Lazarus Project, and then I'll come for you and Calypso.

****

"Okay, Lissen up! You were all warned about what the penalty would be if ya tried to desert to the other side. I know you're not the only ones. I saw the ones ahead of ya. They oughta be runnin inta ma boys at the border about any time now."

At six-foot-eleven-inches, former Delta Force operative Bubba Barnes towered over a group of eight shivering young people huddled together for warmth in the aegis of a large boulder that blocked the biting wind. The landscape was clean and white, as the first snow of the season had come that night. Several of the kids wept aloud.

"What's gonna happen ta ya now won't be good, and I don't have a choice here, so I'll make it quick and painless if I can. If ya believe in God, it might be a good time ta make your peace. If ya don't believe in God, try ta remember somethin or someone ya love."

He snapped a new clip into his trademark .45 caliber United States MK23, Mod O pistol.

"Cuz in the end for all of us, that's all that matters."

Bubba pointed to a boy in the group and nodded to his minions. Two of the four huge guards went over and grabbed the teenager, who began screaming and pleading. The red-haired adolescent, thrashing and begging as guards forced him to his knees before Bubba, could have been no more than sixteen.

"Resistance is futile. Fighting only makes it worse. Pray, meditate, breath slowly."

The boy had yet to develop even the promise of facial hair. A guard at each outstretched arm, he could only move his head. Bubba held his breath, grabbed the mop on the boy's head, placed the gun barrel against the back of his skull and jerked slightly as he squeezed the trigger.

He watched the steaming blood spray a perfect crescent pattern onto the snow in crimson as the boy's neck fell limp and his body shuddered. A guard dragged the still-bleeding corpse to a snowbank fifteen feet away.

"Get me the next one."

Another boy, realizing he was next, made a break for it. Pushing off the girl in front of him, he turned and sprinted away into the darkness with one of the cursing guards following in pursuit.

"He won't get far. Get me another one."

The young woman cried without sound. She didn't even struggle as she knelt before Bubba in prayerful deportment.

"May God have mercy on your black soul."

As she bowed her head in submission, Bubba felt an unsettling sensation in the pit of his stomach. It was the first time he felt such regret for what he had to do, but he had his orders.

"Forgive me."

She was dead before her body slumped to the ground.

"Goddammit! What's takin y'all so long? You should already have the next one over here!"

Bubba hurried through the next three, shooting the struggling third boy through the side of his head. A second bullet was required to finish the job. When he looked over, only two girls remained.

"Bring em over here. Bring em *both* over here."

The girls kneeling before him, Bubba dismissed the remainder of the guards, ordering them to help track down the runner. He looked over at the pile of steaming corpses on the white blanket of snow and then to the girls.

"This is a rough business. And in this business, ya don't get many breaks."

He placed the burning gun barrel against the forehead of one girl, and then on the forehead of the other.

"And even when you get breaks, you don't get somethin for nothin. It's somethin for somethin, nothin for nothin. It's the way things work."

The girls were clenching each other's hands, sobbing, pleading aloud.

"You want a break from me, girls? You wanna live?"

The begging grew louder. The girls' answer was cacophonous, though in the affirmative.

"That's good. Cuz I'm feelin a little *needy* tonight. See, I have the power ta kill you or ta do you some good. My orders are ta kill you. If I don't do it, I put myself at risk. So if I'm gonna put myself at risk and let you go, I hafta ask myself: What am I gonna get out of it? What's in it for *me*? What are you gonna give *me*?"

The first girl answered in fear and confusion.

"I don't know. What do you want?"

The second girl understood.

"You *want* us? You want us both? You can *have* us. We'll do anything you want!"

Bubba smiled, nodding.

"You're two of the finest little bitches I've *ever* come across, here or anywhere else. I noticed that from the first moment we caught you. Tell you what—you spend a few hours with me in my tent, and you make me feel good, I'll personally escort you to the border. I'll personally make sure you get to the other side."

"How do we know we can trust—?"

Her friend had cupped a hand on her mouth to shut her up.

"Of *course* we trust you! We'll do anything you want."

Bubba had not exaggerated the girls' beauty. The first had a burnt copper complexion, a very pretty face with delicate features and a muscular, shapely body. Her breasts were full and firm. Her waist was small and tight, sculpted onto contoured hips and a round, solid butt. Her thighs were taut and smooth.

The second girl's face was stunning to behold. Her piercing green eyes held such innocence, allure and sensitivity. Her cheekbones were high, her lips full, and her skin was clear and creamy white. Her body, like that of the first, was well formed and sensual even in the desert camouflage military fatigues she wore. Upon their arrival at New Lexington, the girls stood out because they were both so attractive.

Bubba conducted both a little over a mile to a tent erected in a shielded recess in the hills. His MK23 was tucked into the waistband of his pants in the front, while he clutched a girl under each well-developed arm. His huge hands had run over their young bodies, clutching, grabbing and rubbing all along the way.

"It ain't much, but it's big enough for three. It's warm. You can take off your clothes inside."

The second girl grabbed the first girl's arm to stop her from ducking into the tent. She hesitated and spoke to Bubba.

"I better tell you this. I hope it doesn't make you mad, but we're virgins."

He smiled.

"All the better."

He pulled her close and snuggled his face into her delicate neck.

"I'll be gentle, for the first go-round. But I wanna remember this night, and it'll be a night that both of you will definitely remember. You'll remember it as the night Bubba Barnes rocked your world."

He left the lantern lit so he could watch the girls undress, so he could watch them lay side by side on their backs in submission and readiness, so he could watch what he was doing. He took the first. For him, it was exciting to watch the second watching him atop the first, with all three knowing she would be next. Then he took the second.

The first "go-round" was slow because Bubba was so large. It took over fifteen minutes just to get inside each of the girls and another fifteen to break each in enough to really get started.

For a man, Bubba had a great body. His neck was thick, his shoulders were huge and bulging, his strong, sinewy arms rippled in tiny waves every time he moved as much as a finger. His waist was tight and the muscles of his stomach were well defined. His hips, butt and thighs, grinding alternately between each girls' raised knees, were powerfully built.

Even his face was handsome. His jaw was square and his features were in good proportion, though his countenance was intimidating. His eyes had a distant and subtly arrogant quality to them even as he peered into the girls' eyes from his place atop each.

Four hours later, Bubba had relaxed into a comfortable pace. At Bubba's insistence, they experimented with different techniques and positions, though it was awkward for the girls. Toward the end, Bubba believed in his mind that the girls were anticipating him, awaiting his re-entry. He interpreted their pained groans as moans of pleasure when, at climax, he plunged as deep as he could, quivering, as he released himself within their bodies.

He told them to get dressed at five a.m. and gave them a day's provisions. By 5:15, their footsteps crunched as they walked, girls limping, on the frozen surface of the snow. Bubba shouted at them, telling them they had better keep up, threatening to kill them if they fell behind. He had changed into white fatigues and wore a large white jacket. Even his headgear and ammunition bag were camouflaged for the snowy terrain. A five-foot sled was strapped to his back.

After an hour, the three went past the New Republic's guard post at the nation's declared boundary line, and an hour after that, they approached a remote stretch along the U.S. Army border.

"Don't try'n go over till I tell you. Their policy is *shoot first, ask questions after.* Give me about fifteen minutes to take out a coupla the guards, and then I'll give you the signal."

The girls sighed with relief, as their ordeal was almost over.

They had learned about New Lexington on the Internet. The whole idea of the New Republic and the freedom it offered intrigued both. New Lexington seemed preferable to life at home with parents for what could be Earth's last ten months, a life with rules and curfews imposed by not only their parents, but by the government as well.

Both had sworn that they would not die virgins. They wanted to go to the New Republic, meet a couple of nice guys, maybe get married and enjoy sex every day until the world ended.

Neither expected conditions to be so harsh. When they arrived two weeks earlier, the weather had turned cold and provisions were running out. For three nights, they managed to sleep in a tent with a friend of theirs from Los Angeles, but then his fourteen-year-old wife got jealous and threatened to shoot them in their sleep if they didn't leave.

Because both were so pretty, they stood out wherever they stopped. When they went to the New Lexington complex, a real creepy guard told them he could get them an actual room, but he said the white girl would have to be Earl Krebbs' girlfriend. *Wasn't happening.*

They stayed with another family for a week and a half while the husband was away, training in the field.

By the end of the second week, they came to the realization that the New Republic was overcrowded and that it was nothing the website promised. Teenagers were being killed for trying to go back home to parents. They came because the New Republic was held out as an idyllic dream. Instead, it had become a horrible nightmare.

"Go! Hurry! You'll have five minutes max. Get over there!"

Bubba had a full body bag slung over his shoulder while he dragged another on the sled at his right side.

"Go home. You got out just in time."

Chapter 29

"The kids—the ones we're gonna send home. They'll be debriefed and sent back in the next coupla days."

"And Krebbs?"

Robert paused and finally nodded.

"I thought long and hard about that one. He's ma family, but he ain't exactly a good man. He ain't even exactly a man I like or trust anymore, but we don't choose our relatives. I don't have a choice in it. I cain't give ya Earl. I just cain't do it. He's family. If anybody's gonna take im out, I will."

Joe Whitmore sighed.

"Listen Robert, I got military leaders and advisors just dyin to blow the New Republic off the face of the Earth, teenagers and all. Earl Krebbs is one man. What's one man's life compared to the welfare of what you call *your whole nation*?"

Robert interrupted.

"You guys come in and get im if you can, but I cain't give im ta ya. It goes against everthang I am and believe ta be proper."

Once again, Robert had flown over to Hill Air Force Base in Utah to meet with President Whitmore. They stood before a huge fireplace as the snow fell outside. The President had a cognac while Robert, his throat sore from a cold, sipped steaming hot lemon tea. Whitmore placed a hand on Robert's shoulder, studying his eyes.

"How firm are you on that?"

"Completely firm. Cain't do it. Be like Washin'ton handin over Charles Lee ta the Brits."

Whitmore turned, wagging his head in regret.

"Well, if that's the case, I suppose the third condition is moot. I take it you won't be returning all government property?"

"I don't think ya understan, Mr. President. Them ones there, they're committed to the New Republic. They're prepared ta die defendin the idea of America, defendin our right ta exist. They wouldn't go back if I ordered it."

Sadly, Whitmore stood in silence for a moment before speaking.

"Then you'll all die."

Robert smiled, his expression reflecting the bitter sweetness of the moment.

"So be it. Then we'll die. We're prepared for that. In the spirit of Patrick Henry: If it's a choice between freedom and death, we choose freedom. This is our finest hour."

The gravity of the situation unsettled Whitmore, who took a seat in one of the leather recliners before the fire.

"There's something else, isn't there? Because I know you didn't risk coming out here just to tell me there was no possibility of us coming to a deal. You could have done that by phone. So why are you here? Is it my daughter?"

Robert continued standing, his head bowed.

"I had my best intelligence guy conduct a secret search. He assured me he'd check the entire state. If she's there and she's alive, we'll find her. Truth be told, since winter come down the mountain, we've lost about forty-four hundred ta the cold. If she was in that number, we wouldn't know."

Whitmore squinted his eyes in suspicion.

"Susan's a very resourceful girl. If she's there and doesn't want to be found, you won't find her, and if anyone was going to die from exposure, it wouldn't be her. She's too smart for that. But you could have told me over the phone you hadn't found her. So I'm still wondering why we're here."

Robert nodded, sipped from his cup and took a seat in the other recliner.

"I appreciate the fact that you're a family man, Mr. President. I respect ya fa that. I have a family too."

"So you want your family out of the New Republic to spare them your fate?"

Robert sighed.

"Naw. Becky and the boys would be proud ta die fa freedom. It ain't that."

He unfastened his ponytail, wagging his head to free his long black hair.

"It's ma Uncle Earl."

"Earl Krebbs?"

"Yep. Last week, he wanted ta kill me. He still does, but he ain't figured out a way ta do it yet. I know im. And I know he ain't above usin ma family, killin ma sons or Becky ta put me in a position so he can do it. I wanna get ma family outa there for their protection and for the good of the New Republic. As a leader, I cain't afford ta hafta worry about em. I'm askin ya ta take care of my wife and kids fer me."

Whitmore stood, extending his hand.

"That would be my honor. How do you plan on getting them out?"

"When we send all the kids back in the next coupla days, Becky and the boys will be hidden in that crowd. She'll be usin the name Betsy Ross. She'll have two boys with her."

Whitmore smiled.

"Betsy Ross? We'll find her."

As Robert stood to exit with the armed guard, he extended his hand, smiling.

"Well, I guess this is it, Mr. President. Don't look like I'll be seein ya again."

"No, I guess you won't."

"Take care of ma wife and boys."

Whitmore nodded, smiling.

"I will."

"So how long we got? How long before ya start bombin us?"

The President looked uneasily at the guards, who were pretending not to listen, and then his eyes met again with Robert's.

"Have a pleasant Thanksgiving, Mr. Lee."

****

The young guard positioned inside the supply yard never heard a thing. He just looked down and saw droplets of bright red blood trailing toward his boots. He felt light-headed and dazed, and yet he felt secure. The strong arms that held him were a comfort in his last seconds of life.

His passing was so quick and silent that his partner on duty never knew anything until his turn came. There were other guards stationed outside, but until they had a reason to burst in, they would remain outside.

Bubba used a lighter to illuminate the map one last time before he set it aflame, dropping it onto the snow. He climbed the backside of the water tower, the side away from the lights at the front of the yard.

The reservoir at the top was large enough to hold eighty thousand gallons of water when full.

As he opened the access door at the top and peered inside, he could see the tank was about three-quarters full, and as expected, there was a problem. The surface of the water in the reservoir was frozen. That meant Bubba would have to climb down the metal rungs of an internal access ladder to the water's frozen surface. In order to deliver the chemical, he would use an ice pick to break a hole in the frozen crust. This could take some time, depending on the thickness of the ice.

Fortunately, for Bubba, the surface ice was less than an inch thick. He was glad he had decided not to walk on it to the middle of the reservoir as Earl Krebbs suggested he should. The ice would have broken. He also decided not to crush the tablets to powder before dropping them into the water, as Earl had also suggested. He was putting them in. That was enough. The main objective of his mission accomplished, he hurried back down the tower to the ground.

When he slipped into the supply yard earlier, he was carrying one of the U.S. Army guards he had kidnapped from the border a night earlier. He had dropped the smaller, terrified man, bound and gagged, next to the dark wall of a building in the yard.

When he retrieved the guard, the man was almost dead from exposure, but that didn't matter. He took his prisoner to a place next to the last supply yard guard he had killed, positioned him in front of the body and untied him. Then Bubba took the pouch containing the last chemical tablet and hung it around the man's neck.

He took the bloody knife he had used to kill the supply yard guards and placed it in the U.S. Army guard's hand. Finally, he took the M-16 from one of the dead guards, fired it twice into the air and once into the U.S. Army guard's forehead.

The gunshots created a commotion outside the yard. It took less than two minutes before a group of ten guards rushed into the supply yard, rifles at the ready. By that time, Bubba was long gone.

The New Republic guards found their two dead colleagues, and they found the U.S. Army guard with the knife used in the assault. Their captain was confused because both guards had their throats slashed, and yet the assailant was dead. The guard who shot him had to be alive when he fired the rifle. So who could have slashed his throat?

He gave orders to a sergeant.

"Secure the perimeter and have a team start searching outside. There was someone else in here, and chances are he's still around."

Then the captain spoke to a second sergeant.

"This is a serious breach. What the hell were they doin in here? We're gonna have to report this to the commander right away."

"That won't be necessary, Cap'n. I already know."

As the startled captain looked up, Earl Krebbs stepped into the light.

"Yer right. It is a serious breach, and it happened on yer watch."

Earl drew the Glock pistol from its holster and pointed it toward the captain.

"We're in a war here. And in war, such breaches are inexcusable."

The captain tried to explain, but Earl ordered him to shut up. Krebbs spoke instead to the other soldier.

"Young man, what is yer rank?"

The soldier stood at attention.

"I'm a sergeant in the New Republic army, Sir! I am committed to protect the lives and rights of our citizens and will fight to the death for freedom and liberty."

Earl grinned as he looked from the condemned captain's worried face to the sergeant's.

"Well Sergeant, looks like this is yer lucky day. How would you feel about makin... Cap'n?"

****

The crowd was larger than critics of the plan expected. Unofficial tallies had the number at ninety thousand, which was forty thousand fewer than the New Republic government had anticipated. A week earlier, the New Republic issued a proclamation, stating that, because MAPS (Militias of the American Plains States) started out as a voluntary militia, those persons wanting to leave to avoid the impending war could do so, provided they left all weapons and belongings behind.

All those leaving were also required to attend the two-day debriefing session at Echo Valley, located in the secure Tump Range, south of Fontenelle Mountain. The decree also urged all persons under eighteen to return to their parents.

The proclamation drew protests in many New Republic cities, with the most ardent demonstrations occurring in New Lexington. Even at Echo Valley, during the first day of debriefing, protesters from New Lexington held a rally outside the camp, enduring the weather to condemn those who were leaving as cowards, traitors and redcoats.

The debriefing session was actually a propaganda campaign, aimed at the American news media and the American public. The situation presented a veiled opportunity to garner public support for the New Republic. Within two days, ninety thousand persons were going to re-enter the former United States of America, armed with the truth about Robert E. Lee and the New Republic.

"For those who call ya cowards," Robert Lee shouted from an elevated podium, "for those who label ya as traitors to the state, here ya have an opportunity to prove em wrong. Here ya have an opportunity ta serve your country like no one else can right now."

He scanned the perimeter to determine where the cameras were positioned so that he could play to them.

"If ya love freedom, go back ta your parents and tell em that the New Republic is the last bastion of freedom in America. If ya love freedom, go ta your congressmen an congresswomen and tell em that the last true Americans on the continent are out here in the freezin cold, sufferin an dyin ta defend your right ta freedom and their right ta exist.

"If ya love freedom and the idea of America, go ta your newspapers and television stations and tell em if they don't do somethin soon, then the federal government's gonna send bombers out here and wipe the last existin Americans off the face of the planet. Ask em about Dr. Helen Engstrom. Why did she just suddenly disappear? And ask the world why we don't have a right ta exist. We ain't hurtin no one out here."

President Robert Lee's forty-minute speech was inspiring to the audience at Echo Valley. He had to stop twenty-six times for applause. Notwithstanding, Earl Krebbs' mysterious absence from the mass debriefing didn't escape the notice of the crowd gathered in the valley. In fact, the non-presence of Earl Krebbs threatened to upstage the news of the debriefing itself.

Since the beginning, Earl and Robert *always* appeared together, especially at important functions, especially when the media would be present. Many knew of a rift that had developed between the two and rumors abounded.

According to insiders, Robert Lee hired a private guard over the past week and never went anywhere alone. Anonymously, one man suggested to CNN that Robert Lee's new security concern was in response to a recent death threat issued by Krebbs.

"If that Earl Krebbs was gone," spoke one bold woman to a reporter, "I'd stay here. He's an evil and disgustin man. He's the reason me and ma boys is leavin."

The first day of the debriefing had gone well. By 6:30 p.m., all official business for Day One was over and the crowds had begun eating their nighttime meals. Some had brought food and other provisions from their homes in anticipation of the journey to the border, but there were vendors spread out all over for those who hadn't.

There were barbeque stands, gyro sellers, Chinese food kiosks and working woks. There was Mexican food, there was someone charbroiling buffalo steaks, and there was an all-vegetarian food court.

For those who weren't stocked on provisions, the New Republic had its own stall, selling provisions for the two-day debriefing and for the journey to the border. The most requested item from any of the vendors: government bottled drinking water.

Robert Lee had dinner in his tent with a security advisor, a political strategist and his media consultant. His guards posted themselves outside the tent and secured the area in a quarter-mile radius.

Lee's guards were unnerved by the unexpected appearance of Bubba Barnes, who had come before the meal and seemed to be lurking on the perimeter. When they told Robert about it, he grew concerned.

Bubba Barnes was, after all, Earl Krebbs' chief lieutenant and the head of his security forces. Opting to confront rather than to be distracted, Robert took two guards and went out to question the menacing soldier.

"What're ya doin out here tanight, Barnes? Earl send ya?"

"No Sir. I came on my own."

"For what purpose?"

Barnes hesitated.

"For protection, Sir."

Robert Lee looked up, studying Bubba's stoic disposition and facial expression.

"Well Barnes, as ya can see, I've already got a guard. Your services ain't needed. You're dismissed."

Thirty minutes later, it was obvious that Barnes ignored the dismissal order. He still lurked at the perimeter, appearing at odd intervals. No one in Lee's personal guard cared to confront the scary man again, and even Lee himself, when informed of Barnes' continued presence, declined to initiate another confrontation.

Barnes made the guards nervous. His reputation for stealth, cunning, cruelty and cold-blooded killing was proven in his actions. The rumors circulating among defected American military personnel at the New Republic suggested Bubba Barnes was a renowned member of Delta Force, a shadowy agency so secretive that the American government disavowed knowledge of its missions.

According to the insiders, Delta Force operatives were selected because they were the elite of the elite, the top one percent of the Army Ranger and Navy SEAL teams, while many operatives had training in both camps. They were supermen. They were ghosts. Because Delta Force missions were so secretive and its agents were spectral, no one was sure about where their orders originated or what agency employed them. The CIA was everyone's best guess.

Bubba was a loner who always spent his nights in seclusion. He pitched his portable tent in remote locations far away from the populated camps scattered throughout the hills and plains. No one had ever seen him asleep or vulnerable. He never even ate in public.

Sometimes he disappeared for days at a time and sometimes soldiers would stumble across his extinguished fires in dreary, unthinkable, uninhabitable locations.

To those who feared or respected him, he was super human. To Earl Krebbs, he was just another dumb nigger. A bad ass, yeah, but still just another nigger.

If his true purpose there truly *was* to protect the leader of the New Republic, then no one would be able to get to Lee. But if he was there to assassinate Lee, the guards feared he would start picking them off through the night, one by one. The call went out for reinforcements, and six additional armed guards arrived, but they were all nervous.

When the chef ran out of water and asked two of the men to hike back to get some from one of the provisions stands in the camp, guards were slow about volunteering. When Barnes approached and insisted on hiking back to get the water himself, no one, including Robert Lee, objected. It was only water, after all, and it was a welcome break from the menacing presence of Bubba Barnes.

Chapter 30

"How long's she been back?"

Aaliyah poured herself more tea from the kettle at the center of the dining room table. She watched the steam rise, drew a deep breath of jasmine and sighed before answering.

"Oh, I'm not completely sure. Yesterday, I think."

He sipped his tea.

"And she came by to see *me*?"

"Yes. She told Dexter she wasn't up to talking, but she said she really wanted to speak with *you*."

Jonah shrugged, perplexed.

"So you have no idea what she wanted?"

"Yes. She wanted to talk to you. She wanted to talk about testifyin in church tomorrow."

Two weeks earlier, when Jonah Williams heard that sixteen-year-old Brenda Brown had run away to New Lexington in Wyoming, he breathed a huge sigh of relief. He heard a week later that Dexter had planned on going with her, but he changed his mind in the end, thanks to Megan. When the Reverend realized how close he had come to losing yet another son, he felt he had dodged a bullet. But now she was back. And she wanted to testify?

"What in God's name is she up to?"

Jonah Williams was nineteen years old when he got married for the first time. His eighteen-year-old bride, the former Ernestine Clinton, was his high school sweetheart and a member of his Snow Lake, Arkansas congregation. A year later, their union was blessed with the birth of a healthy son, whom Jonah named Theodore, meaning "gift from God."

Ernestine was a devoted, loyal wife and a quiet, protective mother who doted on the boy from early on. Her life revolved around the child, especially since Jonah was away so much of the time.

When Theodore was less than a year old, Jonah was accepted at John Brown University over in Siloam Springs, which was a major commute from Snow Lake. He attended John Brown for seven years, earning a Bachelor of Arts degree in theological studies, *summa cum laude*, while he minored in Biblical Studies. Postgraduate work earned him a Master of Business Administration degree (M.B.A.) three years later.

The education he gained at John Brown served him well, but it came at a great personal price. In order to attend the college and perform well, Jonah rented an apartment in Siloam Springs, leaving Ernestine and Theo first with her parents for three years and then in a house he and Ernestine bought in Snow Lake.

Ernestine always dreamed of being married to a preacher, so she complained little about his busy schedule. She was lonely during the week, but she had Theo around to keep her company. During the week, Theo was the "little man" in her life. She took him everywhere she went and bought him everything he wanted.

By the time Theo was three, he was spoiled. He screamed and yelled and hit people when he didn't get his way. He threw temper tantrums, he locked himself in his room and he refused to eat and go to bed.

Where Ernestine begged him and made deals with him, Jonah took off his belt and spanked the boy's butt. The difference in parenting tactics could not have been more extreme, and this difference resulted in Theo abusing his mother's kindness and patience while he began to hate his father.

Theo was eight years old when Jonah finished at John Brown University. He was a third-grader in a private Christian school, though the school's board had sent a letter requesting that the Williams not enroll him for the fourth grade. According to the letter, Theo had "serious behavioral problems that don't seem to be getting attention outside the school."

Jonah was concerned and embarrassed, so he took it upon himself to instill respect, discipline and godliness in his son. Unfortunately, his desperate attempt at fathering came too late.

Over the next seven years, Theo was constantly in trouble, being asked to leave one school or another and challenging his father's authority. At fourteen, he shoplifted at a five-and-dime and got arrested by the police just to embarrass his father at church. He seemed to beam with a sense of accomplishment when he smiled for the arrest photo, which found its way to the front page of the Sunday paper.

Ernestine, feeling guilty that she had spoiled him, made excuses for his egregious behavior, and she was always there to take up for him. Her unconditional support for Theo further aggravated the angry, contentious relationship between the boy and his father.

One day when Theo was fifteen, Jonah came home from the church and caught him cutting school and smoking marijuana in the house. Angry, he went outside, cut a peach tree switch and thrashed the boy who, crying and cursing, told Jonah he hated him. He swore he was leaving and was never coming back. When Ernestine got home from shopping and heard about the incident, she went out to search for Theo.

A week later, she called Jonah and told him that she had rented an apartment and that Theo was living with her. At that point, it was useless for Jonah to demand that she choose between him and the boy. She had made her choice. Jonah never talked to his son again, but he warned Ernestine.

"My dad always said it, and now I understand. *Too good is no good*. You ruined him by being so good to him, Ernestine. Eli learned too late. Remember what happened with Eli."

A month later, Jonah got a call from the police at five a.m. The fire started because Theo was smoking in bed. The flames burned six units in the apartment complex. Eight people had to be hospitalized, including three children. Four persons had been burned to death. Ernestine and Theo were probably the first to die.

Although the Snow Lake Christian community mourned with Jonah for the tragic loss of his family, he became despondent and depressed. He blamed himself for not being there when his family needed him, for not being a part of their lives through transition and growth, for being too busy to spend quality time with them.

Living in Snow Lake with reminders of Ernestine and Theo and their loss before him proved too much. A fellow minister at a congregation in Los Angeles announced during Sunday service that he would take an indefinite leave of absence to begin treatment for colon cancer. He called the next day and asked Jonah if he would like to fill in for the duration of the treatment. Once again demonstrating faith in God and his purposes, Jonah left Snow Lake forever to relocate in Los Angeles.

The Los Angeles congregation accepted him with great enthusiasm and requested him to stay after it became clear their terminally ill pastor would not return. He also met Aaliyah Crawford, the former pastor's daughter. Aaliyah was a pretty twenty-three-year-old who had recently graduated from UCLA's business school. Jonah was thirty-five. They were married within one year, and Dexter was born a year and a half after they were married.

Benefiting from the misfortunes of his earlier marriage, Jonah worked hard to be *there* for his wife and son as a husband and father. This time he had his priorities in order. The Lord came first, his family came next and his own needs and ambitions came third. His family life had been in complete harmony until Dexter turned fifteen and became interested in young Brenda Brown.

Brenda seemed nice enough when she was younger, but as soon as she and Dexter developed a romantic interest, she became a bad influence. She was a year older than Dexter and streetwise.

Her parents were questionable Christians from Inglewood whose over-drinking was the subject of gossip in the congregation from time to time. Her father was an engineer at Lockheed and her mother was a part-time actress.

Because they were too busy to raise their daughter, they spoiled her by buying her expensive clothes and a shiny, new red sports car. She was only sixteen, but she dressed and behaved like a thirty-year-old woman. Simply put, Brenda Brown was out of Dexter's league.

"Did she say what she wanted to testify about?"

"No, but I'm just about sure it has something to do with her running away. She seemed really affected by something. She seemed sad, different."

Jonah looked up, cutting a glance toward his wife.

"Different? How?"

"Just different. You'll see when you talk to her."

****

On a bleak, snowy, blustery morning at Echo Valley, south of Fontenelle Mountain, the agonizing cries for help and wails for comfort went up in vain, the sound of myriad desperate voices drowned out by a howl from the wind that resonated through the crystallized, frozen mountains.

Obscured in the blizzard, thousands of tightly bundled men, women and children stood outside tents in the camp, mourning the profound loss of human life. Outside almost every tent were inert bodies with mourning families standing by, while before other tents, there was no one attending. There were no survivors. All told, there were an estimated forty thousand victims.

By nine a.m., the grief and sadness had become frustration and anger. Unquestionably, there was something sinister going on, with so many dead in a single night. It wasn't the weather, as New Republic officials initially suggested it was. These victims hadn't frozen to death.

Many of the bodies were still warm. It wasn't the food, as the majority in the camp had brought in their own meat and vegetable provisions. It wasn't an airborne bacterial agent like anthrax because, while everyone was outdoors for the debriefing, some were affected and others were not, and death came suddenly, with only a few hours between the onset of symptoms and death.

Many of the victims, before dying, complained about severe stomach cramping. Survivors recalled "a bitter almond smell" on the victims' breath. Some threw up blood, suggesting ingestion of some toxic substance as the most likely cause.

By ten o'clock, the survivors had put it all together. Whatever nefarious agent had been used to poison tens of thousands in the camp had come from the bottled water provided at New Republic provisions stands. Doing everything they could to suppress their anger, leaders among the survivors once again began to press New Republic officials for answers.

An official announcement went out at eleven a.m., and it was read over the loudspeakers:

Be advised that the New Republic is currently aware of sodium cyanide contamination of the water used to fill bottles provided at provisions stands for Echo Valley Debriefing Camps Alpha, Beta and Gamma. If you are in possession of any water taken from any one of these stands, do not drink it. Bring it immediately to the guard post nearest you. I repeat: If you are in possession of any water taken from provisions stands for Debriefing Camps Alpha, Beta and Gamma, do not drink it. Bring it immediately to the guard post nearest you.

Be also advised that a full-scale investigation is still underway. Until such time as the investigation is concluded, no one will be allowed to cross the border into the former United States of America as planned. You are in no danger if you do not drink bottled water provided at provisions stands for Debriefing Camps Alpha, Beta and Gamma. In the meantime, a safe, freshly tested water supply will be available to you by noon.

Per instructions by officials, all the dead bodies were brought to a central location, stacked and recorded. At Lee's request, the U.S. government dropped wooden pallets and plastic wrap to aid the counting and storage effort.

By noon, eighteen thousand bodies had been counted and wrapped for shipping, while the line of people and trucks bringing additional bodies stretched for miles. In the cold, the bodies froze quickly, making stacking and storage easier.

The freezing temperatures also eliminated insect pests, corpse predation by animals and decomposition. If the poisoning had happened in the summer heat, the stench from thousands of fermenting, rotting, maggot-infested bodies would have been nauseating, but the cold lessened the impact of the sheer number of souls lost.

By three p.m., twenty-five thousand bodies, mostly teenagers and small children, were counted, processed and wrapped. As the process continued through late afternoon, the real impact of the mass poisoning began to set on the crowds gathered at Echo Valley.

News reporters for CNN, Fox News and ABC were in Cheyenne to cover the mass exodus of America's teens leaving the New Republic. There were many more hopeful parents waiting in Wyoming's capital city and at the Army's Dugway Proving Ground in Tooele County, Utah, longing to be united with children lost and out of touch since late August. Families had planned reunions and celebrations. Television stations had scheduled interviews. It was to be a national day of celebration.

But as rumors about the mass poisoning began to reach ears beyond the New Republic demarcation line, the gentle, buoyant spirit of jubilation was transformed to a tsunami of fear and horror that surged out in all directions across the country. Initial reports suggested that more than ninety thousand were dead, but that number was adjusted within an hour to thirty-four thousand and counting.

The poisoning was a profound tragedy shared by the United States of America and the New Republic. President Whitmore phoned Robert Lee to offer personal condolences, federal aid and to arrange transfer of the dead bodies to waiting relatives. Robert Lee reluctantly allowed New Republic-friendly reporters in, though he refused to answer questions. He told observers and commentators they would be allowed to cover a landmark speech planned for later in the evening.

Robert, who seemed unstable and grieving, told no one the subject of his proposed speech in advance, leading some to believe he was ready to concede the New Republic over to the United States government. The speech was set to begin at eight p.m. Mountain Time, so reporters and the audience were unprepared when the loud, dissonant feedback screeched from loudspeakers at 7:30.

"My fellow Americans of the New Republic, loyal Americans residin in the former United States of America and elsewhere, it is with a heavy heart and soul I come bafore ya. Fer many of ya grievin and worryin out there, I share yer sorrow. I found out jus minutes ago that ma own boy is dead. Ma precious young son was murdered by some diabolical monster who caught us with our guard down. Ma boy was slaughtered by a demon who saw fit ta send someone in here ta poison our drinkin water supply."

As cameras began to roll, the attention of the world fell upon the ruddy face of the squat man who stood at the microphone on a platform perched on a hill overlooking the crowds.

"Ya all know me. Ma name's Earl Krebbs. I'm a colonel in the New Republic army. I'm the exclusive foundin father of the New Republic of America."

He removed a handkerchief from his pocket and wiped his eyes.

"I lost ma son taday. In spite of that, I spent mosta the day trackin down those who are responsible fer this dastardly deed. And I got news fer ya. We *know* who's responsible."

He paused, waiting for the commotion and the murmuring to subside.

"Jus this mornin, it came ta ma attention that we had a security breach at one of our supply bases night bafore last. Three of our guards was killed in the attack on the base. Bafore one of em died, he managed ta shoot and kill one of the United States government's special agents responsible fer this tragedy."

One of Bubba's men dragged a body onto the platform, the body of the first U.S. Army guard kidnapped from the border, the same man Bubba untied and shot in the forehead two nights earlier.

Earl smiled. After all this time, after all these years, the people were all finally listening to him. He had the attention of the world. He had the attention he deserved. Raising his voice, he continued.

"This was one of the agents the federal government, led by Whitmore, sent over ta poison our water. We know that, cuz after he was shot, we searched im."

Earl reached into a satchel strapped over a shoulder and pulled out two chemical tablets, raising them.

"And this is what we found!"

The crowds reacted with surprise and shouts of anger.

"Yeah, we tested em with our scientists. It's the same sodium cyanide we found in the water. The federal government and Whitmore are responsible! Forty thousand dead, and the federal government's ta blame! They been sayin all along they wanna take us out, and now look at what they did! Forty thousand dead! Lord have mercy on their souls! They lured us all out here ta kill us! *All* of us!"

It became clear that the frustrated, anguished and angry crowd was with Earl, ready to follow where he would lead. He paused a moment and spoke in a subdued, low voice.

"And sadly, my fellow true patriots, it gets worse."

Dead silence fell on the crowd as he continued.

"Errin on the side of caution, I figured maybe this assassin wasn't actin alone, so I sent out a search team just in case. What we fount was something that should make us all rethink the way we look at the federal government. Bubba? Bring im on."

Bubba Barnes dragged up the second kidnapped guard, who stumbled onto the stage, crawled a few steps and fell onto his back, struggling to breathe. Earl continued.

"We were lucky ta lose only forty thousand. Try six hundred thousand or more. That first bastard only managed ta contaminate one of the water towers, the one at the base of Fontenelle Mountain. But we caught this one carryin five times the amount the first one used. They meant ta poison our main water supply at New Lexinton jus like Jake Stanton said they would back in September. They wanna weaken us, and then they wanna take us out. This is what we found in this man's bag!"

Earl held up another satchel, opened it and poured two dozen or more chemical tablets onto the platform. Earl shouted as Bubba grabbed the squirming guard and held him before the outraged crowd.

"This is the man who snuck out in the dark and poisoned ya instead a fightin ya honorably. This is the man who ain't thought twice about poisonin yer wives an yer mamas. Here is the man who stole the breath of life from thousands of yer kids!"

Earl bowed his head in silence.

"Ya know, when I think about what he did ta ma boy, I just wanna take ma gun and shoot the bastard right between the eyes. But that would be selfish, cuz he ain't hurt jus me. He's gotta answer ta folks other'n just me! Fer killin forty thousand of yer families, yer loved ones, yer countrymen and women, he's gotta answer ta alla y'all!"

He nodded to Bubba, who took the man to the edge of the platform.

"So I ask alla y'all! Da y'all *wanna* punish this bastard?"

The valley floor roared in the affirmative as the crowd surged forward toward the base of the hill on which the platform was perched.

"Da y'all want his blood? Da y'all want justice for what he did ta ya?"

The crowd growled even louder, chanting, urging Bubba to throw the U.S. Army guard off the platform. Earl signaled.

"Then he's all yours."

Bubba ripped the clear heavy-duty tape off the struggling man's mouth, elbowed him in the stomach to take his breath, lifted him and pitched him into the sea of swaying arms and groping, snatching, flailing hands, hands that became bloody as the man's body disappeared in the frenzied mass.

Earl yelled into the microphone.

"Was that enough fer ya? Y'all satisfied? He was *only* one man. Was there any real satisfaction fer any of y'all in punishin that one man when ya know he ain't truly responsible fa what he did. He was actin under orders from the federal government. He was an instrument of Whitmore and other wicked men who plotted evil against more'n forty thousand decent Americans, forty thousand poor fools who came out here because they trusted the federal government ta play fair and keep their word. They fooled us all, and if they had their way, we'd *all* be dead."

On television sets across the nation and around the world, many people were hearing Earl Krebbs speak for the first time. Until that moment, he was just an icon of evil, whose name was synonymous with red-necked ignorance and savagery.

"There's a sayin I heard alla ma life. *Fooled me once, shame on you. Fooled me twice, shame on me.* Shame on the federal government! Shame on the president! They lied ta us. They told us ta trust em and send the kids under eighteen back inta United States territory. But we did em one better. Ta demonstrate that we ain't holdin no one here gainst his will, we said anyone else who wanted ta go back could. Then when they got us isolated out here, they poisoned our water supply. Time fer us ta dummy up. We cain't let em fool us a second time."

On the inset inserted in the television feed, cameras panned the snow-covered field in Echo Valley where all the bodies were stacked and wrapped, like codfish in a Newfoundland fish yard. There were four mile-long rows stacked five feet high. At one end, forklift drivers were loading full pallets of frozen corpses onto Army trucks. The temperature had dropped and the wind had picked up, causing blinding snow flurries.

"Last night, the federal government killed more'n forty thousand true Americans. Ain't no dispute about that. Back when bin Laden and his terrorists blew up them Twin Towers, killin bout twenty-eight hundred Americans, the world considered it an act of war. So whadaya call it when someone comes in and kills forty thousand of yer people? Forty thousand of yer countrymen, forty thousand of yer brothers, sisters, mamas and babies? Y'all know it. It's a unmistakable, unrefutable act of war."

In spite of the fall in temperature and the freezing wind, the audience stayed with Earl, demonstrating their acceptance of his new leadership role in the New Republic.

"Now they called a lotta y'all cowards fer wantin ta go back. They said ya was fools ta trust the federal government fer as far as ya could spit. Well, they was right about one thang. Ya were fools ta trust the federal government, and forty thousand of ya paid the price. It's either fools or cowards. So, were ya a fool, or are ya a coward? All I can hope is that every one a y'all out here is a wised-up fool. There ain't no goin back now. The New Republic of America is at war with the federal government."

Half the spirited crowd on the white-covered valley floor roared in agreement, while the other half remained silent, still in shock about the recent events and revelation.

"This is a war about freedom. Now the federal government might have us outnumbered and they might have us outgunned, but we're fightin on the right side. We're fightin on God's side. They're at war ta oppress us, while we're fighting fer the freedom of America. We agree with the outnumbered American militias that fought fer America's freedom the first time, them fighters from Virginia, from Carolina and from New Hampshire, who meant it when they said: We live free or we die fightin!"

The crowds did not cheer at the end of Earl Krebbs' speech. Instead, Echo Valley became eerily quiet. The wind seemed to stop swirling and a grave sense of soberness fell on the congregated multitudes along with feathery, gossamer floating snowflakes.

Two days earlier, many had imagined warm hearths, big family reunion dinners and a restored sense of security and sanity. Now there was only death, freezing temperatures and the stark realization that none of them would ever see their homes or their families again.

****

"Is she under yet?"

The green-masked anesthesiologist glanced toward the instruments monitoring the patient on the table and nodded.

"Sleeping like a baby."

"Very well. Bring in the recipient."

It seemed like a simple, ordinary procedure, but it was in every detail the result of a twisted, convoluted, carefully negotiated deal.

Under emotional pressure and turmoil, Layla agreed to allow an obstetrician to remove the growing embryo from her womb, with the provision that it would not be destroyed. Instead of being discarded, it was to be placed in the womb of a surrogate, who would carry the pregnancy to term. Ironically, the pregnancy's due date was July 4, Reggie's birthday. The single component that clinched the deal was a stipulation that the government would make a way for Reggie and the child to live out the rest of their lives in the Crypt instead of dying in the aftermath of the impact on August 7.

Isabel hesitated as a negotiation tactic, and then she feigned a difficult concession. When Layla signed the agreement and the preselected, preconditioned recipient was notified, the process moved rapidly. Within three days, she was on the table and the process of removing the growing life within her had begun.

The process was straightforward. It involved surgically removing the embryo from Layla's uterus and attaching it the uterine wall of a healthy, compatible surrogate. The doctors' focus involved the pelvic regions of both women.

The first hour involved procedures required to examine, evaluate and physically remove the four-week old embryo from Layla's womb. The next four hours were spent finalizing preparations for the recipient's uterus and body, administering necessary shots (including one for Rh factor, additional hormone injections and boosters of vitamins and antibiotics), attaching the embryo to the recipient's uterine wall and performing a battery of tests and careful monitoring.

When the procedure was complete, doctors considered the womb-to-womb fetal transplant an expected success. In an observation area abutting the operating room, Dr. Isabel Benoit watched the entire process from start to finish with great interest.

Chapter 31

It had been years since Reverend Jonah Williams felt so many butterflies in his stomach on a Sunday morning, years since he felt so unsure and unsettled about what sense the flock would make of the testimony that would come before them. It had been years since he had to put the value of scriptural precedent and the value of the potential message before his own personal interests.

With every fiber of his being, he was dead-set against allowing Brenda Brown to testify before his congregation and before the world, but she had a scriptural right to come before the congregation and testify. Beyond the scriptural right, Brenda had testimony that had to be shared, a witness about Robert E. Lee's New Republic that the world had to hear.

Two days earlier, on Friday afternoon, November 22, the news of the mass poisoning of teenagers in the New Republic shocked and stunned the nation. According to the official count, 41,223 were dead at Echo Valley and thousands more were sick or still suffering from the debilitating effects of the cyanide poisoning. The tragedy touched millions of American families, who in anger and frustration looked for answers.

Earl Krebbs' broadcast response to the poisoning was aired and re-aired on televisions across the nation for thirty-six hours until Jettson Turner, Whitmore's National Security Advisor, banned its broadcast. Jett was concerned that the combination of the tragedy, national grief and Krebbs' incendiary language and mischaracterizations might make the American public more sympathetic to the New Republic's appeal for recognition and autonomy.

Early reactions to the speech proved Jett Turner right. Krebbs, who during the summer had been a symbol of redneck ignorance and anarchy, was becoming a powerful voice for freedom and for mistrust of the federal government, especially in rural areas of the country.

A Gallup poll taken right after the speech indicated that only forty percent of Americans believed that Nostradamus would cause the degree of damage the government predicted it would. Sixty percent were certain the government had a secret agenda that involved an alternative and less severe scenario.

Some suggested no one could be sure about the degree of damage that would result from the collision with Nostradamus, and still others were skeptical about the certainty of any collision at all.

Public distrust was fueled by a group of radical American and Australian astronomers who in November published an article titled "The Glancing Blow Theory," as opposed to the direct impact scenario. These scientists suggested that due to the curvature of the Earth, in the worst case, an incoming object the size of Nostradamus could only achieve "a glancing blow or an indirect impact" against the Earth. The theory was ridiculed in the scientific community, but it gave hope to many, who over the previous four months had none.

The timing couldn't have been better for Earl Krebbs to take over the New Republic's leadership. His words resonated with millions across America who distrusted the federal government and who believed a secret agenda would best be served only by the worst-case scenario. These were people who criticized the government for not working hard enough to achieve any manner of a solution, people who criticized the federal government for offering too little hope.

If nothing else, the mass poisoning of teenagers in Wyoming changed America's attitudes about the New Republic. Because Earl Krebbs had been at least partially successful at blaming the government for the worst massacre in history, many were able to put aside his record of bigotry and savagery and to re-evaluate the role of the New Republic in America's affairs for the upcoming year. The most revealing polls involved attitudes toward the New Republic and the federal government's plans to bomb the New Republic's headquarters at New Lexington.

Before the poisoning and before Earl Krebbs announced his vitriolic murder charges against the federal government, eighty percent of Americans polled believed it was necessary for the government to take action against the self-declared nation. Seventy-three percent believed the New Republic represented a threat to America's national security, and sixty percent approved of bombing as a means to minimize that threat.

However on November 24, two days after the poisoning, America's opinions had changed radically, with only thirty percent feeling government action against the New Republic was required, fifty-eight percent believing the New Republic threatened national security and only twenty-five percent supporting bombing the complex at New Lexington.

****

On Saturday, November 23, Brenda Brown spent four hours before the church board trying to convince members of her need to testify before the congregation on Sunday. With every retelling of the account of her nightmarish ten days at New Lexington, another member was convinced, until only one person remained opposed to letting her testify, and that was Jonah Williams. As pastor of the church, Jonah's voice carried weight. It was unlikely that Brenda would go up before the congregation unless Jonah changed his mind.

After a break for lunch, the board entertained another visitor. Jonah and other members listened to this secret visitor's appeal with great caution and skepticism. First of all, he wasn't a member of the church, and second, he was a high-profile government official, a Cabinet member involved in the matter only to advance the government's agenda.

According to the story National Security Advisor Jettson Turner told, he interviewed Brenda shortly after her escape from the New Republic, and he had personally arranged to return her to her grateful parents.

The day after Brenda escaped, more than forty thousand people at the debriefing camp in that Tump Range valley in Wyoming were poisoned to death. If she hadn't gotten out, she likely would have been one of the casualties. She had been on the edge, close to the action, and from that perspective, she was able to provide information about the events leading up to the mass poisoning in more detail than anyone else had to date.

When the church board asked why she hadn't gone to the media with her story, Brenda replied that there were details about her experience that she didn't want to share with ungodly reporters and strangers. She said her testimony was meant to come before God and the elders of her congregation. Between sobs, she read from the Bible.

"Is any sick among you? Let him call for the elders of the church; and let them pray over him, anointing him with oil in the name of the

Lord: And the prayer of faith shall save the sick, and the Lord shall raise him up; and if he have committed sins, they shall be forgiven him."

After hearing Brenda read humbly from the scriptures, Jonah sighed and admitted that although his heart was still set against her testifying, the scriptures gave her a right to confess before the members of her congregation.

So on Sunday, November 24, Brenda stood before the congregation and the world with a trembling Bible in her hand, reluctant to begin. Though she struggled to maintain composure, her voice broke.

"Brothers and Sisters of Greater Faith, I come before you and the world as a poor and lost soul, as a poor and pitiful wretch who, like many in these last days, lost her way, lost her faith in our Lord and Savior, Jesus Christ.

"Selfishly, I pursued the world and the things in the world and nearly lost my life. I should have been dead. I watched young people who stood beside me being shot in the back of the head by Earl Krebbs' men for trying to escape from the New Republic. I would have been in the debriefing camp and been poisoned if Jesus hadn't saved me at the last minute. Yes, through his Grace, Jesus saved my life, Brothers and Sisters, but I didn't escape punishment."

Her eyes welled with hot tears that began to stream down her face.

"I'll have to live the rest of my life with the horrors I witnessed and experienced in the ten days I was at New Lexington, horrible memories and terrors burned in my soul that are with me every time I close my eyes, memories that make me wish I were dead. But Jesus saved me for a reason. He redeemed my life and my soul so I could come before you as his witness."

Brenda's curly black hair hung down a little past her shoulders. She read from a page in a binder she had placed on the podium, clutching the front of the stand to steady her nerves.

"Through the Grace of Christ Jesus I was saved so I could speak to all the families who lost loved ones at Echo Valley. He saved me so I could bring them the comfort that comes with knowing the truth, even though that truth is sometimes painful to bear."

She paused for the transition as she and her mother had rehearsed, and then she turned a page in the binder and continued.

"From the moment I got to the New Republic, I began to hear the stories. They were stories of homesick kids who Krebbs and his men killed for trying to leave. I didn't believe those stories at first, but there were so many, and there was so much detail. They said at first when kids left and didn't come back, everyone assumed they had made it home, but then some began to come back and tell about execution camps. These were camps where Earl Krebbs' men would round up groups trying to go home and shoot them all but one. That one would be sent back as a warning to others. I don't know the number, but hundreds, maybe thousands, were missing."

Brenda looked toward her pastor, seeking an expression of assurance, and for the first time in years, it was there. He nodded in approval.

"Earl Krebbs blamed the federal government for the poisoning at Echo Valley, but I believe in my heart the government had nothing to do with it. No one can put it past Krebbs to poison teenagers who only wanted to go home. He was killing them already."

She swallowed from a dry mouth, preparing to provide a revelation that could potentially change history.

"On the night before I left, in the tent of one of Krebbs' guards, I saw a metal box and opened it. Inside I saw some circular tablets that looked just like the ones Krebbs said was the poison. This was two days *before* the poisoning. And then later, I think this same guard of Krebbs kidnapped a guard from the other side. I think the kidnapped guard was the man Krebbs accused of the poisoning before they threw him off the stage."

Once again, Brenda was crying.

"It wasn't the government. It was Krebbs and his men. They killed America's children. They killed your children."

In the audience, Dexter held his mother's hand, captivated by Brenda's poise and strength. He regretted he hadn't gone with her. He was sure he could have protected her from whatever trauma she had endured. Megan sat at Aaliyah's other side, holding her other hand. The two women whispered to each other on occasion.

Brenda looked toward the center camera and continued.

"When I realized the New Republic was a lie, I wanted to go home. In fact, I wanted to go home so bad that I was willing to risk death for being caught. There were nine of us. One of the boys said he paid eight hundred dollars for a map that would keep us away from Krebbs' guards and get us to the border in three days. We realized later he was working for Krebbs. He led us right to the guards. It was a miserable night."

Brenda was no longer reading from the page. She was reliving a scene that had played over and over in her mind since that horrible night. She no longer needed the notes, speaking from her heart.

"It was cold and it was snowing. As we knelt on the frozen ground, waiting to be executed, we made a pact. We swore to each other that if one of us lived and ever made it back home, that person would pass on messages to our respective parents. The words of one girl stand out in my mind. She was a Muslim named Chari, a very gracious person and a child of God. She said she wasn't scared. She said the only things that mattered to her in her last minutes of life were her peace with God and the love she felt in her heart for her parents and her family."

Brenda stopped to dry her eyes.

"To all the families of children trapped in the New Republic, please know that you are loved. Please know that your children truly miss you and think about you every day. They want to come home to you. To the families of the children who died from the poisoning and died in other ways, please know this: all that mattered to your children in the end was your love and the thought of going home. Regardless of whether or not their bodies come back to you, please welcome their spirits home."

She closed the binder and looked toward the audience. The sound originated in the pit of her stomach, passing through her lungs, trembling up her throat and out her mouth. She shut her eyes and tilted her voice toward the heavens as she sang.

Aaa-muz-zi-ing Grace— How sweet the sound
That saved a wretch li-ike me,
I once wa-as lost but now am found,
Was blind, bu-ut now, I see.

Brenda looked out toward the congregation.
"Please sing with me? Please?"

Twas Grace that taught

my heart to fear.
And Grace, my fears relieved.
How precious did that Grace appear
the hour I first believed.

By the end of the second verse, the vast multi-racial congregation had risen. In an unplanned moment, the men, women and children of the Greater Faith Church stood and were all holding hands, singing soulfully, singing fervently as a witness to the nation and the world.

Through many dangers, toils and snares
we have already come.
Twas Grace that brought us safe thus far
and Grace will lead us home.

The full choir joined their voices for the next two verses.

The Lord has promised good to me
His word my hope secures.
He will my shield and portion be
as long as life endures.

When we've been here a thousand years
bright shining as the sun.
We've no less days to sing God's praise
then when we've first begun.

The church and the nation stopped and listened as Brenda Brown sang the final verse alone.

Amazing Grace, how sweet the sound,
That saved a wretch like me,
I once was lost but now am found,
Was blind, but now, I see.

I once was lost but now am found,
Was blind, but now, I see-ee.

****

"Gaddammit Earl! No bullshittin! I want the truth and I want it now! Was it you or was it someone *else*? Cuz I sure as hell know it wasn't the gaddamned government!"

Earl Krebbs kept his hands up, away from his gun. He was careful not to do anything to worsen the already fragile condition of his nephew.

"So now yer pullin a gun on me? So now ya think I did it? Ya think I poisoned ma own *son*?"

"Your son ain't *dead*, Earl. I already had it checked out. He's back in Fountain with his Aunt Minnie. *My* son is dead, Earl. And so is Becky. I want the truth!"

Earl studied the position of his gun on the table, two feet away.

"I don't understan why Becky and that boy was out there in the *first* place, in a camp fulla traitors."

Robert fired over his uncle's head.

"Gaddammit Earl. Don't even think about goin for it, cuz I'll shoot ya right in your lyin throat if I see ya goin that way. Now for the last time, who *poisoned* the water tower? Who done it, Earl?"

It was the third time Robert Lee had seen his uncle since the night Earl threatened him with the gun in the bunker. Since that night, he avoided Earl, and until that night, he had never been in Earl's presence without two armed guards standing by.

Just that afternoon, he buried Becky. Earlier in the morning, he buried his youngest son, eight-year-old Dayton. The majority of the other bodies had already been shipped out, but the northwest corner of Echo Valley became the final resting place for at least eleven hundred corpses. Robert dug the two graves himself. His hands were blistered and red, a testimony to the fact that the top two inches of the valley soil were frozen solid.

The decision to corner and confront Earl was a rash one, made in a moment of anger. He had just marked Becky's grave. As he contemplated never seeing her face again and never hearing the sound of her voice again, he broke down, falling to his knees, weeping. He loved her so much!

He was asleep in his tent when he heard the cries and wails rising from the valley floor. Ignoring his own security, he rushed out on foot, running non-stop to the area where a guard said Becky and the boys had set up camp. As he walked past the tents, the carnage was overwhelming.

The bleak scene, with thousands of teenagers and tiny children, lain out on the frozen ground with pale faces and eyes wide open, was surreal. At various times in his life, Robert had imagined Hell as a frozen place, but the Hell he envisioned had never been so horrendous and cold.

After three hours of searching, he spotted the bodies of Becky and Dayton, lying together outside a tent, partially covered with snow. In Becky's frozen hand, Robert found a note scribbled by Tyler, his oldest son.

I'm sorry I let you down, Dad. Mama's dead. And Dayton, he almost made it. He was very brave. You would have been proud. It was something in the water. I don't know if it was the government or if it was Uncle Earl, but whoever it was, I'm going to make him pay. I'm going back to New Lexington. I'll see you. I love you.

Robert cried as he stroked eight-year-old Dayton's delicate face. Dayton was always a sensitive boy, probably owing to the way he came into the world. On his last night as a sheriff's deputy, Robert stopped a speeding car and approached the driver with his gun drawn. Robert had been drinking Jack Daniel's all night, so he was drunk. Inside the car, Dayton's real father was excited and anxious, cursing aloud. Beside him, his wife Becky was in labor.

Even years later, Robert wasn't sure how the gun went off, but it did. The bullet entered the left side of Cecil Thomason's head and exploded out the right, sending Becky into shock. Dayton was born in that car fifteen minutes later.

Life was full of ironies, and no one ever expected that Becky would marry the man who shot her husband in the head, but she did, and she loved him. Now she and Dayton were dead.

When President Whitmore and Robert Lee spoke on the morning after the mass poisoning, the men shared each other's grief. Whitmore was certain that if his daughter Susan had been in the New Republic and survived until November 22, she would have been in that camp at Echo Valley, trying to escape. Whitmore offered condolences to Robert and told him that government operatives active inside the New Republic assured him the water tower poisoning was an inside job, intended to undo any potential accord and to accelerate the onset of an all-out war.

From the beginning of the New Republic, Robert Lee and Earl Krebbs always made public appearances together, especially at landmark events. It was symbolic and significant that Earl was absent during the first day of debriefing at Echo Valley. Robert and Earl were at odds about the decision to send the young people and others back.

There was also an ideological struggle between the two about the direction the New Republic was headed. As hours passed and Robert continued to contemplate the poisoning, it became more and more apparent that even if Earl hadn't poisoned the water tower himself, he had engineered it.

Robert planned to address the nation and the world at eight o'clock on Friday night, but Earl upstaged him, surprising everyone by appearing on an Echo Valley platform at 7:30 to blame the federal government for the poisoning. He even produced the two Army special ops agents who supposedly perpetrated the act.

By some media accounts, Earl Krebbs had emerged, after the speech, as the spiritual and ideological leader of the New Republic. Robert was as shocked as anyone by Earl's speech, but still, it didn't add up. Why would the U.S. government poison a bunch of kids headed back home? It didn't make sense.

As he watched Brenda Brown's testimonial from the Los Angeles church, Robert put it all together. The U.S. Army guards were kidnapped. One of Earl's guards had the poison. One of them, under Earl's orders, poisoned the water and framed the kidnapped guards. Earl already said the "deserters" at Echo Valley were "a bunch of cowards who don't deserve life," but this time he had gone too far. Over forty-one thousand were dead, and among these, Becky and Dayton.

In anger, Robert loaded his gun and sought out his uncle. After searching for fifteen minutes, he found Earl in an underground bunker, dug out in a secure area of the Tump Range foothills. He approached the subterranean fortress, dismissed the armed guards posted outside and went in with his gun drawn. Earl was surprised by his nephew's unexpected appearance and only raised his hands. He realized that either he or Robert, and not both, would leave the room alive.

"Course ya know, Earl, that I wouldn't have this gun on ya if I wasn't ready ta use it. You taught me that. So ya gotta know if I don't start gettin answers real soon, I ain't got no choice but ta take ya out."

A trail of sweat rolled down Earl's face as he struggled to find words that would put Robert at ease.

"Swear ta God, Bobby! I ain't poisoned that water. Dayton was ma nephew. And Becky! Ya know I loved Becky. I *swear* it wasn't me."

"Then who was it? I wanna kill who done it, and I know ya know who it is."

Just then, both men heard a distinctive click, the sound of someone releasing a gun's safety switch. Both turned toward the source of the intrusion.

"Family reunion? Why is it that every time ya have a family reunion, some fool's gotta start actin up?"

Bubba Barnes was already in the room, his MK 23 drawn and aimed toward Robert's head. Earl sighed with relief, though he did not move.

"Ya wanna know who done it, Bobby? Yer lookin at im. *Bubba* poisoned that water tower, but he did it cuz *I* told im to. Bubba'll do anythang I tell im to, so I think ya need to lower ya gun right about now."

Bubba had the advantage of aim.

"Lower the gun, Lee."

Robert had no choice. He knew his fate was sealed. His finger tensed as he thought to shoot Earl. That way he could at least take out the man who killed his family before dying. Unfortunately, he thought too long and convinced himself otherwise.

"I said *lower it, Lee.*"

Robert lowered the gun.

"Now throw it over here."

As soon as Robert complied, Earl snatched his own gun from the table and took aim at his nephew.

"Looks like this is it. Told ya not ta go against me. Ya did and ya lost yer family, and now it's yer life. Shoot im, Bubba."

As a *dead* man, Robert had no fear.

"So how's it all gonna go down, Earl? Bubba shoots me and ya shoot him? Say ya shot the nigger who killed the president of the New Republic? Be a hero? Is that how it's gonna be?"

"Shut up, Bobby! Bubba, I said *shoot im!*"

"So what ever happened ta that family tradition, Earl? Ya remember? The one where we kill our own when that time comes? You've got a gun. Why don't *you* shoot me?"

"Gaddammit Bubba! I said *shoot that bastard!*"

Bubba, still aiming, closed in on Robert. Standing next to Earl, he spoke.

"On your knees, Lee."

Robert stood there, defiant. It was an awkward moment that Bubba exploited as adroitly he holstered his gun and grabbed Earl's arm, his hand clutching Earl's hand around the gun. In that instant the gun fired, but Bubba managed to aim the barrel toward the ceiling.

Still controlling the gun, Bubba locked his muscular left arm around Earl's neck, holding him tight. Bubba's unexpected move surprised Robert, but Earl was dumbfounded as he watched his own pistol in his own hand being turned on himself.

"Bubba? What're ya doin, Bubba?"

Bubba answered as he struggled with Earl, his right arm forcing the gun toward Earl's face.

"I owe ya this much, Krebbs. I work for an agency that has a vested interest in keeping your nephew there alive. My only objective here has been to make sure he stays alive and in control of the New Republic. My orders were very specific. They said if you ever tried to take him out, then it would be my duty to take you out."

"Bubba?"

"This is for Jake."

Bubba pressed the soft area under Earl's ear with his thumb, forcing Earl's mouth to open. Hand steady moving forward, he inserted the shaking barrel of the gun into Earl's mouth. Earl's last word was a desperate appeal to his nephew. The word was intelligible.

"Bobba!"

Bubba shifted his body to avoid the bullet's expected exit path.

"I'll see you in Hell, Krebbs, but you might have to wait a few hundred years."

He stared into Earl's eyes, waiting for him to exhale, and he squeezed the trigger as Earl widened his eyes and drew a final breath.

Earl's Glock was an efficient instrument of death. It blasted off the back of his head. His skull void of matter, his open eyes sunk back deep in their sockets.

Robert Lee stood transfixed, in shock. Bubba clutched Earl's body until it stopped twitching and relaxed, and then he let it fall to the floor.

He looked back over his shoulder at Robert just before he slipped out the door.

"This changes the whole equation, Lee. Now Earl Krebbs is off the bargaining table. Now you have to do your part."